The Consequence of MURDER

NENE ADAMS

Bella

Bella Books, Inc.
P.O. Box 10543
Tallahassee, FL 32302

Printed in the United States of America on acid-free paper.

First Bella Books Edition 2014

Editor: Katherine V. Forrest
Cover Designer: Linda Callaghan

ISBN: 978-1-59493-383-7

Dedication

Dedicated to my enchanting partner, Corrie—I love you even though you won't eat cornbread, hate grits, and laugh when my Southern accent slips in. You may be a Philistine, sweetheart, but you're my Philistine.

My death is plotted; here's the consequence of murder.
We value not desert nor Christian breath,
When we know black deeds must be cur'd with death.
- John Webster, *The Duchess of Malfi*, Act V, Scene iv

CHAPTER ONE

"There's a man," said the fresh-faced young woman seated opposite her in the diner booth. "He's causing me problems."

Mackenzie Cross nodded and remained silent while the waitress delivered cups of coffee accompanied by slices of the best damn pecan pie in the state of Georgia, bar none. Outside the diner, a steady stream of rain pattered against the window, spreading a wet, misty haze over her view of the parking lot.

"Okay, you have a problem with a man. What of it?" Mackenzie asked when they were alone again. She put a dollop of half-and-half in her coffee, took a sip and added two packets of sugar. She tried another taste and grimaced. The sweetener hadn't helped.

The young woman tossed her head of long, glossy blond hair. Her mouth formed a pout. "You owe my daddy big time, so I want you to help me out."

"At the risk of sounding clichéd, who's your daddy?"

"I'm Kelly Collier." The young woman pushed away the plate of pie untouched. She clearly expected to be recognized, and frowned when Mackenzie made no comment. The frown changed to a smirk. "Paul Collier's daughter. You know, he's the pastor of the First Baptist Church of Jesus Christ Our Savior and King, and if I'm not mistaken, Ms. Cross, he's also your landlord." The smirk turned into a self-satisfied smile.

"True. I rent office space from Mr. Collier."

"And I'm engaged to Tucker Dearborn," Kelly went on with an air of triumph. She held up a hand, pretending to look for flaws in her French manicured nails, the better to flash the engagement ring on her third finger. "I'm sure you've heard of him. We're getting married after graduation, and he's taking me to the Bahamas for our honeymoon."

While Kelly spoke, Mackenzie lifted her fork and savored a bite of pie: sweetened with local honey instead of corn syrup, bursting with fresh pecans, and with a crust so flaky it must have been made with lard. Her arteries would never forgive her, but her taste buds sang a glorious hallelujah, reminding her why she tolerated the diner's lousy coffee.

"Tucker Dearborn is the Burton Lemoyne High School football team's star quarterback. His father, Jacob Dearborn, owns half of Antioch," Mackenzie murmured after eating half the pie. "Mr. Dearborn is the pastor at the United Methodist Church on Apple Street, right across from your father's church," she continued. "You and Tucker getting together isn't likely to spark a Baptists vs. Methodists feud, is it?"

Kelly shrugged. "Me and Tucker aren't Romeo and Juliet, if that's what you mean. Daddy and Mr. Dearborn get along okay. Daddy says we all worship the same God and live by the same book. Everything else is unimportant."

"Your father is a wise man." Mackenzie finished her slice of pie, hesitated, and finally pulled over Kelly's abandoned plate. Waste not, want not. "Why'd you call me?"

"Because you fix things, right?"

"My business is finding unusual, rare and obscure items for clients on commission. I do antiques valuations, too. Neither of these things usually requires 'fixing' people's problems, so why come to me with your man trouble?"

"Daddy wouldn't ask you to do anything to repay him, but he's spending all that money on your office. The least you can do is a simple little favor for me."

Mackenzie weighed the merits of the argument.

Mr. Collier owned the building that housed her office. Last month, after a violent storm, he had arranged for repairs to be done when gale force winds and an aging roof hadn't proven the best combination. A fundamentally decent man, he wasn't raising her rent, he hadn't delayed the work, and he'd offered to reimburse her for any expenses incurred because of the construction. He hadn't even so much as hinted at favors owed.

She figured whatever his daughter wanted regarding this mysterious man, she might do it provided the request wasn't illegal, immoral, or too inconvenient.

"Look, this is just a stupid misunderstanding," Kelly burst out, startling a couple at a nearby table. She glanced around and lowered her voice to an insistent whine. "I didn't do anything wrong, and I don't see why I'm supposed to let him get away with it—"

"Just stop right there," Mackenzie interrupted. "You told me over the phone that this is an emergency, right? So I need you to stay calm, begin at the beginning, and tell me exactly what happened. Can you do that?"

Kelly took a deep breath. "I was in the park today," she began hesitantly.

The rain shower ended while she spoke. A break in the clouds sent a ray of sunshine beaming through the window. Radiant light poured over Kelly, turning her hair to spun gold, her skin to porcelain smoothness, and her cornflower-blue eyes luminous. Beautiful as an angel, Mackenzie thought, but she had better sense than to be dazzled by appearance.

She motioned with her fork for Kelly to continue. Across the room, she caught the waitress holding the coffeepot aloft in a mimed inquiry. She shook her head.

"I was in the park with Mr. Dearborn. He's a widower, and Tucker's all the family he has left, and he wanted to talk to me about the wedding," Kelly got out in a rush. "And there's nothing wrong with that at all."

"Naturally."

"Well, we met Reverend Wyland in the park. You know him?"

"He runs the Covenant Rock Church of God with Signs Following."

Kelly's upper lip curled in scorn. The expression didn't suit her pretty face. "A bunch of Pentecostal snake handlers up on Sweetwater Hill. It's not even a real church, just an old shack in the middle of the woods. Anyway, Rev. Wyland saw us together. Now he says…"

Mackenzie ate the last bite of pie, considered washing it down with a swig of coffee, and decided the poor pie had never done anything to her so terrible to warrant such brutal treatment. "What does Rev. Wyland say?" she prodded.

"He says he wants Mr. Dearborn to resign from the church."

"Why?"

"Because he says we're sinners, but that's not true!" Kelly slapped the tabletop with the flat of her hand. The diamond ring winked. "And you have to make him stop."

At last we come to the point. "Let me make sure I understand the situation," Mackenzie said. "You and your future father-in-law were in the park—I assume you mean Stubbs Park—when you were accosted by Rev. Wyland, who now insists that Mr. Dearborn resign from the United Methodist Church."

"Yes, that's right."

"And you and Mr. Dearborn were discussing your upcoming nuptials with his son."

"That's right."

"Has Wyland told you what he'll do if his demand isn't met?"

Kelly opened her mouth, closed it, and opened it again after a moment to say tightly, "I don't know what that crazy man wants. Maybe he's been bit by snakes once too often."

"Why did Wyland call you sinners? You said it was a misunderstanding."

"I don't want to talk about it," Kelly said abruptly. She rose and sidled out of the booth. "You don't need to know. It doesn't matter. Can you help me or not?"

"You want Wyland to...what? Stop threatening you?" Mackenzie dropped her fork beside the empty second plate. "Be very specific, Ms. Collier," she warned. "I don't want there to be any more misunderstandings."

"Just...just make him leave us alone. That's what I want."

"Why can't you ask your father to take care of it? Or Tucker, for that matter."

"I don't want to bother them."

"Let me be clear: I'll talk to Wyland. That's all. And if that's not good enough—"

"Just make him stop!" Kelly's voice rose to a shrill shriek.

The diner fell silent.

Aware of a dozen pair of eyes on them, Mackenzie listened to the sizzling of hamburgers and bacon on the grill in the kitchen and pretended not to notice the sudden, fascinated interest. For a moment, Kelly's angel's façade cracked, showing a glimpse of darkness beneath, something petty and mean.

Before Mackenzie could decide what to make of the slip, Kelly went on in a more normal tone of voice, "I'll tell Daddy you're helping me out. I'm sure he'll be happy." She flipped her hair over her shoulder and stared down at Mackenzie as if defying her to refuse.

The other diner patrons resumed their buzz of conversation and clattering silverware.

"All right," Mackenzie said. "I'll call you when I know something." She wiped her mouth on a napkin, crumpled it up, tossed it on a plate and signaled the waitress, who came bustling over.

"You do that," Kelly said.

She glided her slender, athletic form down the aisle with the self-confidence of a young woman who knows she's prettier than everyone else in the room and expects to be treated accordingly. Mackenzie watched through the window as the young woman climbed into a brand-new, white Corvette Stingray convertible and screeched out of the parking lot.

"Check, please," Mackenzie said to the hovering waitress, taking out her wallet to leave a generous tip.

Pie that good deserved a reward, she decided, though if she'd had her druthers, she wouldn't have given one thin dime for the cup of swill masquerading as coffee, nor would she have paid a plugged nickel for the unwanted company.

CHAPTER TWO

The downtown area of Antioch, Georgia—population 5,424—seemed to breathe more deeply after a rainstorm, Mackenzie thought on her way to the office.

Main Street, so broad it boasted a parking strip in the center, gleamed as blackly as if the asphalt had been shellacked. The late-nineteenth century brick buildings looked refreshed, as did the young hickory trees planted in rows along the pavements on both sides of the street as part of the city's downtown renewal project.

The sense of freshness wouldn't last long, Mackenzie knew. Just until the heat cranked up and the humidity turned the air oppressive. At that point everyone would curse the goddamn storm front that dumped so much water in the air, leaving them to stew.

She managed to wedge her car between two other vehicles in the central parking zone and climbed out, making sure to display her parking permit on the dashboard. She frowned at the police cruiser parked in front of her business, housed in a single-story building much longer than it was deep. She rented one of the three available spaces.

What was a cop doing parked here? she wondered. The Antioch police station had its own lot two streets over close to the courthouse, city hall, other government buildings, the Mitford County sheriff's office and the downtown parking garage.

Mackenzie inhaled deeply, detecting the delicious aromas of sugar and yeast. Today was Thursday. The bakery next to her office made Hawaiian sweet rolls on Thursday. Hawaiian sweet rolls were Sheriff Newberry's most favorite thing in the world excepting his teenage son and daughter and the University of Georgia football team.

The explanation eased the tension in her shoulders. Just a deputy dispatched to pick up a batch of rolls for the sheriff, she thought, a theory which lasted up to the moment her door opened and a man in a Brooks Brothers suit walked outside.

Alarmed, she hailed him and hurried across the street. "Jimmy, what the hell are you doing?" she asked. "Do you have a search warrant?"

"No—" he began, but she interrupted.

"The next words out of your mouth had better be why you have cause to search my place of business without a warrant," she declared, "or I swear, Detective James Austin Maynard, I will kick your ass so hard, you'll taste shoe leather for a solid seven days."

"Good afternoon to you, too, Kenzie," Maynard replied calmly. He didn't quite smile, but the wrinkles at the corners of his eyes deepened. Her cousin was only a couple of years older than her and took after the worst traits of his mother's side of the family—dark, dour, rangy, and about as much fun as listening to a golf game on the radio. "I'm doing fine, thanks for asking. My ulcer is much better and it's been a week since I quit smoking."

Mackenzie flushed, half in annoyance, half in chagrin at having her rudeness pointed out by the person who used to dump frogs down the back of her dress in grade school. Now that they were adults, she always suspected he was secretly laughing at her. She'd rather have dealt with the frogs. "Do I need to ask a lawyer to come over here, Jimmy?" she asked.

"Not unless you want to tell me about the dead woman in your wall," he said.

She went cold. "What?"

Maynard told her that the construction crew hired by Collier had been removing water-damaged drywall in her office and discovered a woman's corpse hidden between the wall studs. "Still waiting for the medical examiner, who's at lunch," he concluded, "but judging from the condition of the body, our victim's been here a good long while."

"How long?" Mackenzie's voice cracked. She cleared her throat. "I mean, when was she killed?" What she really meant was, *How long have I been sitting behind my desk with a dead lady's eyes staring at me?* but she managed to conceal her creeping horror.

"No idea. That's for Dr. Hightower to decide. But at a guess, I'd say the victim's been there a few decades at least." His cell phone rang. Holding up a finger, he answered the call, walking away a few steps for privacy.

Seizing the opportunity to satisfy her morbid curiosity and view the damage herself, Mackenzie slipped past his turned back and went inside where she spotted her friend, Deputy Veronica Birdwell, speaking to members of the construction crew huddled together by the water cooler. The men looked spooked. Veronica looked…well, like herself, as usual.

She considered Veronica a very good person: kind, thoughtful, polite to a fault, compassionate, not to mention pretty and brunette with a complexion like milk and roses— just the type of woman who made her southern charms tingle. Unfortunately, Veronica was also as straight as a carpenter's rule and oblivious to boot.

Mackenzie sighed. She hadn't a prayer in hell of starting anything with Veronica and she'd known the sad fact for years. Just as well, she said to herself. Why rock the boat when she and Veronica had a perfectly decent friendship already? Nevertheless, gazing at the lush curves packed into that unflattering brown deputy's uniform only depressed her further.

So close, and yet so far.

"Hi, Ronnie," she said to attract Veronica's attention.

"Hey, Mac, what are you doing here? Did you hear what happened?" Veronica asked, turning around to focus huge, bright green eyes on her.

"Cousin Maynard gave me the scoop on the body, said it was okay for me to grab some files from the office," Mackenzie answered with a pang of guilt. She hated putting Veronica on the spot by lying, but Maynard would never let her into "his" crime scene and she wanted to see the no doubt grisly discovery the workers had made.

"Oh, sure," Veronica replied. She glanced out the plate glass window at Maynard, still talking on his phone.

"Tell you what, I'll run back there real quick for the files. Won't be a minute."

"Just don't touch anything, okay?"

"Sure thing, Ronnie. Thanks." Mackenzie stepped around a pallet of materials, hopped over abandoned tools and made her way to the back of the room.

The front half of the space she rented from Pastor Collier acted as the public face of her company, *Finders & Keepers, Inc.* Although most of her business was conducted by phone or over the Internet, she'd still decorated the waiting area with colorful abstract prints on the walls, comfortable chairs, potted Swiss cheese plants, a receptionist's desk and an impressive, custom-made, copper monstrosity of an espresso machine.

Never mind that she hadn't needed to hire a receptionist, and only fired up the espresso machine once a year for the volunteer fire department's charity spaghetti supper, bake sale and sock hop. In the business world, appearances counted for a lot.

Mac, my girl, don't you ever forget to shine your shoes, put a ribbon in your hair and wear your best dress, no matter if you ain't got a pot to piss in or a window to throw it out of, her daddy had said when she was fourteen years old, returning home in tears after failing to sell any band candy. *If you look successful, people will treat you like you're about to hand out hundred-dollar bills. If you look like a bum, they'll spit on you. That's the way it goes.*

She dismissed thoughts of her father to concentrate on her company.

The worst damage had occurred in the waiting area when the big front window shattered under the onslaught of wind and rain and took out a Swiss cheese plant. She hadn't been here, staying holed up for the storm's duration in her apartment with a six-pack of beer, a meatball sub and a new copy of the Shooter's Bible.

The second room she used as a private office had also suffered a few minor problems like a ceiling leak and water-damaged drywall. Fortunately, her computer equipment and prized sixties Rock-Ola jukebox escaped unscathed.

She opened the door to her private office. Stale air rushed out at her like an exhaled breath, carrying a dry, musty smell that reminded her of a months-old dead mouse moldering behind the wainscoting. A glance at the wall showed she wasn't far off.

A piece of drywall had been removed and discarded in pieces on the floor. As Maynard had told her, a desiccated human corpse was crammed upright between the wooden wall studs, looking like a prop in a Hollywood horror film.

Mackenzie took in the dry skin, gray with dust and warped to the bones so tightly it had split in places. The lower jawbone hung open in a parody of a yawn. Long hairs clinging to the top of the skull appeared to confirm the victim's sex.

She had been renting the office for three years, ever since she started the business. The victim had to have died and been hidden here before she took possession. Who was this unknown woman? How had she died? Why had her killer stuffed her in this particular wall?

Taking her cell phone out of her pocket, Mackenzie began snapping pictures of the body from every angle. She zoomed in the camera to take more detailed shots. The sound of voices outside the door made her hurry.

When Maynard burst inside the room, she'd already returned the phone to her pocket and stood in front of the jukebox nonchalantly brushing drywall dust off the glass front.

A muscle twitched in his cheek. She could tell he wasn't amused this time. "What do you think you're doing?" he asked, the words rumbling deep in his chest. "Goddamn it, Kenzie, this is my crime scene."

Mackenzie pointed out, "You won't find any evidence here, Jimmy. I had the wallpaper stripped, the walls painted, and the floor redone before I moved in. If there *is* anything, it's in the wall with your victim, which I didn't lay a finger on."

"Damn it to hell and gone," Maynard said, but she saw him deflate slightly. He flapped a hand at her. "Go away, Kenzie. Go home. Go do whatever. Just go."

Mackenzie hurried away, eager to study the pictures she'd taken. Veronica gave her a sad, hurt look as she walked past on her way to the front door. *Shit.*

She paused on the threshold. "Sorry, Ronnie. I didn't mean to get you in trouble."

Veronica nodded and smiled. "It's okay, Mac. Detective Maynard doesn't stay mad long and I really don't mind when he yells."

Feeling like the world's worst asshole, Mackenzie left.

CHAPTER THREE

Instead of returning to her car, Mackenzie walked around the block to her favorite coffee shop—independently owned and operated, not part of a national chain. Even with her fast metabolism and perpetual scrawniness, after two slices of pie at the diner, she wanted nothing to eat, but a cup of coffee that didn't taste like scorched cow manure would suit her down to the ground.

Mighty Jo Young's seemed busy all the time, filled with students from the high school, employees from the courthouse and government buildings, and shoppers taking a break from spending their money in the Straightaway shopping center a few blocks away.

As usual, the tables were full, though conversation was subdued. The loudest noises came from a commercial espresso machine, a stainless steel monster which let out long, steamy, angry-sounding hisses at regular intervals. The exclusive operator of the machine was Josephine Joanna Young herself, proprietor and if necessary, bouncer, currently decked out in a sweet rose-pink dress with a white collar, a white belt and a full, flouncy skirt.

Mackenzie tipped an imaginary hat to the feminine and frilly Jo-Jo, a friend since high school and the largest woman she'd ever known. Jo-Jo wasn't just tall. She was built along Amazonian lines, big-boned and broad-hipped, busty enough for watermelon comparisons, and owning biceps the size of cannonballs. Nobody messed with Jo-Jo twice. She'd left Antioch after school to become a star on the women's professional wrestling circuit. After her triumphant return, she could still tie a man's arms in knots behind his head.

"Oh, Kenzie, honey, I heard the police are searching your office!" Jo-Jo cried from her station at the espresso machine without pausing in her scooping, frothing and pouring.

Going to the counter, Mackenzie leaned an elbow on the wooden surface. She avoided the gaze of a barista who appeared too bored to take her order and replied with deliberate casualness, "The construction boys found a body hidden in the wall."

Jo-Jo shrieked and nearly dropped a cup on the floor. "Good Lord! You poor baby!" She flew out from behind the counter to squash her in a hug.

Mackenzie appreciated the gesture as much as she enjoyed having her face enveloped by huge, soft, pillowy mounds of breasts that smelled of talcum powder and Fair Trade Ethiopian coffee. In high school, she and Jo-Jo had tried the sex thing once after getting drunk under the bleachers, but in the harsh light of mutual hangovers, decided it wasn't for them. Still, she felt almost nostalgic at the sensation of suffocation by the nicest breasts in town.

At a certain point, however, she had to breathe or risk passing out. A tap on Jo-Jo's arm had the much larger woman taking a step backward to release her.

Mackenzie grinned. "Thanks for the mammaries," she murmured, an old joke.

Jo-Jo responded by blowing a raspberry, but quickly became serious. "What do you need? A place to stay?" She glanced around and added in a whisper, "A lawyer?"

"I don't think I'm in trouble," Mackenzie said. At Jo-Jo's frown, she added, "You know if I did kill somebody, you'd be the first person I'd call for help moving the body."

After patting her helmet of flaming red curls—the color matched her fingernail polish—Jo-Jo smiled. "Well, as long as you're okay." She adjusted the apron spreading over her generous bosom. "Let me fetch you something to drink. Did you eat lunch yet?"

"Pecan pie at Sampson's Diner. Two pieces, in fact, but I had a meeting with a client."

"Honey, that is *not* a proper lunch. You're going to waste away if you don't get some meat and vegetables in there." Jo-Jo prodded her in the stomach with a long finger. "I'll send D'Ante over to the luncheonette for sandwiches."

When Mackenzie began to protest, Jo-Jo gave her a quelling look. "Hush. You need to eat. That's all there is to it. Mama Jo has spoken."

Mackenzie subsided, knowing further objections were fruitless. Besides, her skinny physique brought out the nurturer in some women who apparently suffered an obsessive need to stuff food down her gullet. When it came to Jo-Jo, she didn't mind.

"Fine," she said. "But I don't like pimento cheese."

"I know," Jo-Jo said mildly. She retreated behind the counter. A few moments later, a young man darted out of the shop.

Scouting around for a place to sit, Mackenzie spotted a table miraculously free of customers. About thirty seconds later, a perfectly made cup of cappuccino was deposited in front of her by a barista. She picked up the thick, white china cup and lifted it to take a sip. Just as the foam touched her upper lip, it felt like something bumped the bottom of the cup, sending hot coffee surging over the rim and spilling down her front.

She didn't quite yell, but the startled curse that shot out of her mouth must have been louder than she thought. Jo-Jo seemed to materialize out of thin air, looming over her with a concerned expression while applying a kitchen towel to her ruined blouse.

"Was the cup too full, honey?" Jo-Jo asked.

"No, I don't…I don't know what happened," Mackenzie answered, trying to recall if she'd imagined the bump. "Got the dropsies today, I guess."

"There's a T-shirt of mine in the back if you want to change."

Mackenzie plucked at her coffee-soaked blouse, lifting the fabric away from her skin. "Yeah, okay, that's a good idea. I want to drop this off at the dry cleaner in a bit."

Five minutes later, she emerged from the ladies' room wearing Jo-Jo's oversized T-shirt. Not only was the garment a lurid pink and printed with daisies, the hem ended well below her knees. She felt like a little kid playing dress up in her mother's clothing.

She reminded herself to be grateful, mouthed "thanks" to Jo-Jo, and resumed her seat. A second cup of cappuccino arrived at the same time as D'Ante delivered her sandwich.

Peeling apart the waxed paper wrapping, Mackenzie was delighted to discover a Miss Laverne's Luncheonette's famous fried chicken sandwich: a crispy breast of buttermilk-marinated, double-fried chicken smothered in Laverne's special family recipe coleslaw and served on a bun with a homemade dill pickle on the side. A cocktail toothpick pinned a small strip of paper to the top of the sandwich.

Mackenzie freed the paper. Laverne Crawford was a devout Christian spinster who believed in spreading God's word far and wide. No sandwich left her shop without a Bible verse tacked to it. The typewritten words on the paper strip read: *And as it is appointed unto men once to die, but after this the judgment. Hebrews 9:27. Jesus saves!*

She set the paper aside.

While she ate the sandwich, she checked the photographs of the body she'd taken with her phone. The resolution on the cell phone's display wasn't great, but the shots remained pretty gruesome. She didn't know why she'd taken photos in the first place. The difficult task of identifying the victim and her killer fell to the police, not her.

In the corner of her eye, she registered movement across the table. She flicked a glance sideways, expecting to see Jo-Jo or someone else she knew. Instead, a strange woman sat in the chair, staring back at her.

"Excuse me," Mackenzie said around a bite of sandwich while trying to hide her mouth behind a raised napkin, "but I'm not—"

In the space between one heartbeat and the next, the woman disappeared.

Mackenzie blinked. She absently swallowed the mouthful of chicken and coleslaw, drank the rest of her cappuccino and licked the foam off her lip. In her experience, people didn't wink out of existence like a blown candle flame.

Could someone be playing a trick on her? How? Why?

She fixed the woman's image in her memory. Her main impression was a lack of color, just silver, gray and black—pearly skin tinged with gray, darker gray lips, sloe eyes lined with black lashes and thick black hair drawn back from an oval face. Not unattractive despite the lack of color, but the woman's unsmiling expression had been cold.

No, not just cold and unfriendly, she decided. Positively frigid.

Her empty coffee cup rattled in the saucer for a second and fell over, the rim cracking with a sound like a gunshot.

Jo-Jo's exclamation carried clearly above the noise of the espresso machine.

Mackenzie rose hastily, left a tip for D'Ante, and hurried out of the coffee shop with her soiled blouse clutched under her arm.

CHAPTER FOUR

Mackenzie crossed the street quickly, feeling chilled despite the heat. What the hell had happened back there in the coffee shop? An image of the gray woman, especially that flat, black gaze, sprang to mind. Cold. Unfriendly. Almost menacing.

She told herself to stop being silly.

Fact: people did not vanish into thin air.

Fact: coffee cups did not spontaneously break of their own accord.

Fact: eyewitness testimony was unreliable. Human memory was fallible, the senses imperfect, the brain given to filling in blanks with fantasy. Just because a person claimed to have seen something did not mean they actually saw it. They just *believed* what they saw, a subtle but important distinction.

The inevitable and reasonable conclusion: she had spilled coffee on herself, become flustered and caught a glimpse of someone—maybe a woman seated elsewhere—which her agitated brain had imagined as a ghostly figure that subsequently disappeared. Afterward, she'd jerked in surprise or bumped the table, breaking her coffee cup.

Satisfied by the logical explanation, she entered the dry cleaners and dropped off her blouse. By the time she reached her office, the event had become a memory of clumsiness and her own embarrassing suggestibility. Tomorrow she'd have to apologize to Jo-Jo for making such a fuss over nothing.

Maynard was still at her office, supervising the removal of the mummified remains into a black station wagon illegally parked in front of a fire hydrant. He'd been joined by Dr. Hightower, a tubby, short, balding gastroenterologist from the hospital over in Trinity, a town about a half hour away. Hightower acted as Antioch's part-time medical examiner at need.

"Don't make faces at me, Jimmy. I spilled coffee on my shirt and Jo-Jo let me borrow one of hers," Mackenzie said when she approached. "I need to change."

Maynard shrugged. "Not my problem. See that yellow tape? Do not cross."

"You know I live above the bakery next door. I'm not snooping. I want to go home. There's a shower with my name on it and a shirt that isn't covered in flowers."

"What did you hope to accomplish by sticking your nose in my crime scene, Kenzie?" he asked, giving her a decidedly evil eye. "You could've compromised evidence."

She returned his glare, though her heart wasn't really in it. "I call shenanigans, Jimmy. There's no evidence and you know it. We already had this argument. As I recall, I won."

"We'll see about that."

"Besides, it's my damned office. I have files in there, things I need to have so I can find things for my clients and make money. I make money, I pay my taxes. Your salary is paid by my taxes. See the way it works? The circle of life. Now do we still have a problem?"

Looking irritated, he waved her through without another word.

Mackenzie sidled past Dr. Hightower. She unlocked a green painted metal door set into a narrow wall between the building that housed her office and the bakery next door.

A fluorescent light flickered on when the door closed behind her, revealing a flight of cement stairs sandwiched between the outer brick walls of the two buildings. The space was claustrophobically small, airless, and hotter than outside. The air was redolent of baking, scented with cinnamon and spices, sugar, yeast and chocolate.

Mackenzie trudged up the steps, trying not to brush her borrowed T-shirt's sleeve on the stained bricks. Another metal door at the top of the stairs—this one painted peacock blue— yielded to another key, and she went inside her apartment, blessedly cool since she'd had the foresight to leave the air-conditioning set on seventy-five degrees that morning.

She dropped her keys on a small table, added her wallet and cell phone and kicked off her shoes before going to her bedroom.

In the act of pulling the oversized pink T-shirt over her head, Mackenzie paused when she caught her reflection in the mirror above the dresser, half expecting to see a silver-gray woman. She relaxed when the mirror only showed familiar amber eyes gazing back at her, set in a face that resembled her maternal great-grandfather more than her mother or father. She'd seen pictures of the stiff-backed old man, long dead before her birth. He'd been a quarter Cherokee and a quarter Creek and two-thirds son-of-a-bitch according to her grandmother. His complicated ancestry lent her complexion its reddish-brown tint, as well as the prominent cheekbones and chin that gave her face a proud aspect.

She changed into a worn cotton shirt and shorts, and ran a brush through her thick, coarse black hair. Moisture in the air had made her naturally kinky hair more unruly than usual, puffing it up into a frizzy mare's nest. Gathering the mass together, she secured the ponytail high on her head with an elastic band to keep it off the back of her neck.

In the living room, she flopped down on the L-shaped sofa and reached for the remote control, which should have been on the side table. When her groping hand closed around nothing, she grimaced, trying to remember where she'd left the remote control. Not on the coffee table. She checked the floor, the chair, even the bookshelves lining the walls. Her search unsuccessful, she returned to the sofa. Where had the remote gone?

She stuck her hand between the sofa cushions, coming up with two dollars and forty-nine cents in change, a silver bracelet she thought she'd lost last week, a handful of popcorn kernels, a ballpoint pen and a lint-fuzzed peppermint. At last, her fingers closed around a solid plastic shape. The remote! Smiling, she drew out...her cell phone.

What the hell? She frowned, certain she'd left her cell phone on the table in the hall.

Mackenzie rose and padded barefoot to the hall. On the little ebony side table with the malachite top, a bijoux French antique and a thrift store find, were her wallet and keys, apparently undisturbed. Yet she clearly remembered leaving her cell phone here, too.

Am I going crazy? The skin on the back of her neck prickled. Goose bumps swept over her arms. Mackenzie inhaled. For a second, she could have sworn she detected the faintest hint of a dry, dusty scent that reminded her of the dead mouse smell in her office. She exhaled and returned to the living room, deciding she had better adjust the thermostat before she froze into a popsicle.

In the living room, her gaze zeroed in on the remote sitting on the side table next to the sofa, exactly where she recalled putting it last night.

"I must be losing my marbles," she muttered, thinking about a few weeks ago when she'd misplaced her car keys in the refrigerator of all places. She carefully put the phone on the coffee table in plain view, sat on the sofa and used the remote to turn on the television.

The screen flared to life, but she was only able to press the button for the next channel before the television clicked off. She turned it back on. As soon as the picture appeared on the screen, she tried to change the channel. Again, the television cut off.

Mashing the ON button did nothing. The remote was dead.

"What the hell?" Must be something wrong with the batteries.

Growing annoyed, Mackenzie heaved herself off the sofa and stomped to the kitchen for fresh batteries. When she returned and replaced the remote's batteries, the television remained stubbornly off when she pressed the remote's ON button several more times. She turned on a lamp, confirming the electricity in the apartment was working. The problem must be with the television itself.

She knelt on the floor to check behind a bookcase for the electrical outlet, making the baffling discovery that the television wasn't plugged in. But it had turned on twice, hadn't it? Stretching her arm as far as possible, she grabbed the cord, plugged in the television and sat back on her heels to use the remote.

Nothing happened. She scowled.

Her cell phone rang.

She retrieved her phone and answered, "Cross speaking."

"You ever hear of Annabel Coffin?" Maynard asked without preamble.

"Who?" she replied.

"She was buried behind your office wall."

Mackenzie crossed to the sofa and sat down. "Don't know her."

"Doc Hightower found a charm bracelet on the body when it was being moved," Maynard said, the line crackling slightly with static. "One of the charms was inscribed with that name. I'm trying to find out if anyone knew her."

"And you called because you miss hearing me talk? I told you before, Jimmy, I moved into the office three years ago. The body must've already been there. Why would you think I'd know anything about this dead woman?"

"I called because I want you to ask your mother about her."

Mackenzie's stomach lurched in alarm. "What does Mama have to do with any of this?"

"According to another inscription on a different charm, the victim attended high school in the same year as your mother. It's possible she'll recognize the name."

Put that way, how could she refuse? "Fine, I'll go over there tonight," she said. "Although I don't know why you can't just talk to Mama yourself."

"Let me know what you find out." He terminated the call.

She stared at the phone in her hand and snorted. Putting down the cell phone on the coffee table, she went to grab the remote, only to find it gone.

After a brief, internal debate, she walked to the hall. Sure enough, the remote sat on the ebony and malachite table.

Unbidden, memories of campfire stories and family legends sprang to mind. Her great-uncle Stapleton swore he'd seen a ghost in an abandoned funeral parlor when his friends had dared him to peer inside the window. And great-grandmother Beryl Rose had maintained to her dying day that the spirit of a child haunted a well on her property.

Like many small Southern towns, the city of Antioch had its share of strange happenings. As a child, she'd heard about the ghostly motorcycle rider on Conklin "Haint" Hill, the crying stone angel in the old Oak Grove Cemetery, the ghost of a headless woman who groped along the railroad tracks near the Weatherholtz Bridge on full moon nights and other restless spirits. She hadn't believed a grain of truth existed in the stories until now, when she was forced to reconsider her skepticism.

The more she tried to find an explanation for the television becoming unplugged and the remote and her cell phone shifting places without human intervention, the more she came to the reluctant conclusion that the cause might—just maybe—be supernatural.

Cold dread settled heavy in her guts. Feeling foolish as well as apprehensive, she returned to the living room and cleared her throat. "Uh…is anybody there?" she asked aloud, praying she wouldn't receive a reply.

After several minutes of waiting, no answer seemed forthcoming.

Sighing in disappointment mingled with relief, she turned away, only to violently start when the television came on with a blast of sound that left her deaf to her own scream.

CHAPTER FIVE

Her nerves shattered, Mackenzie fumbled with the remote and finally turned off the television. She found the sudden lack of sound more unsettling than the noise, but feared putting on the stereo or her computer. Who knew what else might happen next?

She threw the remote on the coffee table and fixed her gaze on it. If the device moved so much as an inch, she'd see it. She stared until her eyes watered, but the remote remained in place, sitting close to a stack of magazines she hadn't had time to read.

Blinking to clear her blurry vision, she thought she caught movement close to her face. She shied away from a long, luminous, silver-gray blob that vanished when she looked directly at it. Lowering her eyelids, she glanced at the spot obliquely. The blob reappeared, resolving into a woman's gray-skinned hand reaching for the magazines.

Mackenzie made the mistake of trying to focus on the outstretched hand. Exactly as before, the second she put the apparition in the center of her vision, it disappeared.

The stack of magazines toppled over and fanned out across the table's surface, exactly as if someone had pushed it. Mackenzie's heart knocked against her ribs. She didn't know what to do. Screaming and running away seemed like a good idea, but to where?

One of the magazines lifted into the air, the pages flapping like a bird trying to take flight, and in the next second, hurtled across the space to slap the wall next to her head.

Abruptly, Mackenzie lost her temper. The situation reminded her of school, when her petite, perpetually thin, flat-chested physique made her a target for bullies. Being called names like "Olive Oyl," "Skinny Minnie," and "Ironing Board" had hurt. She'd learned to ignore such taunts as the rantings of unintelligent ass clowns who ate boogers for fun. Physical threats and violence against her, however, were met with instant retaliation.

She stood. "All right, that's enough!"

In the corner of her eye, she caught sight of a woman standing beside the coffee table, the same pearly gray, black-haired and black-eyed woman she'd seen in Jo-Jo's coffee shop. By this time, she'd figured out not to scrutinize the strange figure too closely.

The woman sneered, her dark gray lips lifting to show shiny white teeth.

"I'm serious," Mackenzie warned. "I'm sick of this shit. If you wanted my attention, goddamn it, you've got it."

The dry, musky smell she associated with the body grew stronger. She shivered. Without warning, something hit her on the head, bounced off and clattered to the floor. Cursing, she glanced down to find her cell phone at her feet.

"Lady, you keep doing that, I swear I'll get an exorcist in here," she snapped. "Baptist, Methodist, Pentecostal, Episcopalian, Catholic…whatever your flavor, I reckon I've got you covered. If that don't do it, there's a Buddhist temple and monastery on Copper Ridge and the Wiccan coven meets on the second Tuesday of the month at Myrtle Johnson's house."

The cell phone's display lit up, showing a picture she'd taken of the body in the wall. She heard a soft hissing that seemed very close to her ear, and at the same time very far away, like the muffled sound of a radio playing in another room.

The hiss resolved into whispers, at first unintelligible, but definitely an attempt at deliberate communication. Mackenzie concentrated. The whispers became clearer.

Know me? the ghost asked slowly at last.

To Mackenzie, the "voice" wavered in and out. She fixed her gaze on a spot about two inches above the apparition's head, which seemed to work as long as she didn't focus closely. "I think you're Annabel Coffin, or at least that's what the police believe." She paused. "You don't know who you are?"

Why?

"Why what?"

The cell phone rattled on the floor. *Who?*

"I don't understand what you're asking. I also don't understand why you're haunting me," Mackenzie said. "I didn't do anything to you and you certainly didn't die here."

Why? Annabel repeated, her gray hands clenching into fists, her black eyes filled with icy animosity.

"Why did you die? I don't know. You were murdered, though, unless you managed to commit suicide after burying yourself behind a wall."

Annabel let out a wail that climbed the scale to a soprano shriek making Mackenzie's eardrums pop, and then the ghost abruptly winked out of existence.

Mackenzie turned on her heel to survey the entire room including the ceiling. Nothing. The troublesome and apparently confused Annabel was nowhere to be seen.

"Was it something I said?" she asked into the silence.

All at once, her bravado crumbled. She hurried to her bedroom, put on a pair of jeans and sandals and grabbed her keys on the way out of the apartment. Screw the cell phone. If anyone needed to speak to her, they'd leave a message on her voice mail.

When she exited at the bottom of the steps to stand on the pavement outside, she discovered Dr. Hightower's station wagon was gone. So was the patrol car. Scowling, she noticed someone—probably Maynard, that pain in the ass—had fastened more bright yellow crime scene tape across her office's front door.

She decided to leave the tape for now. Crossing the street, she shoved the events with the ghost to the back of her mind. Some things didn't bear close examination, not until the shine wore off, as her father used to say. She got into her car and hightailed it east toward her mother's neighborhood.

A South Carolina native who'd moved with her family to Antioch as a young woman, Sarah Grace Cross née Maynard still lived in the same white, two-story, wooden clapboard house where she'd married and made a home with her husband and only daughter.

In Mackenzie's early childhood, her father had extended the front porch to stretch across the entire width of the house, but otherwise the structure remained much the same as what her grandfather had purchased after returning home from World War II.

Mackenzie parked her car under the shade of a pecan tree. The moment she turned off the engine, and with it the air-conditioning, she began to sweat.

"Hey Mama," she called when she exited the car and walked up to the porch.

"Hey baby," Sarah Grace replied in her low, slow, gliding Charleston drawl that drew out the vowels to a maddening degree. She reached up to tip her watering can over a hanging basket filled with drooping pansies, the gesture so graceful, she didn't spill a drop of water on her light denim shirtwaist dress. A stray breeze ruffled through the mop of cropped, coarse gray curls covering her head. "You want a glass of iced tea?"

"Sounds good. I swear, it's hotter than two rabbits making babies in a wool sock. I feel about to melt." Mackenzie pressed a kiss to her mother's wrinkled cheek. The powdered and lightly rouged skin felt impossibly soft against her lips.

Sarah Grace set down the watering can and turned toward the screen door. She moved on her house slippers in a perpetual cloud of Chantilly, her favorite perfume. "I guess you'd better come in and tell me what you want."

"Mama, can't I just want to see you?" Mackenzie asked, following Sarah Grace's finely boned figure inside the dim, still house. The screen door swung shut behind her.

"Baby, I know you 'cause I made you myself." Sarah Grace's sharp blue gaze arrowed straight through Mackenzie, daring her to protest. "You never visit unless I call and ask, or unless you've got a bee in your bonnet about something. Out with it." She led the way into the kitchen, opened the refrigerator and removed a pitcher of tea.

"All right, all right, if you must know, Cousin James asked me to talk to you."

"James Austin, my brother Dillard's boy."

"No, Mama. He's Uncle Anse's son with Aunt Ida Love."

"Oh, yes. That's right. He's a police detective, I recall. James Austin, I mean, not my oldest brother Anderson. A good boy, that nephew of mine. I like him. He doesn't need an excuse to visit his favorite aunt."

"Yes, ma'am."

Sarah Grace filled two glasses with ice cubes from the freezer, added lemon slices and poured tea to the brims. She placed a glass in front of Mackenzie. "And what does James Austin want from me that he couldn't ask his own self?" She sat at the kitchen table, her spine straight despite the years evident in her liver-spotted hands.

Mackenzie took a sip from the glass, almost shuddering in pleasure at the balance between sweet tea and bitter lemon captured on her tongue. The chilled liquid slid down her throat, cooling her from the inside out. "Well, you know my office is having some repairs done," she began, only to halt when her mother held up a hand.

"I know about them boys finding that poor woman's body in your office," Sarah Grace said, giving Mackenzie a disapproving look.

"How'd you know about that? The story won't be in the paper until tomorrow and I'm sure it ain't on the news yet."

"I had to hear about it from my hairdresser, Mrs. Dewey Broom. She called me a few minutes ago. Her eldest son, Charles, is married to Edna Stafford's daughter, Loretta, who's a dispatcher at the Antioch police department, but you could have called me yourself, you know," Sarah Grace scolded, her expression smug.

The Internet had nothing on the small town telephone tree when it came to information dissemination, Mackenzie thought, shaking her head. "The police think the dead woman may be Annabel Coffin," she said as her mother continued giving her the stink-eye. "Jimmy wants to know if you or Daddy knew Annabel when y'all were in high school. Do you remember anything about her?"

She didn't say a mumbling word about the ghost, mostly to avoid unwanted advice. Despite being a devout Episcopalian and much involved with the church, Mama loved anything to do with spiritualism. Mention the haunting, and she'd veer off on a tangent regarding communicating with spirits according to the latest television psychic.

For several moments, Sarah Grace sipped her tea, clearly considering the question. "Your daddy and I knew a girl named Ann Coffin in our last year of school," she finally said. "Good heavens, that was a long time ago. Nineteen fifty-seven, I believe. We were hardly more than children then. Well, me and your daddy were seventeen. Ann was our same age."

Mackenzie tried not to fidget, hoping her mother's reminiscences weren't about to delve too deeply into "good old days" territory that had nothing to do with her query.

"Kindly pay attention, since you asked me in the first place," Sarah Grace said sharply.

"Sorry Mama."

"As I was saying, we were all so young. Ann Coffin was going with a boy on the baseball team...let me see, what was his name? Oh, yes, I do believe it was Franklin Follett. Bless his heart, Frankie died in the Vietnam War, you know. Blown to pieces, so I heard."

"What happened to Annabel?"

"Ann took up with an unsuitable beau." Sarah Grace's frown deepened. "I don't rightly recall his name. He looked like Marlon Brando in *The Wild One*. Very handsome. All the girls in town were a-flutter, but Ann caught his eye. She couldn't drop Frankie fast enough, which I think is why he never married before he passed on, bless his heart."

"The Marlon Brando look-alike, do you know anything about him?" Mackenzie asked, anxious to prod her mother back on topic.

Sarah Grace made a face, but went on. "This boy—I suppose I ought to call him a young man since he was our age, I just can't remember his name—ran a still somewhere in the mountains and sold moonshine out the back of a truck. He didn't go to school with the rest of us. He quit his schooling young, I heard, and used to run around wild with those no-account Gascoigne brothers, who never did a lick of honest work in their lives."

Mackenzie nodded encouragement.

"Ann was smitten, I tell you, completely smitten with her young man. She wouldn't hear a word against him. Not from her mama, her daddy, her pastor, her family or her friends. I didn't know her very well, but I tried talking to her after communion one Sunday. Her family and ours both went to All Saints' Church." Sarah Grace sniffed. "I don't mind telling you, Ann gave me what-for. She called me names that no lady ought to know, let alone speak to another lady. She said I was just jealous 'cause she'd caught the handsomest boy in town. And I was already engaged to your daddy at the time!"

"That little heifer," Mackenzie murmured, affecting an appropriate degree of shock.

Huffing, Sarah Grace sat back in her chair, crossed her arms over her chest, and glared down her patrician nose at Mackenzie. "You can put that attitude away right this minute, my girl. If you'd rather be doing something else than listening to an old woman's rambling, I have some chores to do before my program comes on."

"Sorry Mama."

"I mean, if you can't even show your own mother a little respect—"

"I really want to hear about Annabel, I promise. I'm sorry."

"Fine. But there's no need to speak to me that way."

Mackenzie bit her tongue and tried her best to seem repentant.

At last, Sarah Grace nodded. "Don't do it again."

"Yes Mama."

Sarah Grace let her stew for five long minutes. Mackenzie drank half her iced tea and thought about crunching an ice cube between her teeth, but that would be too cruel.

"Needless to say," Sarah Grace said when she deemed Mackenzie had learned her lesson, "the whole thing with Ann ended in tears. Ann's parents forbade her to see the boy. They got the sheriff, who at the time was Mrs. Coffin's brother-in-law, to run him out of town. I heard a couple of deputies beat him up pretty bad and drove him over the county line. It wasn't right, but that's how things were done back then. To my knowledge, nobody from Antioch ever laid eyes on Ann's young man again."

"How'd Annabel take it?"

"About how you'd expect. She swore she'd run away and find him, but nobody believed her. Young girls make big talk sometimes. Doesn't mean anything. After he was tossed out of town, everybody figured she'd get over him and take up with Frankie Follett again, but instead, she disappeared one night."

Mackenzie's interest was piqued. "Did she run away? When did it happen?"

"Oh, a few weeks after graduation. She ran away, all right. Everybody assumed Ann had gone after her no good boyfriend." Sarah Grace's voice dropped to a hoarse whisper. "She'd been pining, poor girl. The night she ran away, she looked pale as death and sick as a dog. I know because I overheard Mrs. Coffin talking to my mother in church. My mama would have smacked me senseless for eavesdropping if she'd known."

Sarah Grace fell silent, her gaze far away. Mackenzie joined her mother in reflecting on Grandma Maynard—a dainty, soft-spoken, iron-willed, terribly frightening woman who'd ruled like a despot over her brothers, her husband and her children.

Sarah Grace roused herself. "Mrs. Coffin said that Ann packed a suitcase and must've climbed out her bedroom window in the middle of the night. Nobody saw her leave town and nobody ever saw her after that either. She might as well have dropped off the face of the earth. And then, of course, Mr. and Mrs. Coffin died in a terrible car accident later in the year. Drunk driving, so they said, him being a little too fond of the bottle. In all the fuss with the double funeral and such, I suppose Ann and that boyfriend of hers were forgotten."

"Did the Coffins have other children?"

"No, Ann was an only child. Maybe that's why she was so willful. Spoiled, I should say. Her father's princess, her mother's despair."

"Thank you. I'll be sure to let Cousin Jimmy know everything you told me, Mama. If you remember anything else—"

"When you get to be my age, the past comes to mind more easily than the present," Sarah Grace said, pushing back her chair and standing. "I'll think on it some more. Are you done with your tea?" She didn't wait for an answer, but took both glasses to the sink. "By the by," she remarked over her shoulder, "your aunt Ida Love is having hip replacement surgery on Saturday at the hospital in Trinity. I want to visit her and I want you to go with me some time." The statement came out in the familiar steely voice that brooked no arguments.

"Yes Mama."

"Ida Love used to babysit for us when you were a little girl and your daddy and I went out for an evening at the drive-in. She took you to the county fair, too, and on that trip to Memphis that one time, so I expect you to be good to her, is that clear?"

Mackenzie recalled Aunt Ida Love's fresh peach cake with fondness, as well as her generosity in buying fair treats like corn dogs, unlimited rides passes and extra tickets for the midway games. She agreed to drop by on Monday to pick up her mother for the trip to Trinity, gave her another kiss, and left the house.

In the car on the way back to town, she turned on the radio. The latest pop hit blared from the speakers. Grimacing, she turned down the volume.

A tunnel loomed ahead, a dark hole faced with faded brick, cutting over fifteen hundred feet through the squat bulk of Old Briar Hill. She flipped on the car's headlights just before driving into the semidarkness, lit only by the openings at the entrance and exit.

Suddenly, a darker shadow flitted in front of the car. She gasped, her heart in her throat, automatically stomping on the brakes and jerking the wheel to one side. The bumper scraped along the tunnel wall, making a terrifying screeching noise before she managed to bring the car to a shuddering halt.

Mackenzie remained rooted to the spot, breathing hard, her hands fixed to the wheel in a white-knuckled grip.

After a while, the ticking of the cooling engine cut through her thundering heartbeat. She debated whether to get out of the car and survey the damage—and risk being hit by another car from behind—or drive out of the tunnel and off the road before stopping.

She opted to check now despite the danger. *Something* had jumped in front of her car. She hadn't felt an impact, but that might have been masked when she scraped the bumper on the wall. If she had hit an animal, it could be lying in the road or under the car, injured or dying. The shadow had been too small for a deer. A rabbit maybe? Or a fox.

Weak in the knees, Mackenzie almost fell over getting out of the car. She quickly regained her balance and went to the front of the car. The bumper was scuffed, but that appeared to be the only damage. Thank God she drove her late father's classic 'seventy-two Datsun 510. The vehicle might be a poor man's BMW, but it was solid.

Both headlights still worked, illuminating an empty stretch of road. She glanced in every direction. No animal present, unless she'd grazed it. No, she decided a moment later, no blood on the asphalt either. But she could have sworn she'd seen...

An icy prickling swept from the nape of her neck to her breasts.

Mackenzie turned around to find a pair of cold black eyes staring at her.

CHAPTER SIX

"Damn it!" Mackenzie exclaimed, sagging back against the car's hood. All these frights were giving her a hell of a cardiac workout "You nearly got me killed, Annabel."

I remember, Annabel whispered.

"You remember what?"

Him in the woodshed.

"Who? Your boyfriend? The one who looked like Marlon Brando?" Spotting a truck approaching from a distance, Mackenzie straightened. "Can you ride with me? Because I'm not about to be flattened and become a ghost myself." She got into the car and carefully pulled out of the tunnel. After driving down the road about five minutes, she asked self-consciously, "Hey, are you there, Annabel?"

No answer.

Trying a second and third time yielded the same result—nothing. It occurred to her that just an hour or so ago she'd fled her apartment in a sweating terror because of Annabel, and now she was annoyed and worried that the ghost wasn't responding to her calls.

On the way to her apartment, she passed Stubbs Park, an irregular and lush green triangle set across the street from the courthouse. The grass and trees looked cool and inviting. Acting on impulse, she made a U-turn, parked, dug in her pocket for change for the meter and walked into the park.

The clock on the cupola of the courthouse struck five. A few minutes later, a steady stream of office workers exited the buildings, most headed toward the parking garage two blocks away. No one entered the park and no one appeared to take any notice of her.

Mackenzie took a seat on the fountain's cement rim and stayed a while, enjoying the chill, wet spray that sprinkled her skin every time the wind blew her way, bringing with it the smell of wisteria from vines trained across a trellis surrounding a nearby bandstand.

From her position, she had a good view of the police station if she turned her head. The place seemed quiet until the front door opened and a white-haired old man stumbled outside and down the steps, followed by a uniformed deputy.

She recognized Veronica Birdwell and sat up straighter. If it had been anyone else, she'd have assumed the deputy shoved the man, but she knew Veronica would sooner strip off in public and dance the hoochie-coochie than harm a senior citizen.

Mackenzie left the fountain and walked over to the police station, arriving in time to hear Veronica speaking to the old man.

"Rev. Wyland, please go home," Veronica pleaded. "If you need a ride, I'll be happy to take you in the patrol car, but you can't proselytize in the park, sir."

Wyland gazed at her solemnly, his dignity intact. "My dear sister in the Lord," he said in a rich, unctuous, cultivated baritone more suited to a politician than a preacher. "There are lost souls right now crying out to be saved. How can you expect me to pay no heed to the spiritual needs of my brothers and sisters? How can I deny them the good Word of God?"

"Reverend, I appreciate that you have a right to freedom of speech." Veronica took a handkerchief out of a pouch on her duty belt and used it to wipe her sweaty face. She had clearly been debating with Wyland a while. "However, Sheriff Newberry wishes to remind you that by city statute, you may only practice your right of free speech in—"

"I know my rights, sister," Wyland interrupted with a slight smile. "I know the laws as well. Thank you for the reminder."

"If you continue breaking the law, I'll have to arrest you on a public nuisance charge."

"Then I will be a martyr for Jesus," he replied without turning a hair.

"You will be booked, sir, and sit in the holding cell over the weekend, and on Monday, be brought before Judge Prescott for arraignment," Veronica said, her tone dry. "Judge Prescott has to attend a microbrew tasting party hosted by her husband's boss on Sunday. Her gout's been acting up. She hates beer, but she'll have to play nice. The judge won't be in a pleasant mood come Monday morning. She might deny bail or set it at a million dollars. Who knows? However, Reverend, if you want to take a chance…" Her voice trailed off.

Wyland's white eyebrows lowered. He appeared to ponder what Veronica had said, but Mackenzie read capitulation in the downward slant of his narrow shoulders. "Very well, sister. I understand you're bound to render your duty unto Caesar—"

"I believe you mean Sheriff Newberry, sir," Veronica interrupted with such an air of innocence, Wyland blinked.

"Be that as it may," he continued after a moment, a touch of asperity entering his voice, "it is clear to me that neither you nor the sheriff have been born—"

"Beg pardon, sir, but that would be news to my mother."

"Born *again*, Deputy. Baptized—"

"I was baptized, sir, some years ago in the Methodist faith."

Wyland went on doggedly, "Baptized with the Holy Spirit. But I see that it is past time I return to tend my small flock. I will pray for you and the sheriff. Don't forget, sister, it is written that the wicked will be held with the cords of his sin."

"Thank you. Have a good day, Reverend," Veronica replied politely.

Confronted by Veronica's mask of bland sincerity, Wyland couldn't take offense. He had no choice except to abandon the effort to intimidate her and make a stately retreat.

Veronica watched him go. She said to Mackenzie, "Rev. Wyland is very devout. A good man, I'm sure."

"You just wish he'd go and be a good man somewhere else," Mackenzie replied.

"Amen." Veronica sighed, and finally turned to look at her. "Hey, Mac, did you need something? Detective Maynard's out of the office but I can call him if its urgent."

"No, that's okay, Ronnie. He asked me to talk to my mama about the victim, which I did, but she didn't tell me anything that can't wait until tomorrow." Mackenzie paused. Should she tell Veronica about the ghost of Annabel Coffin showing up? Better keep it to herself. No need to cast doubt on her sanity. Veronica was her friend, but the tale sounded far too fantastic to be believed.

"Well, I'd better get back to work." Veronica hesitated. "Mac, would you like to have dinner with me tonight?" she finally blurted.

For a split second, Mackenzie's heart leaped with astonishment and joy. A moment later, reality struck like a punch to the gut. Veronica wasn't asking her on a date.

She stood on the sidewalk, baking in the heat and coming to the bitter realization that Veronica had just wanted to ask her very best *friend* to their very first girls' night out at a sit-down restaurant, goddamn it. She felt sick, but hid her disappointment. "Sure, Ronnie," she replied with all the fake perkiness she could muster, manufacturing a smile until her jaw ached. "Where'd you like to go?"

Veronica flushed pinker to the tips of her ears. "Um...I thought...well, how about Swine Dining? That new place over by the railroad. You like barbeque, right? The *Antioch Bee*'s restaurant critic gave it a four-towelette review."

"Sounds good to me," Mackenzie replied, puzzled by Veronica's anxious glances. What was going on? Was something wrong?

"They have fried pickles. You told me you liked fried pickles. Oh! And I called over there today to ask about the black bean cake on the menu, because I thought that sounded kind of odd, but it turns out the cake isn't dessert. It's like a vegetarian burger thing."

"Are you okay?" Mackenzie ventured. "How's everything?"

"Peachy," Veronica said overly brightly. "I'll pick you up in an hour. Is that all right?"

The bottom of Mackenzie's stomach dropped out when Veronica touched her arm and then snatched her hand away and practically ran inside the station. The warm touch had felt good on her skin, like sunshine after a storm. Closing her eyes, she imagined how wonderful it would feel if Veronica offered her more than just a fleeting gesture. If Veronica hugged her, for example. Or kissed her, those soft pink lips parting under her mouth…

She crushed the fantasy before it could go any further.

Get over it, she told herself with a mental shake. Veronica wasn't romantically interested in her, or any other woman for that matter. *Ronnie is straight. Falling for a straight girl will only end in heartbreak. Besides, it's just dinner, for cryin' out loud. Don't mean a thing except Ronnie's hungry, craving smoked pig, and doesn't want to eat alone.*

Why did her perfectly good, perfectly logical reasoning seem like bullshit?

CHAPTER SEVEN

Following a lukewarm shower, Mackenzie tied back her flyaway hair with a red kerchief, put on a pair of khaki cargo pants and a sleeveless plaid shirt, added worn work boots and met Veronica outside her building when she drove up in a new Ford truck.

She opened the passenger side door and began climbing into the cab, only to stop and stare in bewilderment.

Veronica looked exceptionally smart in a navy blue, off the shoulder silk dress that seemed more suited to a cocktail party. A discreet string of pearls gleamed around her neck. She'd arranged her brunette hair in a smooth French twist and applied makeup with a subtle hand, just mascara, a smudge of eyeliner and a sheen of lip gloss. The style suited her.

Mackenzie glanced down at her own outfit, which at best might be described as hobo chic, and felt the lack of fashion keenly. "We're still going to Swine Dining, right?"

"That's right," Veronica replied, giving her a smile. "Don't forget to buckle up," she added when Mackenzie sat down on the bench seat. "Safety first."

"That's a beautiful dress, Ronnie," Mackenzie said when the truck pulled away from the curb. "The blue color suits you."

"Thanks, Mac. I don't get the chance to wear it often."

Ah, that explains the fancy getup. Mackenzie relaxed slightly. Veronica was using their dinner as an opportunity to be a pretty woman for once instead of a sheriff's deputy. Still, the contrast between her own careless, casual clothing and Veronica's stunning dress and pearls made her feel as out of place as an atheist in church.

Swine Dining was housed in the former Antioch railway station, a modest, turn-of-the-century building that had remained unoccupied since the highway came to town in the fifties. To Mackenzie's amusement, the owner had done some sympathetic restoration work on the exterior and then spoiled it by adding a huge neon sign in the shape of a bright red pig running away from a barbeque fork stuck in its rear end.

Mackenzie exited the truck and joined Veronica, who wobbled toward the restaurant. She soon discovered the reason for the unsteadiness: the parking lot was covered in a layer of gravel rather than asphalt and Veronica wore impractical high heeled shoes that made her legs seem longer and more luscious.

The dress hugged Veronica's curves in flattering ways. Mackenzie's mouth watered from more than the scents of burning pecan wood and barbequing pork and brisket wafting around the air on puffs of smoke. The low neckline exposed Veronica's shoulders and chest down to the tops of her round breasts, as nice as Jo-Jo's in quality, if not quantity.

Mackenzie took a moment for naked admiration before controlling herself. Letting Veronica see how much she'd love to throw her down on one of the parking lot picnic tables, rip off that navy blue dress, mess up that perfect hairdo and lick her all over would only make the evening awkward. She offered an arm to Veronica for support while they crossed the gravel expanse to the restaurant's front door.

After being seated and placing an order for an appetizer platter and Snakehead Brown Ale, Veronica faltered. "It is nice, isn't it?" she asked plaintively.

Mackenzie gazed around at the whitewashed walls hung with license plates, piggy collectibles, bizarre antique tools, vintage car parts and beer signs. "So far, so good," she said, taking pity on Veronica, who appeared ill at ease.

The waitress returned soon, bearing bottles of ale and an oversized plate of fried pickles, burnt ends of brisket, hot wings drowning in sauce, chunks of house smoked sausage and fried green beans with blue cheese dip.

Thoughtfully trying a crunchy, tangy pickle, Mackenzie decided a restaurant like Swine Dining would be wasted on vegetarians and supermodels. The only salad she'd seen on the menu was composed of chopped iceberg lettuce with a fried green tomato on top.

Veronica picked at the food, avoiding the hot wings altogether—a wise move, Mackenzie considered, as the chef dished out hot sauce by the pint. Strangely out of character, Veronica also didn't speak to her or even glance at her, but polished off a bottle of brown ale in a few gulps and ordered a second from a passing waitress.

Mackenzie sipped from her bottle despite the urge to chug-a-lug just as quickly. "How long has it been?" she asked, desperate to end the painful silence.

"What?" Veronica's green eyes grew impossibly wider, as if Mackenzie had asked an unexpected and unwelcome question. "Well, I…I don't…I mean, I do, but…" she stammered, her expression panic-stricken.

"How long has it been since you moved to Antioch?" Mackenzie clarified.

"Oh! Yes, yes, a couple of years already," Veronica replied, flushed and blotting sweat with a paper napkin. "I was glad to leave the Savannah force. They were real good to me and I enjoyed living there, but I was doing more paperwork than policing. Antioch suits me fine."

The brief spurt of conversation ended. Mackenzie's dwindling appetite fled. She and Veronica were friends. They knew each other better than casual acquaintances, which was why she found the uncomfortable atmosphere between them alarming…

Veronica gratefully snatched a fresh bottle from the waitress' tray, and ordered a pulled pork platter and another Snakehead ale.

Mackenzie placed her own order and came to the conclusion that she'd better nurse her single bottle of ale since she'd be the one driving them home tonight if Veronica kept drinking like her liver was her worst enemy.

"Um…hey, Mac, I have something to tell you," Veronica said, still not looking at her, but focused on picking the label off an empty bottle.

"Are you okay?" Mackenzie asked, reaching out to still Veronica's nervous fingers.

"I'm fine, but I—"

"And your family? Everything good?"

"Yes, Mac, they're okay, only I think you should know that I—"

An explanation suddenly occurred to her for Veronica's atypical drinking, the uneasiness, the dinner invitation, the perplexing silences and the skittish glances.

"Oh, God, you're sick, aren't you?" Mackenzie blurted. "Is it cancer?"

"What? No! No," Veronica said, lowering her voice and jerking her hand free from Mackenzie's grasp. "Why would you think that?"

Because I'm an idiot, Mackenzie thought, blaming a childhood fondness for her mother's soap operas on her habit of assuming the worst. She blushed and mumbled a lame excuse, wishing the dinner from hell would end so she could leave and tend to her psychological bruises in private. The waitress swept in with their dinner platters before she could manufacture a plausible excuse that would get her home.

The pulled pork was delicious—moist and not too fatty, laced with a sharp, spicy, vinegary sauce—and the sides of baked beans, corn bread, collard greens and sweet potato casserole were tasty. However, Mackenzie found it difficult to enjoy her dinner with Veronica when the woman kept staring at her so surreptitiously.

At last, after an agonizing amount of time, Veronica pushed her half-eaten platter away. "Do you want dessert? They've got peanut butter pie, bread pudding with bourbon sauce, peach cobbler and 'nanner pudding. Or maybe a cup of coffee."

"No, thanks, I'm pretty full," Mackenzie said, ignoring the muted howling, whining and gurgling as her stomach protested the lie. She'd hardly eaten a thing "Think I'll call it a night, if you don't mind."

"Really? Was the food that bad?"

No, the company, Mackenzie almost said. She kept the mean-spirited observation to herself. "Everything was good, Ronnie. I'm just not that hungry. I'll ask the waitress for a doggy bag. That leftover pork will make a nice sandwich tomorrow for lunch."

"I'll add mine to yours. When you're ready to go, I'll drive you home."

"I don't think so. You've had four Snakeheads since we got here. I'll drop you off at your house. Call me in the morning and I'll run your truck over there."

Veronica looked crestfallen. "Did I drink too much?" she asked in a heart-wrenchingly small voice.

"No, not at all," Mackenzie hastened to say. "I had a wonderful time, Ronnie. I just don't want you to get in any trouble if we're stopped by a state trooper. You know those breathalyzers will pick it up if you're even a fraction of a hair over the legal limit."

"That's true." Veronica appeared to rally, squaring her shoulders as though getting ready to face a challenge. "I'd be honored if you drove me home."

Mackenzie flagged the waitress and asked for the check. When it arrived, she started to take out her wallet, but Veronica stopped her.

"My treat. I asked you out."

"But—"

"Please, Mac, I got this." Veronica opened her purse, fished out a credit card and gave it to the waitress.

Mama would have argued until the crack of doom about who paid the check, Mackenzie thought, but she had made up her mind long ago not to play that pseudo-polite tug-of-war game over a few dollars. Even on a date, she'd offer to split the check. If her offer was rejected, so be it. She wouldn't turn down a free meal.

In the truck on the way home, with Veronica slumped on the passenger side holding the bag that contained her leftovers, Mackenzie recalled an unfinished bit of business.

"What did you want to tell me?" she asked.

Veronica started, the bag on her lap almost toppling over. "Huh?"

"In the restaurant, you said you had something to tell me."

"Oh."

Mackenzie waited a full minute before she prodded, "Well?" The word came out a little more pointed than she'd intended.

Veronica's face looked gray and pinched. "It's not important," she said at last.

"You sure?"

"Yeah."

Shrugging, Mackenzie continued to drive. She sensed something was wrong, but Veronica didn't seem to be in the mood to talk.

Later, she told herself. She'd figure out the problem later, and then she'd fix it. She could do no less for a friend.

CHAPTER EIGHT

The next morning, Mackenzie slapped the alarm silent and rolled out of bed with a groan. She'd been up half the night with heartburn and indigestion, reduced to sitting in the dark on the sofa in front of the television, watching infomercials—to her relief, the remote control and television behaved themselves—and swigging Pepto-Bismol from the bottle. The thought of eating leftover barbeque for lunch did not sit well.

She shuffled into the bathroom, took a hot shower, belched acid, and brushed her teeth. After contemplating her bleary-eyed reflection in the mirror, she ran a comb through the rat's nest of her hair and dragged her feet to the bedroom.

Thinking about the mess in her office gave her a headache, but she decided not to work from home. She got dressed and followed the smell of coffee into the small kitchen. Thank God for whomever had invented the programmable coffeemaker.

She poured a cup of strong brew into her favorite mug, added a splash of half-and-half and carried the coffee with her to the front door.

Delicious smells rose from the bakery below, including a whiff of hot oil. Mackenzie grinned and opened the door to find a small box sitting at the top of the stairs. As per the rental agreement, the bakery's owner provided her with fresh baked goods every morning. If her nose was correct, today's offering was—she picked up the box and lifted the cover—a deep fried cinnamon roll drizzled with maple glaze and bits of crunchy bacon.

Happy to the depths of her greedy soul, she padded back into the kitchen carrying the box. She unfolded a small vintage card table made of Danish birch, a flea market find, and sat down on a red painted wooden chair to enjoy her unhealthy breakfast.

Just as she took the first bite, she heard the glass coffeepot rattling behind her.

"Go 'way," she said indistinctly, her mouth full of sweet, crunchy, salty deliciousness. Whatever Annabel Coffin wanted could wait until she finished her treat.

The rattling grew louder and more ominous.

Annoyed, Mackenzie put down the half-eaten cinnamon roll and started to turn in her seat. A silver-gray streak flashed in her vision seconds before the coffeepot exploded, showering her with glass splinters. She managed to get an arm up to shield her face. Her short-sleeved T-shirt protected her torso, but the rest of her exposed skin stung from dozens of tiny cuts. She lowered her arm and glared sidelong at the space in front of the counter.

Annabel didn't appear as a full-body apparition this time. Instead, the ghost remained a smoky smudge with no visible features.

"I can't believe you did that," Mackenzie said, switching her glare to the glittering carpet of glass fragments on the wood laminate floor. "And I can't believe I'm going to have to walk barefoot to get the broom, damn it."

When she scooted the chair back from the table she saw that her breakfast was ruined too. She grabbed the bakery box with the ruined cinnamon roll and stuffed it into the trash.

By the time she minced to the broom closet, leaving a small blood trail behind, and cleaned up the glass, Mackenzie was furious. She disinfected various minor cuts and stripped naked so she could shake out her clothes over a spread newspaper.

After retreating to the bedroom to change into a green cotton blouse, denim capri pants and a pair of sneakers, she returned to the kitchen and said with heartfelt conviction, her hands on her hips, "That's it. I'm done, Annabel. You can go to hell."

One of the cabinet doors creaked open and slammed shut with a tooth-jarring bang.

Mackenzie ignored the provocation. "Goddamn it, what do you want from me?"

The woodshed.

"You said that before. What does it mean? Where is this woodshed?" Blowing out a frustrated breath, Mackenzie tried to will away the knot in her chest. "What do you want?" she repeated, suddenly more tired than hostile.

What happened? Where's Billy?

"You were killed a while back, I think. I'll let you know what I find out. Who's Billy?" At least Annabel had grown a little more coherent since last time.

Billy Wakefield.

"He's the boy you ran away with?"

Annabel took a long minute to answer. *I love him*, she said slowly at last. *We're going to New York City.*

Mackenzie had never heard of Billy Wakefield, or any Wakefields for that matter, living in Antioch or one of the nearby towns. Was this the name of Annabel's young man, the budding Romeo her parents had had run out of town? She'd ask her mother. "Okay, you were supposed to meet Billy in the woodshed so y'all could run away together to New York. What else do you remember?"

*I went to the woodshed, and...and...*Annabel broke off with a wail that sounded like the mosquito whine of a dentist's drill with the volume amped up to eleven.

"Christ!" Mackenzie stuck her fingers in her ears, which helped dull the sound of Annabel's crying, but not by much. "Could you tone it down a little, please?" she begged.

Where's Billy? Annabel sobbed. *Billy, Billy, Billy…*

A stainless steel fork lifted from the dish drainer next to the sink. Mackenzie flinched, expecting the utensil to fly at her, but it landed on the kitchen table as though tossed underhand. The fork's tines were now bent at several angles and the shaft twisted in a spiral.

When she lifted the fork, the shaft snapped in half.

"Will you get hold of yourself?" Mackenzie shouted when another mangled fork joined the first. "Damn it, Annabel, if you don't stop wrecking my silverware—"

Where's Billy?

"I don't know!"

The eerie crying ended abruptly. *He promised.*

"I'm doing my best here, but you aren't helping by pitching conniption fits." Mackenzie took a deep breath, striving for calm. "Just try to remember what happened."

In the woodshed. A noise. And then it ended.

"What ended?"

Everything.

Mackenzie suppressed a shiver. Sounded like Annabel had been killed in the mysterious woodshed she kept talking about. "What kind of noise did you hear?"

Noise.

"A gunshot? An explosion?"

Behind me.

"Do you know how you…uh, how you got in the wall?"

I ended.

"Well, where have you been all this time?"

Annabel's eyes appeared first, as black as pitch and filled with sadness, no longer cold. The rest of her face and body followed. Mackenzie focused her gaze above the ghost's head to keep her in view, noticing for the first time that Annabel, an attractive young woman, wore a simple belted dress with a Peter Pan collar and a full circle, A-line skirt typical of the fifties. A charm bracelet shone on her left wrist.

Maynard had mentioned finding a charm bracelet on the body, she recalled.

Annabel replied after a pause, *I woke up. Billy gone. You were there. I went with you.*

What had she done to rouse the ghost of the murdered woman? Mackenzie wondered. Had taking pictures of the body stirred things best left undisturbed? No, she realized a moment later. Maynard must have had deputies and crime scene technicians in her office snapping photos and processing the scene. Why had Annabel become attached to her?

She asked and was unsurprised when Annabel didn't provide an answer.

"I really can't put up with you breaking my things all the time," Mackenzie said. She felt sorry for Annabel, but that didn't mean she enjoyed being terrorized.

Annabel remained silent, watching her.

The overhead light flickered three times.

Mackenzie considered the ghost stories she'd read, or seen on television or at the movies. A solution seemed at hand, if the writers weren't lying. "If I help you, if I find out who killed you and why, and what happened to Billy, will you go away? Can you go away?" she added when the thought struck her that perhaps Annabel was stuck somehow, caught between this world and the next.

Tell me, Annabel demanded, her gaze zeroing in on Mackenzie with frightening intensity. *Tell me and I'll go.*

"Deal!" Mackenzie exclaimed.

From the doorway came the sound of someone clearing her throat.

"Hey, Mac...who are you talking to?" Veronica asked hesitantly.

When Mackenzie cast a frantic look toward the counter, Annabel was gone. She buried her face in her hands, asking herself if the day could get any worse.

CHAPTER NINE

"Mac, is everything okay?" Veronica asked, coming into the kitchen

The gentle tone, the same as one might use to calm a spooked horse, got on Mackenzie's last nerve. "Everything's hunky-dory," she snapped. "Can't you tell?"

Veronica's gaze drifted to the coffeemaker. "Did you break your pot?"

Mackenzie sighed. "Something like that."

She eyed Veronica, dowdy as ever in a sheriff's department uniform. The polyester/rayon blend trousers were truly abominable, a color of brown normally associated with baby poop, and the button-down shirt was an insipid tan that washed out her gorgeous complexion. The thick, heavy-duty belt didn't do much for her either.

"Would you like to get breakfast before I go to work?" Veronica leaned a hip against the counter, gazing down at Mackenzie with a smile on her pink, well-scrubbed face. Not a trace of last night's makeup remained. Her brunette hair had been scraped back into a tightly pinned and very serviceable bun at the base of her neck.

Recalling the ruined pastry with regret—and recalling last night's dinner debacle—Mackenzie shook her head. Maybe they needed a little time apart to let the inexplicable awkwardness fade. "Sorry, Ronnie, I've got things to do in the office and I was hoping to get an early start. I want to head over to Sweetwater Hill later today."

"Oh? What do you need on Sweetwater Hill?"

"I'm doing a favor for a friend."

Disappointment briefly flickered in Veronica's expression, but in the next second, she smiled. "If you need anything, you call me, yeah?" Her tone softened. "And Mac, about last night... I'm real sorry if I made you uncomfortable."

Mackenzie didn't know how to respond. Why was Veronica apologizing like she'd done something wrong? Sure, dinner at Swine Dining hadn't gone well, but that was no reason to act like it was her fault.

"No problem. I'm not mad or anything about it," she ventured. "Stuff happens."

"I'm glad to hear you weren't offended."

"Why would I be offended?"

"I was drunk."

"You had a bit too much to drink, that's all. Not like you were slobbering all over me or anything like that. God, that would have been the worst!" Mackenzie's laugh sounded tinny and slightly hysterical to her ears.

Veronica flushed an ugly shade of red.

Feeling as if she'd made a gaffe, Mackenzie asked, "Are you okay?"

"You know me. I'll be fine." Veronica's smile turned brighter and more brittle. "Like you said, everything's hunky-dory."

The wattage of Veronica's grin didn't fool her. Mackenzie had seen that toothy-white crescent when Veronica had faced a drunk armed with a shotgun. Her smile not touching her eyes, she'd strolled up to the guy, grabbed the shotgun's barrel and wrenched the weapon out of his hands just as he pulled the trigger. Thank God the weapon hadn't been loaded.

Then, like now, Mackenzie felt a cold looseness in her lower belly at the sight of Veronica's stony green gaze. To have that distant glance, that false friendliness, that lack of true warmth aimed at her hurt like an open-handed slap.

Screw waiting and time apart, she decided. Clearly, for some unknown reason their friendship had suffered a rupture. She needed to fix this right now.

"How about lunch?" Mackenzie offered. "We can eat in the park. Forget leftovers. I'll spring for that potato thing you like from Shapiro's Deli."

"Knish," Veronica said stiffly. "Actually, I've got to catch up on my paperwork. Thank you kindly for the invitation, though. I'm sure I'll see you around, Mac." She left, holding her spine so rigid, Mackenzie's back ached in sympathy.

Well, wasn't that the most polite rejection she'd ever been given? Mackenzie sat back in the chair, wondering about Veronica and why she had the niggling suspicion that she'd put her foot in her mouth at some point during their conversation.

She replayed the events of the morning and decided to focus on work at the moment. Speculating on her friend's mood swings wouldn't pay the bills—nor would her own bad temper, another inheritance from her late great-grandfather—and she couldn't think of an immediate solution anyway. Her decision made, she picked up her keys and wallet from the hall table on her way out the door.

She walked downstairs and went to the building next door where she tore the crime scene tape off her office door and let herself inside. Her nose wrinkled at the mess the construction workers had left. Not just the workers, she realized, glancing at the floor and the dirty footprints of sheriff's deputies who hadn't bothered wiping their shoes on the mat.

If she had her carpets shampooed and presented a bill to Sheriff Newberry, would he pay it? She thought not, so she settled for grumbling under her breath. Come election time, she knew who wasn't getting *her* vote.

At least her private office remained relatively undisturbed if she didn't count the gaping hole in the wall. She sat at her desk, powered up the computer and checked her email.

A client had contacted her about locating a 1931 Bugatti Royale for sale. She recognized the man's name, a multibillionaire oil sheik from Abu Dhabi. He'd given her work in the past and now sent her a definite challenge.

A few minutes of research on the Internet revealed that only six cars, one of each model, had ever been produced by Bugatti. She frowned. The Limousine Park-Ward, Coupé Napoleon, Berline de Voyage and Cabriolet Weinburger were in museums. The fifth car, the Coupé de Ville Binder, was owned by Volkswagen AG. The sixth car on the list would be her best bet. Ownership of the Kellner was speculative, but not impossible to track down.

Her reply to the email stated the conclusion she'd drawn, along with a statement of her fee if successful. Typing the string of numbers transformed her frown into a smile. In 1987, the last time the Kellner had sold at auction, it brought eight point seven million dollars. Given the vehicle's rarity, the value had to have appreciated since then. Her commission of one percent of the sale price would put a pretty penny in her bank account, provided she could locate the owner and persuade him to sell.

She sent her reply and scrolled through the rest of her inbox, finding junk, junk, more junk, and a joker asking to hire her to find the heart he'd left in San Francisco. Typical. After clearing out her inbox, she pulled up a file containing her ongoing cases.

The rest of the morning was spent making long distance phone calls and hunting clues about the '31 Bugatti Kellner and doing Internet searches on behalf of current clients who hired her to locate objects, usually rare or unusual collectibles, on their behalf.

Most of the items were fairly prosaic: a vintage toy tractor, a certain model of Coke vending machine for a collector in Atlanta, boxing gloves signed by little known champion boxer, Greg Page. Not worth huge amounts of money, but every bit helped pay the rent.

"Yes, I know Martin," she said into the phone at one o'clock, speaking to the owner of a sports memorabilia shop in Las

Vegas, "I know Page died in 'oh-nine, but his signature isn't worth nearly as much as Ali's. I'll be damned if I let my client pay more than a couple of hundred bucks for the gloves and that's a gift. Uh-huh, you get back to me. Bye."

She hung up, satisfied with the deal. Martin would sell. She'd never known him to turn down a fair offer, though of course he'd try to bump up the price if she let him.

Rising from her chair, she put both hands on the small of her back and stretched out the kinks. She'd had a productive day so far. Now she had to shift her focus to Kelly Collier's problem with the Pentecostal preacher, Reverend Wyland.

The drive to Sweetwater Hill cleared her head, the fresh air and sunshine chasing the last of the stuffiness away. She turned off the main route to follow a gravel access road up the hill, driving slowly around the potholes. The recent rainstorms hadn't been kind, and the road's surface was still muddy and very bumpy in patches.

She pulled her car over when she reached the Covenant Rock Church of God with Signs Following. As Kelly had told her, the structure was hardly more than a wooden shack. Looking at the sagging roof, she wondered how the church remained standing.

A half-dozen older model cars, mostly Fords and Chevys, lined both sides of the road—members of Wyland's flock, no doubt, gathering for one of their thrice weekly meetings to take up poisonous serpents and test their faith in God. Mackenzie thought the practice was tempting fate in the most flamboyant way possible.

She got out of her Datsun and took a moment to glance around.

The sun-blasted grass around the church had been recently cut to the tree line. Beyond the cleared area grew a thick tangle of crab apples and wild North Star cherry trees, and beyond them rose taller pines and clusters of hornbeams. In the distance, she glimpsed the blue-gray peak of Laxahatchee Mountain brushing the clouds, with the lower Big Brother and Little Sister Ridges spreading out on either side.

An odd sound intruded on her reverie, a kind of buzzing that didn't come from a bumblebee. Mackenzie glanced down and froze, her mind going blank with horror.

Coiled close to her shoe, a huge diamondback rattlesnake opened its jaws wide to show wickedly curved fangs, and its tail rattled a second warning.

CHAPTER TEN

Mackenzie dared not move. Through an effort of will that tightened her muscles until her body ached under the strain, she denied the instinct to leap away.

Eastern diamondback rattlers were aggressive, dangerously unpredictable and quick to strike, with some of the biggest fangs and venom sacks of any poisonous snake. This particular specimen looked about seven feet long. Unless she suddenly developed instant levitation or teleportation, she wouldn't be able to get out of its strike zone fast enough to avoid being bitten. If she remained calm, the snake might retreat.

The door of the church opened. A teenage girl came outside. She wore an ankle-length white cotton dress and her long blond hair hung loose to her waist.

"Stay back!" Mackenzie croaked.

As if resenting her warning, the rattlesnake's flat, triangular head, as big as a man's fist, darted at her calf, a lightning feint that nearly caused her to scream. The snake's nose struck her, but the fangs didn't penetrate her skin. While she tried to remember how to breathe, the snake coiled itself into a compact, hostile ball, its tail rattling continuously.

"Jesus will be there with you if you call on Him," the girl said, her bare feet skimming the grass as she drew closer. "Remember God is good. Have faith in the Lord. 'Behold, I give unto you power to tread on serpents and scorpions,'" she quoted from the Gospel of Luke. "'And over all the power of the enemy: and nothing shall by any means hurt you.'"

Before Mackenzie could to do more than make an aborted negative gesture, the girl bent and picked up the snake, grunting as she lifted the long, heavy length into her arms.

"Jesus Christ Almighty," Mackenzie said, afraid to move lest she trigger the snake to strike the girl, who swayed and crooned a melody, her crystal pale eyes focused on a spot far away. From within the church came the faint strains of music.

The rattlesnake stretched out its length to lay its huge head on the girl's shoulder beside her ear. Its thin, black tongue flickered out. Mackenzie fought not to scream. A snakebite on or near the artery in the girl's throat, and she'd be dead in minutes.

A man exited the church, a lean figure dressed in a dusty black suit. She recognized Reverend Wyland by his mane of white hair. He approached them with quiet confidence, his gaze moving from the girl to Mackenzie and back again.

"Does the Spirit stir you, Alafair?" he asked the girl.

"Yes, sir," she replied in a dreamy voice, beginning to rock on her heels. The snake remained quiescent.

"Go inside, child," he said in his rich baritone. "Go inside and bring the Spirit of the Lord to your brothers and sisters in Christ."

The church door remained open. A dozen voices lifted in a hymn, "I'm Going Home to Be with Jesus," accompanied by a piano and a guitar. Carrying the rattlesnake across her shoulders like a living boa, Alafair drifted across the grass and disappeared inside.

As soon as she was free to do so, Mackenzie confronted Wyland. Her heart still pounded, but this time in fear for the teenage girl. Her errand for Kelly Collier flew out of her head.

"How dare you encourage that child to handle dangerous snakes! I have a good mind to report you to the police," she said to him indignantly. "If she's bitten—"

"Alafair is not only a child of God, she's my daughter in the flesh," he said mildly. "I have the greatest care for her since her mother's passing."

Mackenzie was surprised Wyland had a daughter that young. She'd thought he was about her mother's age, but as Meemaw Cross used to say, *Ain't no bull so old he can't catch a cow and make a calf.* Of course, modern medicine hadn't invented Viagra in those days.

"She slept with snakes in her cradle," he went on. "Handling serpents is evidence of her salvation, her moral purity and her obedience and trust in the Lord's will. Besides, no harm will come while the Lord's Spirit dwells within her."

From inside the church, a man's deep voice shouted, "Bless Your holy name, Jesus!" followed by a chorus of thanks, praise and amens.

Mackenzie wanted to call Wyland on his bullshit, but his hooded gray eyes, set deep in nests of wrinkles, were lit with the fire of true belief. Arguing with him would be futile. She grudgingly settled for saying, "Your daughter's too young to handle rattlesnakes. It's not against the law. You and your adult congregation are free to practice your religion as you see fit, but I'm fairly certain Sheriff Newberry takes a dim view of child endangerment."

He nodded. "You must act as God wills."

"Unless you want Family Services out here—"

"I will speak to Alafair."

Mackenzie paused, aware of the church service continuing while the pastor patiently waited on her with his hands clasped in front of him, his head cocked to one side. She had made her point. Time to move on. "I was asked to talk to you by Kelly Collier."

Wyland assumed a disapproving expression. "I am familiar with Miss Collier," he said. "Miss Collier and Mr. Dearborn know one another, may God forgive them."

"What do you have against Mr. Dearborn and Kelly? Why do you want him to resign from his church?" Mackenzie asked, genuinely puzzled.

All of the religious institutions in and around Antioch, including the Catholic church in Trinity, got along fine. Even the Wiccan coven had become a little more accepted in recent years, or at least not denounced so often or so thunderously from the various pulpits.

The Holiness Pentecostals were a small sect of a small sect within a Christian sect—in fact, members of the Church of God with Signs Following preferred to think of themselves as nondenominational, believing splitting Christianity into denominations was not commanded by God, but invented by man and therefore demonic—but she'd never heard of a feud between Wyland's people and Dearborn's Methodists.

Wyland laid a hand over his heart. "Jesus saves and the Lord forgives the sinner, though he be dyed in the deepest black to the depths of his soul," he intoned.

Growing frustrated by the lack of answers, Mackenzie asked him bluntly, "What did you see that day in Stubbs Park, Reverend? What were Kelly and Mr. Dearborn doing that's made you take against them so?"

"Only God can pronounce judgment on them as deserves it," he said piously.

"Well, it seems to me like you're doing your damnedest to judge them yourself, sir, considering you've made threats against Mr. Dearborn," Mackenzie countered.

"That man doesn't deserve to shepherd good Christian people," Wyland said, an edge creeping into his voice. "He should step down."

"That's not your call." Mackenzie took a breath, letting her irritation at his vagueness recede. "I'm asking you politely to leave Kelly and Mr. Dearborn alone."

A loud voice issued from the open door of the church, a woman crying gibberish at the top of her lungs. *Speaking in tongues*, Mackenzie thought.

"The Holy Spirit begins to move," Wyland said, "therefore I must be brief. Tell Mr. Dearborn that I will take no action against him now, for what's to come is God's will and lies between him and the Lord. You may say I will pray for him to gain wisdom and the moral strength to do what's right. I will pray for the girl also."

Although Mackenzie had the promise she'd hoped for, she remained unsatisfied. "What *did* you see in the park, Reverend?"

Wyland turned and began walking to the church, pausing halfway to stop and speak over his shoulder. "Sin," he said and continued on his way without uttering another word. He went inside the church and closed the door behind him.

"Damn it," Mackenzie muttered. Try as she might, she could make no sense of Wyland's animosity toward Dearborn.

She decided the matter required further investigation, if only to satisfy her curiosity. Perhaps Dearborn had done or said something to Wyland that Kelly knew nothing about. She'd go and talk to him today before she went home for dinner.

Or maybe Kelly was suffering from pre-wedding jitters and seeing man-eating tigers instead of kittens, she thought. Either way, she'd find out the truth.

CHAPTER ELEVEN

Returning to her car, Mackenzie drove back to Antioch. On the way, her cell phone rang. Although she shouldn't be talking on the phone while driving, she checked caller ID and answered the call. "Hey Mama."

"Hey, baby," said Sarah Grace. "Are you out and about?" In her Charleston accent, the word sounded almost like "aboot."

"I'm in the car."

"That's all right, I just wanted to tell you I was thinking about Ann Coffin and that boyfriend of hers this morning—"

"Mama, his name's Billy Wakefield."

"Gracious, Kenzie, how'd you find that out?"

Mackenzie smirked, though she knew her mother couldn't see her. "I have my ways. Do you know his people? Do they live around here? Is Billy Wakefield still alive?"

"Well, if he passed, he didn't do it in Antioch," Sarah Grace said with the surety of someone who'd lived in a small town for the majority of her life. "You used to find Wakefields yonder to Little Sister Ridge in an itty-bitty place called Emorysville."

"Never heard of it."

"Oh, after the lumber boom petered out, Emorysville dried up like a squashed frog on a hot rock."

"And the Wakefields used to live there."

"Yes baby, but when the mill closed, a lot of folks left town. And of course, there was the murder. Really took off the shine. The town went downhill lickety-split after that."

Mackenzie pulled off the road, put on the car's emergency blinkers and focused her attention on the phone call that had suddenly become interesting. "What murder?"

"It was in the paper, I recall. Terrible tragedy. The whole Wakefield family was killed by a hobo. Or a crazy person, maybe. I don't remember." Sarah Grace fell silent, and then suddenly exclaimed, "Oh! I forgot to tell you. I remembered Billy Wakefield had a tattoo."

With difficulty, Mackenzie shifted mental gears, putting the matter of the murder aside for the moment. "Okay."

"On the back of his wrist."

"Okay."

"Mackenzie Lorelei Cross, are you listening to me?"

Mackenzie sighed as quietly as possible. Her mother had wandered off topic, not unusual for a woman her age. The recollection about Billy's tattoo had no relevance to a murder in Emorysville as far as she could tell. "Yes Mama. Billy Wakefield had a tattoo."

"You young people today…" Sarah Grace released her own sigh in a gust of breath. "Folks were different back then. Tattoos were just for sailors, or men who'd been to jail, or delinquents and no-goodniks. Really, the way you children run around these days covered head to toe in tattoos, looking like a bunch of savages—"

"Mama please," Mackenzie broke in. "Apart from the fact he had a tattoo at all, what was so special about Billy Wakefield's ink?"

Sarah Grace sniffed. "A cartoon girl's head. She wore a sailor's hat. Not what you'd call pretty or even well done. Just crude black lines. I thought you'd like to know."

"Thank you, Mama. Now, you were telling me about a murder in Emorysville."

"I don't remember much. It was summer around nineteen seventy-five, I guess, hotter than a two dollar pistol and my feet were swole up something terrible. Your daddy went into town to buy a quart of peppermint ice cream from the Thirty-Two Flavors store and got a flat tire on his way home. By the time he fixed it, the ice cream had melted all down the seat and ruined his best Sunday shoes." Sarah Grace chuckled. "Goodness, he cussed a blue streak!"

"Mama, the murder," Mackenzie groaned. "Tell me about the murder."

"Oops! I have got to go. My program starts in five minutes. Goodbye, baby."

"Mama don't—" The call disconnected.

She cursed the producer of the soap opera that had become her mother's obsession. Calling back wasn't an option. Sarah Grace hated interruptions and usually unplugged her phone when *Passion's Pastimes* came on.

Nothing to do but drop in at the *Antioch Bee*, she decided, starting the car. The murders in Emorysville might not have anything to do with Annabel Coffin, but maybe she'd find out information that would lead to something more relevant, like what had happened to Billy Wakefield in the years after Annabel's murder.

The town's newspaper occupied a prime piece of downtown real estate, a building on the corner of Main Street and Washington Avenue, almost within a stone's throw of her office. She parked the car on Main in her usual spot and walked the rest of the way, stopping at Mighty Jo Young's coffee shop to pick up two cappuccinos to go.

Mackenzie swung into the *Antioch Bee*'s lobby and up to the antique mahogany counter that had stood in the same place more than a hundred years, ever since the newspaper's founding. The scarred, stained counter looked organic, as if it had grown there.

The newsroom stretched behind it, a haphazard collection of mismatched desks and chairs, but only three of the desks held computers.

A handsome, dark-skinned man wearing a short-sleeved green polo shirt tucked into khaki pants sat in front of one of the computers, using two fingers to rapidly peck on the keyboard. Mackenzie thought his buzzcut was recent. When she'd seen him a couple of weeks ago, he'd been sporting the same short, tidy afro he had worn for years.

"Hey, Little Jack," she called. "You the only one working today?"

James "Little Jack" Larkin, Jr., glanced at her and smiled. "Everybody else had the sense to go to lunch. I wanted to finish the front page story for tomorrow's edition."

"What's with the haircut?"

"My hairline's in retreat. The buzzcut makes it less obvious."

"You look sharp, my man. I brought you an offering." Mackenzie put both coffee cups on the counter. They'd been friends since high school, though he'd been a year ahead of her.

"Bless you, bless you, bless you," Larkin said, rising and crossing to the counter. He pulled the lid off a cup, inhaled the steam and took a sip, closing his brown eyes in bliss. Despite his nickname, Larkin stood well over six feet tall, a fact that always amused Mackenzie considering his father, "Big Jack" Larkin, barely came to his son's shoulder.

"How's Esme?" she asked, referring to his wife, Esmeralda. "She ready to pop yet?"

He drank more coffee before answering. "Any day now. This baby's a real procrastinator. Two weeks late already and Esme's about ready to explode, but I guess you didn't come here to make small talk. What's up, Kenzie?"

"I have a favor to ask you," she said, cracking open her own cappuccino. "You know anything about Emorysville? A whole family was killed back in the seventies."

Larkin shook his head. "Emorysville? Way before my time. I can check the archives and get back to you unless you want to do it yourself. What's this about, anyway?" he added, shooting her a keen glance over the rim of his raised cup.

"Something my mother told me," Mackenzie said hastily, wary of rousing his reporter's lust for a story. "I guess the murder happened around nineteen seventy-five or maybe early 'seventy-six." She drank her coffee while waiting for his response.

"Mmm-hmm." He finished his coffee, pursed his lips and tossed the empty cup into a wastebasket. "Tell you what…I'll do this favor for you and in return, you'll tell me the real reason why you're digging into a murder that happened so long ago. Deal?"

Mackenzie didn't need to think about it. "Deal."

"Then get out of here and let me finish my work. I'll call you later. And thanks for the coffee!" he said over his shoulder as he returned to his desk.

"Wouldn't have to ask if George Wyatt wasn't such a cheapskate and just digitized the archives already," Mackenzie muttered.

Nevertheless, Larkin heard her and laughed. "From your mouth to God's ears, girl, but don't hold your breath."

Mackenzie grinned and made her goodbyes. She'd honor their bargain later, but she had no intention of speaking about Annabel Coffin's restless spirit. She'd keep her information generic, her true purpose concealed.

When she walked away from the counter, she saw a glimmer of silver-gray hovering on the edge of her vision. *Speak of the Devil…*

She stopped and carefully turned her head, but the ghost wasn't there.

CHAPTER TWELVE

What did Annabel Coffin want from the newspaper? Mackenzie wondered. Was she after Little Jack? *Christ, I hope not.*

So far, the ghost had seemed satisfied to haunt her, not transfer that spectral animosity to other people. The thought of Annabel wreaking havoc on her mother or any of her friends made her swallow hard in mingled anger and fear.

"You just leave them alone," she whispered fiercely. "I'm doing the best I can, so you leave everybody else be, or so help me God—" She left the threat unuttered.

Annabel gave no overt acknowledgment, but Mackenzie felt a chill pass through her. She'd have to be satisfied with that, she supposed.

Leaving the building, she made a last-minute decision to appease her growling stomach and went to Miss Laverne's Luncheonette.

"A bit late for lunch, dear," Miss Laverne Crawford remarked above the tinkling of the bell on the door when Mackenzie entered. "Or early for dinner." The elderly woman's makeup was as bold as the bright Hawaiian print muumuu hanging loosely on her plump frame—heavily clumped mascara, violet eye shadow, and blusher the color of tangerines slashed over both wrinkled cheeks. A wrapped purple turban concealed her hair.

"I had a busy morning, ma'am," Mackenzie replied.

"You should eat three good meals a day. You're not on one of those fad diets, are you?" Miss Laverne's orange-painted lips thinned. She pointed a bony finger, the knuckle swollen from arthritis. "You're a scrawny little thing, Mackenzie Cross, skinny as a poor man's wallet. If you want to attract a husband, you need to eat."

"No diets, just not enough time," Mackenzie said politely, minding her manners though she somewhat resented the "scrawny" comment. She was almost certain Miss Laverne knew she was a lesbian—she'd never tried to hide it and dated other women openly—but Miss Laverne probably chose to think she'd get over it if she found the right man. She wasn't really offended. The woman was older than dirt and meant well.

"Well, your mama always hoped you'd blossom, bless her heart, but it wasn't to be," Miss Laverne said. "That's no reason to neglect your health, young lady."

"Yes, ma'am."

Miss Laverne's smile showed unnaturally smooth false teeth.

The luncheonette was tiny, just big enough to hold two small tables with two chairs each, a shelf crammed with potted ferns, a framed picture of the Sermon on the Mount and a long, glass-fronted refrigerator case and counter that rivaled the one at the *Antioch Bee* in terms of age and wear.

Old-fashioned black and white marble tiles covered the floor. The white tiles continued halfway up the walls where they gave way to pale lavender paint and glossy white trim. Years ago, the shop had been an ice cream parlor, the Thirty-Two Flavors store her mother had mentioned earlier—Antioch's homegrown answer to Baskin-Robbins.

"What can I do for you, dear? It's almost closing time, but don't worry, I'll rustle you up something tasty that'll put meat on your bones," Miss Laverne said, donning a pair of thick-lensed glasses and leaning over the counter to peer at her.

The refrigerator case held blue-and-white china dishes of homemade pickles: crunchy dills, pearl onions, bread-and-butter, yellow squash and sweet baby cukes. Jars of chow-chow, green tomato relish and preserved peaches stood next to pocket Bibles with red covers stacked to one side. Mackenzie knew Miss Laverne gave the Bibles away to anyone who came into the luncheonette needing spiritual guidance.

She studied the handwritten chalkboard menu hanging on the wall and ordered a bacon and egg salad sandwich on whole wheat flaxseed bread with chow-chow, lettuce and tomato, plus a side order of preserved peaches.

"Bread's fresh from the Mennonite bakery this morning," Miss Laverne said while she worked, using a knife to shave paper-thin strips from a head of iceberg lettuce.

A thought struck Mackenzie. Miss Laverne was a town fixture who might know more than her mother. "Do you know a boy from 'fifty-seven, Billy Wakefield? Or a girl named Annabel Coffin? Maybe she was your student when you were teaching at the high school."

Miss Laverne put a generous scoop of egg salad on the sandwich. "Oh, that's a lifetime ago, dear. I only taught English for a year before I married and had to quit. Let me see…no more Coffins around here, I'm afraid. That whole family's gone to Jesus. The Wakefield boy does sound familiar. I do believe he had people in Emorysville."

"That's right," Mackenzie said. "Do you know anything about a family being murdered in Emorysville in the mid-seventies?"

"I'm sorry, I didn't pay much mind to such things in those days. My boy was just back from the war in Vietnam minus his legs. Land mine, they said. He needed so much help at home, I hardly had time to catch my breath, let alone keep up with the news," Miss Laverne replied, adding a large spoonful of chow-chow to the top of the egg salad and pressing it down well. She piled on bacon, tomato slices and shredded lettuce while she rambled on, "You know, right after I married and left the school, I worked as a part-time secretary under old Pastor Rush at the First Baptist Church before he retired. After his son went to prison, he was hardly the same man. Just broke his heart. He went off to do missionary work in Africa. I practically had to run the church by myself until we found a new pastor. My husband wasn't too happy, but what can you do? The Lord gives us no burden we aren't strong enough to bear." She cut the finished sandwich in half with a flourish of her knife.

Mackenzie suddenly saw a flash of silver-gray in the corner of her eye. Annabel was trying to call her attention to something Miss Laverne had said, she believed.

She thought about the conversation while Miss Laverne secured a Bible verse to the top of the sandwich with a toothpick, added a dill pickle and wrapped the whole package in wax paper before fetching a small plastic tub for the preserved peaches.

Surely Annabel didn't care about Miss Laverne's job as a church secretary, so her interest had to do with Pastor Rush or his son. Mackenzie ventured a guess. "Excuse me, did you say Pastor Rush's son went to prison? I hadn't heard about that."

Next to Miss Laverne's left elbow, a silver-gray fog coalesced slowly into the form of Annabel Coffin. Mackenzie fought not to stare, but she watched the ghost sidelong, hoping nothing would happen. If knives or pickles began flying around the place, she doubted she could convince Miss Laverne it was the Holy Spirit at work.

"Yes, dear, I was smack-dab in the middle of things at church, what with Isaac being arrested and everything coming out at the trial. Who knew a doctor had it in him? But let's not speak ill of the dead." Miss Laverne passed her a full paper bag. "That'll be six dollars, dear."

Mackenzie dug out her wallet and handed over a ten-dollar bill, receiving the bag in return. She waved away the four dollars change, which Miss Laverne folded and dropped into a plastic box marked *Donations for Lake Minnisauga Bible Camp* that sat on the counter.

"When did this happen?" Mackenzie persisted, horribly aware of Annabel's cold black eyes focused on her, demanding more. "What was Isaac in jail for?"

A deep, vertical line bisected Miss Laverne's creased brow. She removed her glasses and looked disapproving. "Sorry, dear. There's been a great deal of water under the bridge since then and my memory's not what it used to be."

Disappointed, Mackenzie didn't press further. She thanked Miss Laverne and walked to the door. When she opened it, the bell sounding irritatingly cheerful, the old woman spoke.

"Best to let the dead rest in peace, dear," Miss Laverne said.

I wish, Mackenzie thought.

A sudden wind rushed through the luncheonette, rustling the wax paper squares piled behind the counter. Miss Laverne exclaimed and made a grab for a Bible verse that flew into the air and wafted over to Mackenzie to land at her feet.

"Shut the door, dear, before we blow away to Kingdom Come," Miss Laverne said.

Mackenzie bent and picked up the Bible verse, reading the typewritten words: *Before I formed you in the womb I knew you; before you were born I sanctified you. Jeremiah 1:5.*

She walked to her apartment and belatedly ate her lunch while contemplating the verse. No doubt Annabel's handiwork, she thought, grateful the ghost hadn't thrown a destructive fit and given poor old Miss Laverne a heart attack. What was Annabel trying to tell her? Why drop these hints instead of speaking to her outright?

Doctor, Annabel whispered in a voice as cold and smooth as a pane of glass.

Mackenzie paused in the act of lifting a chunk of preserved peach to her mouth. "You mean Pastor Rush's son, Isaac?"

Doctor. My doctor.

"What did he do, kill somebody?" She meant it as a joke, but Annabel let out an ear-splitting wail and appeared in the kitchen looking like a whirling thundercloud shot through with streaks of silver lightning.

Mackenzie stiffened. *Oh, shit.*

The half of the bacon and egg salad sandwich she hadn't yet eaten flipped off the plate into her lap, and then the plate itself went soaring through the air to smash against a kitchen cabinet. Shattered pieces of china rained down on the clove-scented preserved peaches that had slid off the flying plate to land on the linoleum.

"At least this time I have shoes on," Mackenzie said grimly, trying and failing to shovel egg salad off her capri pants without making more mess. "That plate belonged to my grandmother, damn it."

Annabel whispered, *My boy. My boy.*

"I'm trying to find out what happened to Billy Wakefield, but it's hard when you act like a three-year-old having a temper tantrum."

My boy.

"Oh, for God's sake, quit repeating yourself!" Mackenzie shouted, her limited patience at an end. She hadn't asked to be involved in this supernatural melodrama and she certainly didn't appreciate the destruction of a treasured family keepsake. "Now if you're done terrorizing the only person who's helping you, get the hell out of here. Go on, git!"

A drawer jerked open. A butcher knife, the well-honed blade glinting in the light, rose to balance on its tip. Mackenzie's breath caught. The knife fell back in the drawer.

The implied threat served to fuel her fury.

"Fuck you," she choked, rising to her feet. Unheeded, egg salad plopped on the floor and smeared her shoes. "Fuck you sideways and goddamn you for being an ungrateful bitch."

As if in answer, the butcher knife rose a second time, accompanied by the rest of the utensils in the drawer.

A bitter laugh escaped from Mackenzie's anger-tightened throat. "Go ahead. Go ahead and kill me, and I swear when I get to the other side, I will kick your ass from here to Hell."

Annabel's form reshaped itself, becoming less cloud-like and more human. She appeared angry, but a gleam of thoughtfulness shone in her black eyes.

The utensils cascaded to the floor in a glittering, stainless steel stream.

Unappeased, Mackenzie turned her back on the ghost. "You have no reason to bust my things or threaten to hurt me. I am doing my best, my very best to figure this situation out for you, but it's been less than a day. If you're so impatient, find somebody else to talk to."

She waited in vain for a reply. Annabel remained visible in the corner of the kitchen, but said and did nothing, simply continued to give her a thoughtful look.

Breaking the silence, the central air-conditioning's hum kicked in.

Mackenzie spun around, her movements jerky. "Fine. Be that way," she said. "I don't care anymore. I'm done with you and your—"

The utensils jumbled together on the floor seemed to leap of their own accord into the drawer, which slammed shut as Annabel disappeared.

"What about my grandmother's plate and the rest of this mess?" Mackenzie called.

No answer. *Of course not. That would be too easy.*

Fetching a roll of paper towel, she managed to get the egg salad off the linoleum and into the trash. Her shoes required more care. She swept up the shattered plate, added the pieces to the garbage can and spent ten minutes cleaning mayonnaise and eggs off her shoes, grateful they were leather and hadn't cost the earth. What else could be done to get rid of the funky smell, she didn't know. She made a mental note to ask her mother, who used to religiously clip the *Hints from Heloise* column from the newspaper.

When she finished cleaning and taking the trash downstairs—the sulphurous stench of eggs had begun to trigger nausea—she fetched her laptop from the bedroom and set it up on the coffee table in the living room, piggybacking off the bakery's Internet connection.

The comforting smell of baking bread surrounded her as she checked her email, finding a reply from Martin in Las Vegas offering the autographed Greg Page boxing gloves at the price she wanted. She sent him a confirmation and made a phone call to her client to deliver the good news. She also put out a feeler to her contact at a prestigious London auction house, inquiring about the current owner of the '31 Bugatti Kellner.

Realizing a faint eggy odor still hung around the apartment, Mackenzie turned off the air-conditioner, opened the windows and left to pay a visit to Jacob Dearborn.

The United Methodist Church on Apple Street was a long walk or a short drive away. She considered her options. The temperature had cooled slightly, a nice breeze was blowing, and she was in no mood to wrangle for a parking spot near the church. Her choice seemed obvious. She donned sneakers, took a reusable water bottle from the refrigerator, grabbed her keys and cell phone, and headed downstairs and out the door.

Mackenzie had gone a third of the distance when she happened to spot Veronica across the street, standing half-hidden off the sidewalk where the side of an empty house for sale was shaded by a magnolia tree, creating a spot not easily overseen by passing cars and most pedestrians. She smiled and waved, but Veronica didn't acknowledge her, apparently absorbed in a conversation with someone.

What's going on? She couldn't get a good look at the second person. Deciding to abandon subtlety in favor of full-blown nosiness, she crossed the street. Halfway there, she realized the other person was an ex-girlfriend of hers, Debbie Lou Erskine—a hard-bitten, hard-drinking, hard-partying, blue-eyed blond with a poisonous disposition. If Barbie were a real woman and smoked two packs a day, thought tube tops were fancy dress and preferred quantity over quality when it came to beer, she'd look a lot like Debbie Lou.

The smile slipped from her face when without warning, Debbie Lou hurled herself bodily at Veronica in an enthusiastic hug that knocked off her deputy's hat. Veronica staggered backward through an oversized gardenia bush, disappearing from view with Debbie Lou clinging to her.

"Oh, hell, no!" Mackenzie growled, marching quickly to rescue Veronica from the clutches of Debbie Lou—forever branded an evil, manipulative, lying cow who had dumped her when she was in the hospital for an appendectomy. Afterward, she'd discovered Debbie Lou had stolen her five-hundred-dollar emergency stash of cash and slept with three men, two women and possibly farm animals, too, while she was being operated on, although she might be exaggerating that last part because she hated the woman's guts.

Arriving at the scene breathing fire and righteous indignation, Mackenzie pushed through the gardenia bush and into a secluded side yard. She came to an abrupt halt when she saw Veronica beneath the magnolia tree, not rejecting Debbie Lou's embrace, but apparently returning it with interest. And tongue, she realized a split second later.

A jolt of shock sizzled down her spine. Veronica and Debbie Lou were kissing. No, not just kissing. They appeared to be devouring each other's faces like they'd been given two minutes to live and only swapping enough saliva would save their lives.

Veronica made a kind of throaty, grumbling moan and clutched Debbie Lou more tightly. Despite her confusion, the sound went straight to Mackenzie's most private parts.

Shock gave way to a pang of regret, which in turn gave way to a renewed burst of anger. How dare Debbie Lou Erskine, liar and cheat extraordinaire, corrupt the finest, purest, loveliest and most innocent specimen of femininity in the state of Georgia?

Before Mackenzie could voice her ire and whisk Veronica away for immediate drug testing—Debbie Lou must have dosed the poor woman with roofies, the only explanation that made sense—Veronica's eyes opened. She sprang free from Debbie Lou's clutches.

"Oh! Mac, I...uh...I didn't see you there," Veronica stammered. "Did you need something?"

An explanation and it had better be a damned good one, Mackenzie wanted to say, but the way Debbie Lou, Grand Bitch of the Universe, stared at her with a gloating smirk on her stupid face made the words stick in her craw.

"No, I was on my way to the United Methodist Church and I saw you here and wanted to say hi," she said to Veronica, forcing her mouth to form a smile instead of a snarl. She turned to Debbie Lou and said through clenched teeth, "How nice to see you again, Deb. It's been a while. Tell me, has that nasty case of syphilis you got in Tijuana been cured yet?"

Debbie Lou's grin turned sickly. "I don't know what you're talking about," she replied. "But you always did get fact and fiction mixed up, just like a crazy person."

"I didn't know you two had dated," Veronica said quietly. She was ignored.

"Oh sweetheart, as I recall, you did some crazy things yourself when we were dating," Mackenzie said, putting on a mask of concern. "Pole dancing and gelatin body shots at the Get-R-Done roadhouse, for instance. Has Ronnie seen the tattoo above your hoo-ha? It's very tasteful," she added to Veronica, who watched her with a flat, unhappy expression. Unable to bear the reproachful look any longer, she returned to needling Debbie Lou. "What was that tattoo again? Oh, yes... 'Tastes Like Chicken.'"

"I was drunk," Debbie Lou said, batting her mascara-laden eyelashes at Veronica.

"Well, I can testify that you do not, in fact, taste like chicken unless we're talking about rancid, rotten chicken from a KFC dumpster," Mackenzie said in her sweetest tone.

"Ladies, perhaps we can—" Veronica began.

"You bitch!" Debbie Lou ground out, reaching for Mackenzie's face with frighteningly long acrylic nails that resembled green and white polka-dotted claws.

Veronica caught Debbie Lou's wrist. "Don't do it," she warned. To Mackenzie, she went on, "I'll call you later, Mac." She cut a glance at Debbie Lou. "Now's not a good time."

Mackenzie had been hoping Debbie Lou would start a fight. She'd have taken great personal satisfaction in whipping the woman's ass while tearing out those cheap, nasty, peroxide blond hair extensions by the handful.

"There's no need for you to be angry, Mac," Veronica went on in a reasonable tone that made Mackenzie itch to smack her too. "Attacking Debbie Lou won't solve anything. Whatever problem you have, I'm sure there's a diplomatic solution."

Her blood boiling, Mackenzie snapped at Veronica, "Well, I can see when my advice isn't wanted. Good luck with your new relationship. Hope you've had your shots."

"Stay the fuck away from Vera and me," Debbie put in, always eager to get the last word. "She's mine, so fuck you, Kenzie. And by the way? You were a lousy lay."

Vera? Mackenzie thought. The situation got worse by the second. "Only because your genital warts and pubic crabs put me off." She started to wade through the gardenia bush, headed toward the street.

"Mac, wait. Come on, let's talk about it," Veronica pleaded.

Hurrying to get away before she broke down and did something irrevocable, like punch Debbie Lou, or Veronica, or both the women who'd betrayed her, Mackenzie marched down the pavement, her heart aching so much she thought she might expire from the pain.

CHAPTER THIRTEEN

Unable to continue to the United Methodist Church, Mackenzie returned to Main Street, got in her car and sped out of Antioch to I-85. She needed to clear her head. A long drive with no particular destination in mind sounded like a plan.

On a whim, she left the interstate after fifteen miles to switch to the lesser-used Jackson Lowe expressway, known to locals as the "Lie Lowe" because of the savage dips the road made as it plowed over a series of steep hills.

"Like a roller coaster designed by the Devil," she remembered her father grousing once when he'd been driving her to summer camp.

The twenty years since his death from cancer had a blurring effect on some of her memories, but she knew he'd been an average man who loved his family and did his best for them. Even now, she felt the warmth of his affection in her heart.

For once, thinking about her father didn't bring her happiness or peace. Instead, she found herself dwelling on Veronica as she drove.

It wasn't fair. Veronica was supposed to be straight.

The day they'd met two years ago, she'd seen Veronica hugging and laughing with a handsome, well-built man. Not merely handsome, but the kind of male beauty that graced magazine covers and catalogs of a much higher caliber than Sears or old Montgomery Ward. Due to their obvious closeness, she had assumed he was Veronica's boyfriend, though she hadn't seen him since and believed they must have broken off the relationship at some point.

She'd never known Veronica to flirt with a woman, go out with a woman, or talk about other women in any way that might signal a less-than-heterosexual interest. Conclusion: Veronica Birdwell exclusively liked men. Period. End of statement.

At one time, she'd have bet everything she owned that Veronica would never even think about sex with another woman and been confident she'd laugh all the way to the bank when she won. Discovering it would have been a sucker's bet came as a blow.

Mackenzie brooded a while longer on how Debbie Lou Erskine, Supreme Empress of Bitchiness herself, could have managed to corrupt Veronica.

She hadn't imagined the kiss and she sure as hell hadn't imagined Veronica's reaction to the kiss. That's what pained her the most, she decided, her fingers tightening on the steering wheel as if she had a strangler's grip around Debbie Lou's neck.

Seeing Veronica embrace Debbie Lou really stung. *She* had been lusting after Veronica since the minute they'd been introduced. *She* had been careful of Veronica's feelings, not wanting to hurt her friend or herself by making inappropriate and unwanted advances. *She* had resisted the urge to take by seduction what wasn't freely offered.

And then Debbie Lou had come along, a tempting serpent in the Garden of Eden.

Regret and jealousy etched acid into her soul. *It should have been me!*

Woodshed, sighed a familiar voice next to her ear.

Startled, Mackenzie almost stood on the brakes. Lacking power steering, the Datsun 510 handled like a tank, but she muscled the car onto the grass shoulder and brought it to a halt. A musty, dry smell crept into the air. Her nose itched. She rolled down the window before turning to regard the empty passenger seat.

Silver-gray fog wavered in the rearview mirror, a reflection from the backseat.

"To what do I owe the pleasure?" Mackenzie asked, not bothering to hide her sarcasm.

Woodshed.

"The famous woodshed where you used to meet your boyfriend. Well, whoop-de-do! You must've mistaken me for someone who gives a flaming rat's turd."

The driver's side door swung open.

Mackenzie swore. "Damn it, Annabel, I'm not shitting you. That stunt you pulled today…no, wait, I tell a lie…all of the stunts you've pulled have really hacked me off. I don't appreciate having my stuff destroyed, so I'm not helping you anymore. Go haunt Maynard. He's the one actually trying to solve your murder. Me, I'm not interested."

The passenger side door flung open violently, bouncing on its hinges.

"And I'm not impressed by your little tantrum, either."

Go see, Annabel said.

Mackenzie crossed her arms over her thin chest and shook her head. "Nope."

The silver-gray fog in the backseat shimmered apart into wisps that floated away.

She blew out a breath, feeling like she'd just avoided a boatload of unpleasantness. Something had to be done about Annabel. She recalled the threat of exorcism she had made yesterday. Perhaps it wouldn't be a bad idea to pay a call on Father Dominic at Our Lady of the Angels. He might have some insight into—

A little shriek escaped her when a bunch of wild roses dropped into her lap, scattering leaves and pinkish red petals everywhere.

Woodshed, Annabel said. *Please.*

The roses might be Annabel's way of saying she was sorry. Or the offering was meant to kill her with the Death of a Thousand Cuts, she thought after scratching herself on a thorn the size of her thumb. She stuck the bleeding finger in her mouth.

"Okay, fine, I accept your apology," she said, gingerly placing the roses on the passenger seat and brushing off the detritus on her jeans. She would have to stop at the gas station on the way home and use the coin-operated vacuum to clean up the mess.

Mackenzie exited the car. A bush rustled to her right. She went over there, feeling on edge. If a bunny rabbit hopped out, she'd probably wet her pants.

The bush stopped moving when she came closer. Farther away, she saw a stand of ferns whipping back and forth. She followed the signs from ferns to trees to bushes. With each step, she wondered if Annabel was luring her deeper into the woods for some terrible purpose, but she went on. At least she had about three good hours of daylight left.

At last, a structure loomed into view, standing off-center in a clearing surrounded by pines: a crudely constructed house, what used to be called a shotgun shack, long since abandoned. The roof had fallen in, the windows busted out and the front door was missing.

Mackenzie nearly tripped over an object half buried in the ground near a rotting log. She bent to sweep away the forest litter and discovered the remains of a copper pot still. To her amazement, the milk can-shaped boiler looked intact, though green with verdigris.

Four hundred dollars easy, she thought, automatically examining the still with an appraiser's eye. Collectors loved this kind of stuff, real authentic Americana.

Why had Annabel brought her here? Was this the woodshed where she'd died?

The leaves underfoot stirred. *My boy*, the ghost whispered.

Understanding dawned. Prohibition had been repealed in 1933, but distilling moonshine was illegal to this day without the proper permits and licenses. That didn't stop 'shiners from running stills and selling Mason jars of one-eighty proof spirit liquor out of their trucks or under the counters of bars and roadhouses throughout the state, mostly to avoid paying taxes and, of course, give the middle finger salute to the federal government.

She reckoned somebody had been cooking moonshine here for sure, likely within the last fifty or so years considering the pot's condition. Did the still belong to Billy and his partners? Mama had said he ran 'shine with the no-account Gascoignes, but the copper pot was impossible to date since the same design and materials had been used for a century at least. For all she knew, another moonshiner had set up operations in the sixties or seventies, long after Annabel's death and Billy's disappearance from Antioch.

If the still dated from the fifties, it was possible Annabel and Billy Wakefield had used "the woodshed" in the middle of the woods as a meeting place.

Now suppose this isn't Billy's still, even if it's contemporary to the time when he and Annabel were an item. If a rival moonshiner had set up a still back then without knowing about the house's frequent young visitors, that might explain Annabel's murder, though not why and how her corpse had been hidden in the wall of a building in Antioch. Moonshiners were known to be quick on the trigger defending their property, but the woods went on for miles. Plenty of places to hide a body where it wouldn't be found.

She needed answers, not conjecture. "Annabel, I want to ask you something," she said, straightening up and walking to the house. "You there?"

Yes.

"When you and Billy used to meet, was that copper still around?"

Yes. Billy's.

Her theory down the drain, Mackenzie peered through the glassless window frame at the house's interior, finding nothing more exciting than bird's nests, piles of animal feces and trash.

A vaguely rectangular shape on the floor might have been a mattress once.

Billy Wakefield made moonshine. He must have had business rivals. She'd have to do further research to learn who might have wanted Billy dead, but only if she couldn't find any further leads. She stood back, thinking. *Why not just ask the victim for clarification?*

"Annabel, you did die here, right?"

No answer.

"Who killed you?"

No answer.

Well, that was as useful as tits on a boar hog. "Did you meet Billy in the woodshed the night you were killed? Just tell me straight out, yes or no."

Yes.

A chill touched the back of her neck like a poke from a cold finger. "What happened?"

My boy.

"Do you mean Billy?"

Doctor Rush.

Mackenzie felt her eyebrows rise in surprise. "Isaac Rush?"

Yes. Annabel began to weep. *My boy, my boy, my boy...*

The sound receded farther into the woods, growing fainter until it was gone.

Mackenzie glanced around. "Annabel?" She received no answer.

A bird began to call from the top of a tree, answered by another bird nearby. The wind rustled through the pines. Her shoulders knotted with tension.

"Well, isn't that just peachy," Mackenzie said to herself. Alone in the woods, abandoned by her guide and no reception on her cell phone. Fortunately, she had a decent memory and a good sense of direction.

As she plodded back to the car, she made a mental to-do list. Talk to Maynard about the case. Find out more on Billy Wakefield, the murders in Emorysville, and why Dr. Isaac Rush had gone to jail and his possible connection to Annabel Coffin.

She added *talk to Veronica* to the list and crossed it off.

Twice.

Feeling more sorrow than resentment, she continued on her way.

CHAPTER FOURTEEN

The next morning, after a night spent in dreamless sleep, Mackenzie awoke feeling tired and sluggish, like some sneaky bastard had tiptoed into her head while she slept and wrapped her brain in cotton wool. A shower didn't help, nor did two cups of coffee—instant espresso until she ordered a new glass carafe to replace the one Annabel had broken.

Opening the front door, she found a warm poppy seed bagel from the bakery. She made a face. She loved bagels, but she'd run out of cream cheese. Since the Winn-Dixie closed last year, the nearest large grocery store was eight miles away. The nearest convenience store that might carry cream cheese was the slightly more upscale gas station three miles away, where she'd stopped last night to vacuum the leaves and withered rose petals out of her car. If only she'd known she was out of schmear then...

Sighing in annoyance, Mackenzie put away the bagel, checked the refrigerator and cabinets and made a grocery list. She'd take a trip to the Little Giant supermarket after work.

While she was in the bedroom trying to decide what to wear—
her prized vintage Hawaiian shirt or a short-sleeved tobacco
brown blouse—her cell phone rang.

She checked the caller ID before answering. "Hey, Little
Jack, I wasn't expecting you to call so early in the morning.
Have you got news for me?"

"I'm a journalist, Kenzie, I always have news," James Larkin
replied, chuckling.

"Very funny. You know what I mean."

"I do indeed, which is why I'd like you to join me for
breakfast at Mr. B's Cafeteria."

Mackenzie made a quick calculation of her funds. She hadn't
been to the bank lately and it wouldn't open for another two
hours. "Your treat?"

"Even unto the New York strip steak and eggs," he said
solemnly.

"I'll meet you there in twenty minutes," she replied.

Ending the call and returning to her bedroom, Mackenzie
ditched the shirts and chose more fitting, business-type attire: a
sleeveless white cotton blouse with coconut shell buttons, worn
with cream linen pants and lipstick-red wedge sandals.

Five minutes later, she rushed out the front door with her
key ring and several bobby pins clenched between her teeth,
using both hands to twist and pin her fuzzy, frizzy, frightful mop
of hair into a loose knot as she navigated the cement steps.

Halfway down, the overhead fluorescent light flickered out.
She felt her way to the bottom and hesitated, her eyes straining
to see anything in the absolute darkness. More of Annabel's
handiwork? When nothing else happened, she went outside,
squinting at the bright golden sunlight pouring through the air
like honey.

She dashed inside the bakery long enough to let her
landlord—Sam with the unpronounceable last name whom
everyone called Bakery Sam—know about the fluorescent bulb
and hurried across the street to the central parking zone and
her car.

Mr. B's Cafeteria on Clovis Street was already full when Mackenzie arrived. She walked inside, scanning the crowded tables. Larkin raised a hand to attract her attention. Dodging the hostess, she went over to him.

"Good grief," she said, sliding into the chair opposite him. "Is it usually like this?"

Larkin handed her a menu, his brown eyes filled with good humor. "Like a stirred anthill, you mean? Most days. The cook makes sourdough pancakes better than your mother's. Try the banana nut. It's almost a religious experience."

Accepting a cup of coffee from the waiter, Mackenzie placed her order. As soon as they were alone, she focused on Larkin. "Did you find out anything?"

"Some." He raised his coffee cup to his lips and paused, staring at her over the rim. "*Quid pro quo*, agreed?"

"Agreed. Now gimme," she said, making grabby motions.

"In nineteen seventy-five, William Wakefield, Sr., a Korean War veteran, shot and killed his family members in the only murder-suicide ever to occur in Emorysville," Larkin told her between sips of coffee. "The victims included his wife, Aurora Wakefield née Stokes, his youngest daughter, Caroline, his other daughter, Betsy, and himself. His son, William Jr., known as Billy, was serving time for armed robbery in the Central State Prison in Macon at the time. He'd been in and out of jail since 'fifty-eight on various charges."

Mackenzie listened as Larkin painted a picture of William Wakefield, Sr., a decent husband and father. Working as a drywall hanger and plasterer for the Young Construction Company and getting fired for drunkenness on the job, he'd apparently snapped, taken a hunting rifle, and shot his wife and daughters before committing suicide. A neighbor had heard the shots and called the police.

"Is that it?" she asked when he gave her printouts of the *Bee's* coverage.

"That's everything." He pointed at the pages in her hand. "If you're looking for a coroner's report or a complete police report, you'll have to go to the sheriff's office."

"No, this is good. Thanks." She skimmed the articles until the waiter returned with plates of banana nut sourdough pancakes served with sausage patties on the side.

She put the printouts away to enjoy her breakfast. As Larkin had promised, the pancakes were delicious slathered in butter and maple syrup. The coffee was good, too, with just a hint of chicory to give it bite.

Almost as soon as Mackenzie finished and wiped her mouth with a napkin, Larkin pointed his fork at her, a deep frown creasing his brow. "Give it up, Kenzie. Why are you asking me about the Wakefield murders?"

"You know some construction workers found a woman's body behind the wall in my office, right?" she asked.

He nodded. "The official statement the sheriff's office put out said the victim's name is Annabel Coffin and she died in the late fifties. No word yet on cause of death."

"That's right," Mackenzie said. "Turns out Annabel Coffin was in high school with my mother. They weren't best friends or anything like that, but you know how it is."

"Antioch was a much smaller town back then. Less than half the current population if memory serves. Everybody knew everybody else."

"Mama told me Annabel was going with a boy named Billy Wakefield and later she mentioned the murders in Emorysville."

"And you wondered if Annabel Coffin's murder and the Wakefield murders were connected," he murmured, looking disappointed. "Kenzie, I can't see how. Billy was in a prison cell in Macon when his father committed murder-suicide and that happened long after Annabel died."

She patted his hand. "You can't win 'em all, Jack. No scoop today."

"At least I can do a background piece on Annabel Coffin." Larkin brightened slightly.

"Oh, hey, when you were looking up the Wakefields, did you happen to find out anything else about Billy?"

Larkin stuck a forkful of pancake in his mouth and reached into his shirt pocket for a small, spiral-bound notebook. He laid it on the table and flipped to a page. "Bill Wakefield was a bad 'un," he said after studying the handwritten lines. "Arrested and convicted of assault with a deadly weapon in nineteen fifty-eight, got out of prison after serving eight years, and promptly picked up a new charge for operating a still and for federal tax evasion. Armed robbery later. Another assault. Looks like he spent most of his adult life in one jail or another. I couldn't find anything after 'eighty-five when he was released from Macon the last time. He just disappeared. A career criminal like that probably got himself killed."

"Good to know, thank you. Um...you know, I was hoping for another favor," Mackenzie said, wincing when he scowled. "I just need access to the newspaper's archives one day real soon. That's it. I'll do my own dirty work."

"You won't find more about the Wakefields and nothing else about the Coffins except a story about the car accident that killed the parents. I know. I already checked."

"This is something else. I need to know about Dr. Isaac Rush."

"Why?" He waved the question away before she could make up an excuse. "No, never mind. I don't want to know. You can come in anytime during business hours. I'll get Melinda to show you how to work the microfilm reader."

"Thank you, Jack. I appreciate it."

"No problem."

"And thanks for breakfast. I didn't know Mr. B's served such great food."

"Ah, that'd be my brother-in-law's doing," Larkin said, rising from his seat. "Owen bought the place last year, hired a new cook and improved the menu. I hope you didn't mind driving out here, Kenzie. It's just that family eats for free."

"I should've known you weren't treating me to breakfast out of your own pocket. Tell Owen those pancakes are to die for," Mackenzie said, following him outside.

She left the restaurant with her appetite satisfied, but no gratification otherwise. The murder-suicide in Emorysville seemed unrelated to Annabel Coffin's death.

Annabel had been killed in the dilapidated house in the woods off the Lie-Lowe, most likely on the same night she disappeared. The murderer remained unknown, as did the motive for her death. A possible connection to Dr. Isaac Rush needed to be explored further.

She still had a lot of work to do.

CHAPTER FIFTEEN

Mackenzie used the rest of the morning to work on her own projects for *Finders & Keepers, Inc.* The toy tractor was discovered in an antique store in Maine and at the right price for her client. Her London contact got in touch with her, but he had no news to share about the '31 Bugatti Kellner. He put her onto a wealthy art dealer in Hong Kong who was rumored to have bid on the car the last time it came up for auction.

Despite the lack of concrete leads, she was pleased. Once interested enough to bid on a one-of-a-kind item, men like Richard Chen usually kept tabs on it if they failed to win. He might lead her right to the Bugatti if she asked the right way.

Her email brought two more clients: a doll collector seeking an early Jumeau Bébé and someone in Utah asking her to locate vintage bowling pins. Those requests took her less than an hour to research and arrange. She wouldn't deliver the information for a few days, however. If she made her work seem too easy, customers wouldn't want to pay her fees.

Her chores complete, she drove to the Burton Lemoyne High School to talk to Kelly Collier. While she parked her car, she recognized Kelly's white Corvette in one of the reserved student's spaces. She knew Paul Collier wasn't church-mouse poor—he lived pretty well and owned a few properties around town—but a fifty grand car seemed way over the top. On the other hand, she'd bet Collier had a hard time refusing his spoiled daughter anything.

When she checked with the principal's office, the secretary let her know Kelly was on the football field practicing with the rest of the cheerleading squad.

Mackenzie walked to the field, avoiding a knot of teenagers huddled beside the bleachers and smoking cigarettes—at least she hoped they were tobacco cigarettes—and texting on their cell phones. Scattered groups of other students sat at the top of the bleachers.

Coach Wilcox "Fighting Cock" Sumter sat on a bench at the sidelines, alternately bellowing instructions and abuse at the football players running up and down the field, or snarling at the gangly, pimply, teenage assistant who sat beside him, clutching a tablet PC.

"Coach," Mackenzie said, giving him a more polite nod than he deserved. She'd considered the Fighting Cock a loud, bullying, arrogant, self-righteous prick when she'd been in high school and her opinion hadn't changed one iota.

Sumter ignored her. She mouthed, "asshole" at his back and moved on to the spot where the cheerleading squad was doing drills.

Kelly appeared even more angelic, not to mention athletic, in a pink T-shirt cropped to bare her midriff and white shorts that showed off her tan. Her blond ponytail bobbed at each movement as she leaped high into the air, her legs spread in a split, and touched her toes. A diamond tennis bracelet on her wrist had joined the engagement ring.

"Very impressive," Mackenzie said when Kelly landed with a surprisingly heavy thump on the grass. The girl was built like a dancer—slender, but muscular and solid. She eyed the bracelet. A gift from Tucker, she supposed. The Dearborns had money to spare.

"What are you doing here?" Kelly asked sharply, going to take a towel from a pile on a nearby bench. She patted her face. "Did you talk to Rev. Wyland?"

"I did and he promised not to bother Mr. Dearborn anymore," Mackenzie replied. "I'd still like to know what set him off, though. What if it was something y'all did—totally innocent, like a hug between future daughter-in-law and future father-in-law—that Rev. Wyland misinterpreted? He might make other trouble if it happens again."

"Why don't you ask him? He's the one who acted like a dick."

"I'm asking you."

Kelly tossed her head. "Forget it. As long as he's doesn't make a fuss, I don't care."

"On your head be it." Mackenzie started to go. She stopped when Kelly spoke.

"If he bothers me or Mr. Dearborn again, I'll let you know," the young woman said.

Mackenzie turned around. "No, you will not," she said, losing friendliness in favor of firmness. "I'm not your employee. I did you a favor. If Wyland threatens you or Mr. Dearborn again, y'all are on your own. I have more important things to do than run your errands."

"You'd better not talk to me like that," Kelly spat. Her chin went up, her expression turning ugly. "When I tell my daddy on you—"

Amazing how quickly an angel turns into a devil, Mackenzie thought, recalling the glimpse of nastiness she'd seen under Kelly's façade during their meeting in the diner. "Tell your daddy what, exactly? That Rev. Wyland saw you and Mr. Dearborn in the park doing something he believed he ought to stop?"

To Mackenzie's surprise, Kelly blanched, her blue eyes blazing with panicked fear in her colorless face. Through stiffened lips she said, "Go away. Leave me alone."

"Are you okay, hon?" asked another cheerleader, giving Mackenzie a suspicious glare. She put an arm around Kelly's shoulders. "Maybe you should sit down."

Kelly jerked away from her friend, her gaze fixed on Mackenzie. "I mean it," she cried. "You stay the hell away from me."

"Did she do something to you?" the cheerleader asked Kelly, who didn't answer.

A perky redhead—from her air of authority, likely the squad's captain—ceased her tumbling run and joined the others. "Is there a problem here?" she asked, watching Mackenzie as if sizing her up for potential felony charges.

Becoming uncomfortably aware that the commotion had attracted Coach Sumter's attention, Mackenzie decided to retreat rather than add to the drama. "No problem. My business is done. And Kelly, you're welcome," she said as she headed off the field.

In the car on the way home, Mackenzie went over what had happened.

Kelly had been downright terrified when she'd said *doing something he believed he ought to stop* in reference to Wyland and the mysterious event in Stubbs Park. In her opinion, the reaction implied that whatever Kelly and Dearborn had been caught doing, it wasn't an activity the young woman wanted to become general knowledge.

From there, her imagination went wild. She reined in her more evil-minded thoughts. Vicious rumors were started by people taking an event that could be interpreted in many different ways and putting the foulest spin possible on it.

Better get the truth from the other horse's mouth, she decided, turning the Datsun around and driving to the United Methodist Church on Apple Street.

The church was locked, the rear office closed. Spotting Dearborn's Pontiac in the parking lot, she walked next door to the pastor's home, a modest two-story house without much of a front yard, just a patch of tended grass and a flowerbed filled with colorful annuals on either side of a short stone walkway that led from the sidewalk to the front porch steps.

When she reached the top of the steps, she saw the front door was open and the screen door closed. She rapped her knuckles on the screen door's aluminum frame, calling loudly, "Anybody home? Hey, Mr. Dearborn, you there? It's Kenzie Cross."

Jacob Dearborn appeared after several seconds, glowering at her through the screen door's wire mesh panel. His shirtsleeves were rolled up. Bits of grass peppered his slacks. He'd been mowing the backyard, she guessed. His usual immaculate coif of iron gray hair was windblown, hanging in disheveled strands around his flushed face.

"How may I help you, Ms. Cross?" he asked in a clipped tone.

The chilly reception made her wonder who'd peed in his Cheerios. "I'd like to ask you about Kelly Collier and—" she began.

He cut her off, his jaw set, his face like granite. "I just got off the phone with Kelly. That poor girl says you're harassing her, even showing up to persecute her at school in front of her friends. This must stop. It must stop right now."

Dumbstruck by the unfair accusation, Mackenzie could only gape at him.

Dearborn went on. "I'd rather not involve the authorities, Ms. Cross, but I will if you don't stay away from Kelly. She and my son are to be married soon and I will not allow you to disturb or upset her. If necessary, I'll alert Kelly's father and advise him to apply for a restraining order on his daughter's behalf. Am I understood? Do not speak to Kelly. Do not call her on the telephone. Do not approach her in any way."

While he'd been speaking, Mackenzie regained her composure. A wave of cold fury swept over her. "Let *me* be clear, sir," she said, biting off each word as if her teeth snapped at his throat. "Kelly Collier asked me to speak to Rev. Wyland on your behalf. It seems Wyland was blackmailing you into resigning your position in the church because he believed he'd seen you and Kelly misbehaving in the park."

"Nonsense," Dearborn scoffed, but he didn't sound confident. "Baseless allegations."

"I'll be more than happy to give the police permission to dump my phone records, which will clearly show that *she* called *me*, not the other way around," Mackenzie said. "And I'm sure Rev. Wyland will be happy to testify that I did speak to him about the issue."

He stared at her a moment longer and dropped his gaze. His manner became almost conciliatory. "Kelly must have been mistaken," he said. "I apologize."

Mackenzie kept her mouth closed.

"Will you please leave the matter be?" he asked quietly. "It's no one's business but our own and I'd think it a Christian act if you were to forgive our offenses."

To push or not to push? Mackenzie asked herself. Clearly, she'd get nothing substantial or even true from Dearborn, who seemed to understand he'd overreacted and gone on the offensive with far more force than the situation warranted.

"I don't bear either of you ill will," she said, "except for the tomfoolery you tried to pull. Frankly, I don't care what the two of you are doing that's so goddamned secret. But so help me God, if I'm pushed to it, if y'all lay false charges against me, everything I know or think I know will come out in court." She leaned closer to the screen to repeat in a low, controlled whisper, "Everything." To her satisfaction, he flinched.

"Then this sorry business is forgotten on both our sides," he said.

"If you like to think so," Mackenzie snapped, still angry. "Goodbye."

She took the porch steps two at a time and made a beeline for her car, her eyes burning with rage-induced tears. Once inside the Datsun, she let out the breath she'd been holding, wrapped her fingers around the steering wheel and let herself shake.

Screw Kelly Collier and Jacob Dearborn, she thought, reaching for a tissue to mop her sweaty face. Attempting to intimidate her acted like a red flag to the bull of her stubbornness. *Mark the pastor down as strike two. I'll have to talk to Rev. Wyland again. He might be willing to let a little more information slip if I play my cards right.*

Mere curiosity had driven her before, but now that she'd been threatened, she was absolutely determined to uncover the truth.

She blew her nose, started the car and pointed it toward home.

CHAPTER SIXTEEN

Loud drums and guitars woke Mackenzie from an afternoon nap. She sat up on the sofa, scowling at her cell phone. Why had she thought "Smells Like Teen Spirit" would be an appropriate or even desirable ring tone?

She answered the call while wiping sleep from her eyes. "Cross speaking."

"Mac, it's Ronnie," Veronica said hesitantly.

Mackenzie's spine stiffened. "Hey Ronnie," she said. "How are you doing?"

"Not so good."

"What's wrong?"

"My best friend's angry with me and I'm an idiot."

"Look, honey, you just don't know Debbie Lou Erskine like I do."

"I didn't know you two used to date," Veronica suddenly blurted, "and I'm very sorry if I hurt your feelings and I won't be seeing her anymore—"

"Slow down, take a breath before you keel over," Mackenzie said, getting worried.

"Fine, but I want to talk to you about Deborah."

"Who?"

"Deborah Louise. Debbie Lou. Anyway, please don't hang up."

"I won't." Mackenzie ran a hand through her hair, trying to work out the snarls left by her nap. Did she want to have this conversation? Not really.

However, she'd cooled down since yesterday and had time to consider the situation more rationally. She and Veronica were friends, period. If Veronica was having a sexual identity crisis or a post-Debbie Lou crisis, she ought to be supportive.

The tightness in her neck eased. She could do this. She could give Veronica a shoulder to cry on, lend an ear and pass the tissues. What else were friends for?

Besides, Debbie Lou was horrible enough to turn a confirmed lesbian straight. God knew what she'd done to poor confused Veronica, who wasn't even bisexual. Hallmark needed to make a "sorry your big gay experiment didn't work out" card.

"Did Debbie Lou want you to do...you know...something kinky?" she asked, recalling a few moments in the bedroom when she and Debbie Lou hadn't seen eye to eye. Or other body parts to other body parts for that matter. "She's not exactly vanilla, if you know what I mean. More like a Neapolitan ice cream sundae with extra crazy sauce on the side."

Veronica spluttered incoherently, finally producing a negative wheeze.

Indignation filled Mackenzie when the obvious answer surfaced. "She broke up with you, didn't she? Hell, I knew she was bad news the minute I saw her skulking around. If she broke your heart, Ronnie, I swear I'll go to her house right now and snatch her baldheaded!"

Veronica made a sound like a choked off laugh. "Really, it's okay," she said at last and paused. "Are *we* okay, Mac?"

"Yes, we are."

"You aren't upset?"

"At you, no. As for Debbie Lou, if she was on fire, I wouldn't p—"

"I get the picture," Veronica interrupted hastily. Another pause. "Can I come over?"

Mackenzie checked the time on her wristwatch and mulled over the contents of her refrigerator. She still hadn't had time to go to the grocery store. Her empty stomach grumbled. The pancakes at breakfast, while appreciated, hadn't lasted long, and she'd skipped lunch.

"I could make us dinner if you don't mind scrambled eggs," she said.

"I could swing by the Chinese place," Veronica offered.

"Golden Buddha? I'm not a fan of their cook. Honestly, I'd rather make a run to the store and whip up something, if you don't mind."

"That sounds nice, Mac. I get off work in an hour. I'll come over then. 'Bye."

When the call abruptly disconnected, Mackenzie pulled the cell phone away from her ear. She considered the looming conversation with a sinking heart and thought about running away or feigning an infectious disease, but Veronica would track her down or break in the door. Better to steel herself for an evening of being Veronica's completely asexual BFF with motives of shining purity. She should be prepared for tears, back patting, sympathizing, possible ranting, and if she was very good, a little platonic hand-holding.

She sighed, depressed by the prospect, and left the apartment.

Twenty-three minutes later in the Little Giant grocery store, listening with half an ear to the classic country tunes piped over the intercom, Mackenzie ran into her cousin James Maynard, the police detective, striding purposefully into the same aisle with a shopping basket over his arm. According to the items in the basket, he appeared to be living on a diet of beer, corn chips and canned chili. *No wonder he's such a miserable so-and-so.*

"Hey, Jimmy, y'all get the autopsy report from Doc Hightower yet?" she asked, reaching for a box of yellow *shi* noodles. Thanks to the Buddhist temple and monastery just outside town, the local stores had been stocking more Asian ingredients.

He glared. "Birdwell been telling tales out of school?"

"Nope, Ronnie hasn't said a mumbling word." Mackenzie pushed her cart to the produce department with Maynard trailing behind her like a morose stray dog in a Brooks Brothers suit. She picked a bunch of green onions and a hand of fresh ginger from the displays. "By the way, I talked to Mama about the victim."

"By all means, Kenzie, do tell."

While making the rounds of the store, she told him what she'd discovered about Annabel Coffin and Billy Wakefield, including the information Larkin had told her that morning. Finally concluding her shopping, she led him to a checkout lane that had miraculously just opened. "I'll try to trace Billy further," she said. "Maybe I can run down some folks who knew the Wakefields when they lived in Emorysville."

"I want you to stay out of the case," Maynard said, scowling and pointing a finger at her. "Thank you for your help. Now you're done, so mind your own business and let the police do theirs."

Mackenzie paused in the act of unloading the groceries in her cart onto the conveyor belt. "Seriously, Jimmy? Is that all you can say to me? I did your job, you know, helping build the victim's profile when I could've been earning money doing other things. You could be nicer about it, show a little gratitude instead of acting like a Grade-A asshole."

"I'm not arguing with you—"

"I mean, I can't help it if you're too chickenshit to talk to Mama yourself."

"That's not fair—"

"*Bwok-bok-bok-bok*," Mackenzie made chicken noises at him. He'd always hated that when they were kids.

The middle-aged cashier giggled.

"Goddamn it, Kenzie, quit that!" Maynard exploded. He stopped, clearly exasperated. "I asked you to talk to your mother, not run around town acting like an amateur private eye."

"Why not talk to Mama yourself?"

"Because I was busy doing other things…"

Mackenzie scoffed. "Really? That's the best you can come up with?"

"I figured if there was a story to be had, Aunt Sarah Grace would know, but this Coffin thing isn't my only case. I couldn't spare the time to run over there, so I asked you. I thought it wasn't a big deal." His sour expression deepened the lines on his brow. "Had I known you'd take it as permission to go all *Murder, She Wrote* on me and imagine you were a real investigator, I wouldn't have bothered."

Mackenzie bristled, ignoring the cashier's guffaw. Maynard always knew the surest way to dump gasoline on the flames of her temper. She caught herself slamming the rest of her groceries on the conveyer belt. Except the eggs. She made a deliberate effort to lay the box of eggs down gently. "You are an inconsiderate dickweed, James Austin Maynard. It'll be a cold day in Hell before I do a favor for you again."

Maynard relented in the face of her withering scorn. "Okay, okay, I wasn't looking for a fight, Kenzie. I'm really sorry. Truce?"

"Ronnie's coming over to my place tonight," she said, angling for a concession. "Can she tell me what's been found out already? To satisfy my curiosity, of course."

"Kenzie..." he sighed. "Fine. Anything that'll be public knowledge soon. No more digging around on your own, you hear?"

Her fingers crossed behind her back, she said sweetly, "Promise."

He stared at her suspiciously, but she smiled, paid the cashier and left.

CHAPTER SEVENTEEN

Dripping sweat from four trips over the street to the car and back to the apartment, hefting grocery bags up the stairs in the dark since Sam hadn't fixed the fluorescent light yet, Mackenzie finally staggered into the kitchen with the last of her burdens. She felt wrung out. Thank God she hadn't planned on anything more elaborate than Szechuan noodles.

She took a quick shower and changed into cutoff shorts and a T-shirt. By the time Veronica rang the doorbell, she'd cooked the noodles, put them in ice water and now stood behind the stove cooking lean ground pork with chilies and ginger.

Going to answer the door, she suddenly felt awkward, not sure how she should act around Veronica. Eating dinner together, just the two of them in her apartment, seemed like the world's worst idea. What if she said something wrong? What if she made an ass of herself? What if Veronica cried? What if—

Enough. She jerked open the door, a smile pasted on her lips.

Light spilled from the doorway to illuminate the darkened stairwell. Veronica stood on the threshold, still wearing her deputy's uniform. She'd released her hair from its usual tight bun, letting it spill in a glossy brunette wave over her shoulder.

"Hey," Veronica said.

"Hey," Mackenzie echoed. The heat outside had brightened the pink in Veronica's complexion, which in turn made her eyes seem brighter, more sparkling, like green glass polished by the sea. "Come on in," she said, stepping aside.

Veronica walked into the apartment, her clunky black work shoes squeaking on the wooden floor. "Something smells good."

"Oh, crap!" Mackenzie ran into the kitchen, relieved to find that dinner hadn't burned.

She added homemade chicken stock to the pan, followed by Szechuan peppercorns, soy sauce, a spoonful of red wine vinegar, a bigger spoonful of tahini from a jar in the refrigerator and a pinch of sugar.

A long, lush body suddenly pressed against her back. Veronica's chin dug into the top of her shoulder. She froze.

"You smell good, too," Veronica murmured in her ear.

Goose bumps erupted over Mackenzie's body. At the same time, sweat trickled down her spine. She twitched. "Uh, I'm trying a new shower gel. Mandarin orange," she said. "On sale. Only five dollars. At Peebles Drug Store. On, uh—" Her mind went blank.

Veronica let out a breathy chuckle.

Mackenzie squeaked, "On Brubaker Street next to the Hot Spot café."

Christ, could she sound any dumber? She savagely poked at the bubbling sauce in the pan, checking the consistency. Almost done. Shuffling away from Veronica, she opened the bag of unsalted peanuts and set it aside. The baby bok choy had been cleaned. The green onions were already on the counter, washed and thinly sliced. All she needed now was—

Something inside the knife drawer rattled.

Mackenzie froze again, panicked thoughts running through her mind: *No, no, no, not now, Annabel, not now, not in front of Ronnie!*

"Did you hear that?" Veronica asked.

"No," Mackenzie replied hastily. Too hastily, she thought, caught by Veronica's confused frown. "I mean, I don't hear anything."

The knives in the drawer jangled more loudly.

"I'm sure I heard something," Veronica said, her hand moving to her hip. Reaching for the gun holster that wasn't there, Mackenzie realized. "Is somebody trying to break in the window?" She spun around, craning to look into the living room.

A quarter-inch at a time, the drawer crept open.

The blood drained from Mackenzie's face.

"Are you feeling okay?" Veronica frowned. "I'm sorry, that's a stupid question. You look like you've seen a ghost."

Mackenzie flinched when Veronica touched her forehead as if checking for a fever. A thin, hysterical giggle escaped her. Her gaze turned to the drawer, visible behind Veronica. It slid shut smoothly, as if Annabel obeyed her frantic mental commands.

"Have you been out in the sun today, Mac? You have, haven't you? Running around on such a hot day, then you came home to cook dinner…can we hold the sauce a while if I turn the fire down? Maybe you should sit in the living room. I'll turn up the air-conditioning a notch and bring you a cold cloth to put on your neck." Veronica tried to take her arm.

A different drawer suddenly shot out of the cabinet, dumping cutlery on the linoleum before flipping upside down on top of the heap with a god-awful clatter.

Mackenzie closed her eyes as Veronica whirled around, waiting for terrified shrieks and the sound of pounding footsteps headed toward the door. Instead, she heard a sharp inhalation of breath, followed by a creak and a thud that had to be a cabinet door opening and closing. Compared to some of the other stunts Annabel had pulled, this one would have seemed mild if it weren't for Veronica witnessing the whole thing.

Afraid to look, she screwed up her courage and forced her eyes open anyway.

Veronica did not appear frightened. In fact, she looked peeved. "You need to stop this right now!" she snapped in a loud whisper, her mouth a grim line. "That kind of out-of-control behavior is totally unnecessary and I won't have it."

"But I'm not doing anything," Mackenzie protested.

"I mean it!" Veronica cast a ferocious glare at an area near the kitchen sink before she turned to Mackenzie, her attitude apologetic. "Mac, I am so, so sorry about that," she said. "I don't know quite how to explain, but I hope you weren't frightened."

Mackenzie made an effort to unstick her tongue. "Me? What about you?"

Veronica shrugged, staying focused on her with flattering intensity. "Please pay no attention to...well, to anything strange because I promise I'm leaving and when I do, the...the strangeness will go with me. And of course, I'll clean up the mess later. And pay for any damages. Again, I apologize. I didn't know I'd be followed tonight."

A stuttering silver-gray light materialized in the corner of Mackenzie's eye and resolved into a familiar ghostly face that just as quickly faded.

Mackenzie groped for understanding. "Do you see Annabel Coffin, too?" she settled for asking, praying she wouldn't come off as a complete lunatic.

"Oh, my God," Veronica breathed, staring at her with huge eyes. She seemed to lose her balance, staggering backward until she collapsed in a kitchen chair. "You see her?"

"Sort of. Not always. But I know she's there." Reality intruded with the aromas coming from the pan on the stove. Panic retreated. "Excuse me a second."

Mackenzie rescued their dinner, turning the heat low to prevent the sauce from scorching, and dumped the cold *shi* noodles into the dish, also stirring in the baby bok choy. A couple of minutes should complete the dish, and then she'd serve dinner, provided Annabel was finished prompting shocks and revelations.

Color flooded into Veronica's cheeks. "Do you see them all the time?" she asked in apparent excitement. *Like me*, went unsaid, but not unnoticed.

"Annabel's my first," Mackenzie confessed. "So...you see dead people."

"I knew you were going to say that." Veronica's smile took the sting out of her words. She stood and started gathering the cutlery on the floor, putting the knives, forks and spoons into the sink. "I've seen spirits my whole life. 'Wait-abouts,' my grandmother calls them. I saw Annabel's spirit hanging around your office when the body was still there, but not since. She didn't try to communicate."

Mackenzie turned off the heat and divided the noodles into two bowls. She added a generous amount of sliced green onions and roasted peanuts to the top of each portion. "You never told me," she said, bringing the bowls to the table and giving one to Veronica.

"People think you're delusional or untrustworthy if you claim to see ghosts," Veronica said. "I tend to ignore them unless…well, unless it involves a case. Mostly, they're confused. They don't know what happened. They can't move on." She tried the dish and nodded enthusiastically. "This is good, Mac. Spicy. What's it called?"

"Dan dan noodles. Szechuan specialty." Mackenzie tasted her own serving. Perfect. "What's Annabel told you?"

"Not much. All I got was she wanted someone named Billy Wakefield—"

"Say no more, Ronnie. I think I'm already ahead of you."

Between bites of dinner, Mackenzie told Veronica everything she'd learned about Annabel Coffin and her boyfriend, Billy Wakefield. When she finished, she concluded bitterly, "And Jimmy, that noxious pain in the butt, has ordered me to stay away from the case. Except he said you could tell me the stuff that's going to be public knowledge."

Veronica slurped a noodle into her mouth, patted her lips with a napkin and set the empty bowl aside. "Sure, I can do that."

Mackenzie crunched a peanut. "You know," she mused, "I wonder how come Annabel came to me in the first place. Apart from her body being found in my office, which is technically not *my* office since I only rent the space, why not someone else? I'm sure Myrtle's Wiccan group would have helped her out."

"I was wondering the same thing," Veronica replied. "You'd think she would've come to me a bit more."

"Oh? Why's that?"

"Because she's my aunt."

Mackenzie stared, her last bite of dinner forgotten.

CHAPTER EIGHTEEN

Veronica continued before Mackenzie had a chance to voice her surprise. "I mean, Annabel's sort of an aunt, I think, or something like that. My mother's got Coffin relations, but as far as I can tell, Annabel's people pretty much stuck around Mitford County. My mother's folks are all over the place. Last night I got hold of Mémé Faillard in Louisiana, who used to be a Coffin before she married Great-Uncle Oscar. She told me I'm related to Annabel through my father's second cousin, though I'm not quite sure how. It's complicated."

"Relatives usually are," Mackenzie said, recalling the near-impenetrable Gordian knots of relationships on her own family tree. *Go back far enough*, she thought, *and almost everybody you meet is related to you somehow.*

The cabinet door opened and banged shut, a reminder of Annabel's presence.

"Do you see her?" Veronica asked.

"Yes and no. If I look straight at her, I don't see anything. But when I sort of focus sideways, or above her head, I see her sometimes. Not always. Sometimes, I feel a chill or catch flashes of silver and gray light when she's around."

"Like a black-and-white movie?"

"Not exactly." Trying to describe the indescribable was frustrating. Mackenzie picked up the empty bowls and went to the sink, where she turned on the tap, retrieved a plastic washbasin from the cabinet below and added dishwashing liquid. "The few times I've actually had a good look at her, she's black, silver and gray, but sharper than an old film," she said over the sound of water gushing from the faucet. "And foggier, too. Blurry, but sharp. Damn it, I know I'm not making sense—"

Veronica stopped her with a gesture. "That's okay, Mac. I understand what you're getting at. You know, what's interesting is how our experiences are so different."

"What do you mean?"

"I see Annabel in color."

Mackenzie's jaw dropped. "No shit! How'd that happen?"

"Beats me. It's always been that way." Veronica rose from the table and joined her at the sink. "You wash, I'll dry," she said, grabbing a dishtowel from the rack.

Up to her wrists in hot soapy water, Mackenzie didn't argue, although her mother would have been horrified by the idea of a guest doing the dishes. "Thanks."

They worked in comfortable silence. The cutlery had been washed, dried and put away when Veronica said, "According to Doc Hightower's report, Annabel died from a cerebral hemorrhage caused by a single blow to the back of her head with an object consistent with a pipe. The angle of the blow suggests the killer wasn't much taller than her. The working theory is that she was killed on or about the same time she disappeared in nineteen fifty-seven, but we don't know who did it or why."

The cabinet door banged twice.

"We'll do everything we can," Veronica went on, "but we have no witnesses, no evidence and no forensics apart from the body itself."

Mackenzie wasn't sure if Veronica was talking to the ghost or her. "What about the charm bracelet? Maynard told me that's how y'all identified her."

Billy, Annabel said, startling her.

Veronica used a towel to dry the cooking pot Mackenzie had just washed. "Did Billy give you the bracelet, Annabel?"

Yes.

"All the charms, too?"

Silence.

Mackenzie frowned. "Can I see the bracelet?" she asked Veronica.

"You'll have to ask Detective Maynard for permission. If I show it to you without his say-so, I'm breaking chain of custody." Veronica neatly folded the damp towel, replaced it on the rack and then did something strange. She reached into the sink, into the dirty, lukewarm water and took hold of Mackenzie's hands. "Now I want to talk to you about Debbie Lou Erskine," she went on, her expression almost bleak.

Mackenzie's heart began to gallop. Suddenly fearful, she tried to pull free.

Veronica let go, but only long enough for Mackenzie to take her hands out of the water before they were claimed again. "Let me talk." She took a deep breath, never shifting her gaze from Mackenzie's face. "I'm not dating Debbie Lou."

"Sure, sure, you broke up with her," Mackenzie replied, laughing nervously. "Good riddance to bad rubbish, as Meemaw used to say."

"I didn't mean to kiss Debbie Lou. She surprised me."

"I could tell." Mackenzie's insides quaked. She wished Veronica would release her, or at least stop staring at her that way, as if willing her to understand. "Debbie Lou is trash. You can do a lot better. Uh, if you're still, you know, wanting to experiment and all that."

Veronica seemed puzzled. "What do you mean?"

Thoroughly unnerved, Mackenzie yanked her hands out of Veronica's grip. "I figured you were curious about lesbians, which is fine, nothing wrong with pushing the boundaries of your sexuality. You know, trying from Menu B for a change, maybe getting ready to mix it up a little with Menu A and Menu B if that sauces your egg roll—"

"I'm confused. Are we talking about the Golden Buddha now?"

"No. We're talking about you being free to explore your potential bisexuality. And Debbie Lou—who is not, by the way, representative of the majority of lesbians, being a kind of sexual black hole from whence there comes weeping and gnashing of teeth—well, Debbie Lou took advantage of you…of your innocence," she plowed on, determined to convey to her friend that one bad experience didn't necessarily mean the experiment was a bust.

To her dismay, Veronica didn't respond. Or rather, instead of thanking her for her insight or telling her to go to hell, she burst out laughing.

For several long minutes, Mackenzie fidgeted uncomfortably in place, wondering if she ought to cure Veronica's hysteria by slapping her. On the other hand, she didn't want to appear abusive either, or give Veronica further bad impressions of lesbians in general.

Finally, Veronica ran down enough to gasp, "My…my…my what?"

"I know Debbie Lou didn't treat you right," Mackenzie said, alarmed by the fiery color of Veronica's face. "But trust me, I'm sure you can find another woman one day—"

Veronica cut her off with a loud honking bray. She sat down, clutching her sides. "Stop, please stop, I'm begging you!" she giggled, her cheeks slick with tears.

While waiting for the giggles, guffaws and gulping belly laughs to die down, Mackenzie emptied the washbasin, rinsed it out, dried it and put it away. She told herself that Veronica wasn't mocking her or being mean, which helped ease a fraction of her annoyance.

Her chore done and the laughter behind her finally ceased, she turned around, intending to demand an explanation, only to find Veronica standing inches away, gazing at her with warmth and affection.

"I think we got our signals crossed, Mac," Veronica said gently, again taking Mackenzie's hands. "Where'd you get the idea I was straight?"

The question sizzled into Mackenzie's mind with the stunning, illuminating force of a lightning bolt. She opened her mouth. Nothing came out.

"Two years, Mac. Two years I thought we were dancing on the verge of something and I've been waiting for you to make a move," Veronica continued, the corners of her mouth quirking. "You gave off such mixed signals! And when I finally work up the courage to ask *you* out, our first real date's a disaster."

"What date?"

"Swine Dining. I know, I'd just as soon forget about it, too."

Mackenzie wanted to deny that their awful dinner at the barbeque joint had been an actual date, but in recollecting the details, she began to see how she'd misinterpreted Veronica from the start. Or maybe not...

"What about the blond guy, Ronnie?" she asked.

Veronica appeared taken aback, but she answered calmly, "What guy?"

"When I first saw you after you moved to Antioch," Mackenzie said, working up a full head of indignant steam, "you were hugging a blond man. A very pretty blond man. Wasn't he your boyfriend? I mean, there's nothing wrong with being bisexual, but you can't blame me for thinking you were straight. The way you two made goo-goo eyes at each other—"

"Him!" Veronica chuckled. "That's my middle brother, Alex. He helped me move. And he did not make goo-goo eyes at me. He's farsighted and too vain to wear glasses."

Brother. Mackenzie deflated. "Okay, I feel like an idiot. I know you have a couple of brothers, but you've never shown me pictures and I had no idea Alex was man candy."

"Man candy?"

"Not important. Point is, I shouldn't have made assumptions about you."

"I thought I'd developed halitosis or really bad body odor. Every time I flirted with you, you pushed me away."

"I didn't realize you were flirting." The humor of the situation started to sink in. Mackenzie snickered. "I really believed you had no idea what you were doing."

"I knew what I was doing, but you made me so nervous! I figured maybe I wasn't your type, but then you went out with Mary Dean."

Mackenzie frowned. "What's special about Mary Dean?"

She'd gone to the movies with Mary a couple of times, visited the antiques district in War Woman Springs and taken her to the drive-in fast-food place for hamburgers, tater tots and strawberry milkshakes. Pleasant outings, but nothing earth-shaking. Mary was sweet and sunny, a curvy brunette with green eyes who, come to think of it, reminded her of…

Oh.

Now she really felt like an idiot.

"Mary looks a bit like me," Veronica said, "and you like being around me. We see each other almost every day. You kept showing up for lunch, inviting me on picnics and drives to the lake. You're wonderful, you're my best friend and I want you so much, Mac, and right now…right now, I'm going to kiss you."

The last two words penetrated the fog of realization in Mackenzie's head.

Something inside her broke, a dam she hadn't known she'd built cracking under the strain. All this time, she'd forced herself to consider Veronica as a friend. Only a friend. Specifically, a straight female friend for whom she shouldn't have wicked, lustful thoughts, because a stupid crush wasn't worth sacrificing their friendship.

Oh, how wonderful to be told she'd been wrong!

Giddy, she leaned forward, her lips already parted, because if Veronica meant to kiss her, by God, she intended to enjoy every second of it.

Veronica came closer and settled a hand on her hip. Mackenzie tingled with anticipation, but before their mouths met, a phone rang.

Not Nirvana. A business-like ringing tone.

"That's me," Veronica said. "I'm sorry."

Coming back to earth with a bump, Mackenzie groaned. "Don't answer," she pleaded, but Veronica shook her head.

"It's work, I have to take it," she said, turning away and pressing the phone to her ear.

Abandoned in the kitchen, Mackenzie huffed and sat at the table, grumbling to herself. Two years of tightrope dancing around Veronica, teetering between desire and disaster, and just when she thought the balancing act was over, another delay reared its ugly head.

"Damn it all to hell and gone," she muttered.

The cabinet door swung open.

She gave it the stink-eye. "Don't *you* start."

Slowly, the door creaked closed.

Mackenzie began to smile in satisfaction. The knife drawer rattled. "Cut it out," she snarled, unwilling to be intimidated by a dead woman.

Veronica returned after a few moments, twin carnation pink stripes blooming on her cheeks. "I'm sorry, Mac, I'm so sorry—"

"You have to go?"

"I don't want to, believe me, I'd rather stay with you, but there's been an accident on I-85 close by the Laxahatchee City exit. Overturned semi. Milk all over the road and traffic backed up for miles. I can't stay." Veronica kissed her chastely on the mouth, murmuring against her lips, "I'll come back, Mac. Soon as I can. Promise."

Mackenzie forced a smile. "We've waited this long. What's a little while longer?"

As soon as Veronica left, she went to the bedroom, buried her face in a pillow and screamed curses until she started repeating herself.

Tantrum over, Mackenzie sat up and blew her nose. Facing the prospect of sitting alone in her apartment with only the idiot box to keep her company, she decided to go for a drive, her go-to panacea for most ills. Maybe head over to Cherry Bomb's restaurant and pig out on a Cookie Monster Sundae: three scoops of ice cream—cookie dough, cookies and cream and chocolate chip cookie—plus lashings of hot fudge and whipped cream ought to soothe the sting.

Or maybe not, since the Cookie Monster was best when shared with someone else. Someone who wouldn't be there on account of spilled milk.

She put on sneakers and went to the hall for her cell phone and keys.

The sky had turned to gold, edged at the horizon with copper and brass as the sun touched the mountains. The temperature had dropped to a comfortable seventy-one degrees or so, but the mugginess had increased to a miserable proportion. Mackenzie felt like she'd been brushed all over with a thin film of sorghum molasses, leaving her dirty and sticky.

She drove with the window down, not set on any particular destination, just going where whim took her. Traffic decreased as asphalt eventually gave way to gravel.

Really paying attention to her surroundings for the first time, she realized she'd come to Sweetwater Hill. She glanced at her wristwatch—eight o'clock—and decided to pay Reverend Wyland a visit. The way she'd been treated by Kelly Collier and Mr. Dearborn still rankled. Perhaps outside his church, Wyland would be more willing to talk to her.

Her phone rang.

"Cross speaking."

"I just wanted to let you know the accident isn't too bad, but the cleanup's going to take a good long while, so I probably won't see you again until tomorrow," Veronica said. In the background, Mackenzie heard a fading ambulance siren.

"I'm out on Sweetwater Hill fixing to talk to Rev. Wyland. Want to meet for breakfast in the morning at my place?" Mackenzie crossed her fingers, hoping for a positive answer.

"I'd love to, Mac." A pause and a groan. "Sorry, I've got to go direct traffic."

"Okay. Be careful."

The call ended. Mackenzie tossed the cell phone on the passenger seat.

About a half-mile north of the church, she found a somewhat dilapidated house built of weathered wood, capped by a high peaked roof that extended on all sides. The structure resembled a small barn, right down to the square hayloft hatch in the center of the upper story.

Alafair stood in the side yard, taking laundry off a clothesline hanging between two trees. Encroaching twilight had begun to haze the air, but some daylight remained, allowing Mackenzie to see the hens strutting and pecking in the grass around Alafair's bare feet.

Mackenzie pulled off the road onto the dirt shoulder and got out of the car. "Hey, Alafair," she called politely. "Is your father home?"

The hens scattered, clucking alarm. Alafair folded a pillowcase and dropped it in a basket on the ground. "No, ma'am. Daddy's checking rabbit snares over to the church."

"Well, I'd better run over there, then," Mackenzie said.

"He'll be home soon. Say, have you found Jesus, ma'am?" Alafair asked after a pause. Even wearing a shapeless cotton shift, with her crystalline eyes and pale blond hair, she possessed a delicate beauty that outshone Kelly Collier. "Have you been saved?"

"Thanks for your help," Mackenzie replied, evading the question.

She'd been raised Episcopalian, but as a teenager about Alafair's age, she'd left the church. Religion didn't appeal to her. She refused to debate the matter. *Arguing about politics or religion, ain't no faster way to lose friends and make enemies,* her father had said.

Leaving Alafair behind, she found a place on the road to make a careful U-turn and drove back to the church.

From the road, the shack housing the church looked as though it would fall down in a mild breeze, but when she parked the car across the road and walked up to the door, she saw that repairs had been made, the sagging roof shored up and new windows installed.

Early evening had slipped further into night. She needed to leave soon, Mackenzie thought. She'd rather not have to navigate down the Sweetwater Hill road after dark. With her luck, she'd get a flat tire and lose cell phone reception at the same time.

A shuffling noise inside the church prompted her to call out, "Rev. Wyland, it's Kenzie Cross. May I speak with you, sir?"

She heard a series of dry scuffling sounds, like footsteps on sand. The church's door was open. She went inside, her hand groping for a light switch and finding nothing.

"Rev. Wyland, are you here?"

Her voice echoed slightly in the room. Metal folding chairs were arranged in a row against one wall. Opposite stood a long table holding a stack of hymnals, several wooden boxes with screen tops and two huge glass jars containing at least four or five gallons each of clear liquid. Strychnine, she thought. She'd heard Holiness Pentecostals drank poison during services when the Spirit took them. Survival was considered proof of salvation.

At the end of the room, a low dais held a pulpit. Behind it, a wooden cross hung on the wall, surrounded by framed, printed slogans declaring, "Jesus Saves!" and "Jesus Never Fails." An upright piano was wedged in the corner.

Mackenzie took a few more steps. "Reverend?"

Weakening light coming from the windows did little to push back the thickening shadows in the corners. Feeling a little chilled, she scrubbed her palms on her thighs, wishing she'd changed from cutoff shorts to jeans before leaving the house.

Suddenly, the silence in the church was broken by a loud buzzing, rattling sound near her sneaker, immediately followed by a stabbing pain in her calf, and two more thumps that felt like a sharp fingernail scratching her skin.

Her heart seized in her chest. Her lungs arrested mid-breath.

Rattlesnake.

CHAPTER NINETEEN

Mackenzie staggered backward, unable to tear her horrified gaze from the seven-foot long diamondback rattlesnake uncoiling from its hiding place under a chair. As if satisfied with its deed, the snake stopped rattling, slithered toward the dais and disappeared, leaving her alone in the church with a leg growing rapidly numb.

Frantic, she started for the door, growing clumsier with each step. She reached the doorway and clung to the frame, raising her gaze at a flicker of movement. Near a pair of cherry trees about a hundred yards away stood a lean figure topped by white hair. Wyland.

"Help me!" Mackenzie cried. "I've been bit!"

Wyland didn't move. She felt his eyes on her—watching, judging, deciding—and then he turned around and melted into the woods.

"Son of a bitch," Mackenzie gritted, doubting he'd gone for help.

She knew she shouldn't move around too much, but if she wanted to live, she needed to reach her cell phone, which she'd left in the car. She managed four steps outside before her leg buckled. She collapsed on the ground.

Her gaze went to her bitten calf, the area already beginning to bloat and turn blue. The two punctures oozed blood that looked dark in the deepening gloom. The other two strikes were probably scratches, impossible to see now with the swelling.

Her arms and lips were numb. Her tongue tingled. Unable to stand on her swollen leg, she crawled over the ground, grabbing handfuls of dry grass to assist herself along. Two of her fingernails broke painfully near the quick, but those were minor sparks in the bonfire of burning pain consuming her, as if her blood had reached boiling point.

Gasping, sweating heavily, grunting out her effort and her agony, Mackenzie made her way foot by foot on sheer strength of will. The car swam in her vision, sometimes impossibly far way, at other times appearing close enough to touch.

The muscles in her face began twitching. Her saliva tasted metallic. Without warning, a flood of thick vomit poured out of her mouth. She choked and spat to clear her airway. The reek of vomit triggered another spasm. She heaved helplessly. When the retching ceased, she felt weak and light-headed. Small, shuddering spasms wracked her frame.

After crawling away from the stinking mess, Mackenzie rested her head on the grass. Maybe she'd lie here, she thought. Catch her breath. The world receded in a haze. In her peripheral vision, shadows stirred. She closed her eyes.

Just rest a while…

A sharp pain shot through her scalp. Someone had pulled her hair.

"Stop," she mumbled.

The sadistic bastard yanked on her hair again.

"Ow!" She raised her head. Her gaze met a pair of eyes like black ice staring down at her from the top of a silver-gray column of light shining dazzling bright in the darkness.

Up, Annabel whispered.

Realization burst over her like cold water. Rattlesnake. Car. Cell phone.

Marshaling her strength, Mackenzie continued her painful belly crawl toward the Datsun. Whenever she stopped, Annabel chivvied her with pokes and pinches until she moved on. She cursed the tormenting spirit with every swear word she knew, but kept going over the grass and finally, on her hands and knees, over the pea gravel road.

Gravel dug into her palms, into her bare knees, sometimes cutting her flesh like little teeth. Spots of blood showed dark and wet against the gray dust powdering her skin.

At last, she came to the car. She stopped and leaned her forehead against the cool metal for a moment, panting and trembling. Her heart felt like a stone fist hammering against her ribs. No matter how much air she took in, it wasn't enough.

In, Annabel ordered, the word whispered right in her ear.

Reaching up to grasp the door handle caused a bright flare of crimson to explode in her vision. Everything went black, like a television signal suddenly cutting off. A vicious pinch on the flesh of her upper arm wrung a yelp from her. Consciousness returned in a rush.

"Damn you, Annabel," she tried to say, but her lips and tongue wouldn't work properly. The words came out in a garbled wheeze.

Sheer stubbornness got the car door open. Her searching hand scrabbled over the part of the driver's seat she could reach. No cell phone. She sobbed in frustration. Goddamn it! She was *not* going to die here. She was *not* going to die today.

Summoning the strength to continue from deep inside, Mackenzie reared up on her knees and grabbed hold of the steering wheel with both hands. Her uninjured leg pushed for purchase against the road as she heaved her body into the driver's seat. Pain flared, turning her muscles to lumps of lava under her skin.

Her vision stuttered, making it hard to see even though the interior light had come on. She made a grab for the cell phone on the passenger seat and jabbed a finger in the direction of speed dial. The phone slipped from her sweaty grasp and fell next to the brake pedal. In the shadows, she saw the phone's display glowing like an oversized firefly.

Exhausted, Mackenzie pressed her forehead on the steering wheel. From the phone on the floor, she heard Veronica's voice, faint but distinct.

"Hey, Mac, I'm still at the scene…Mac? Hello? You there?" Veronica sounded harried. "If this is one of those pocket dialing accidents—"

Mackenzie croaked and stretched an arm down, but she couldn't reach the phone. Her fingers scrabbled uselessly at the plastic case. She attempted a scream. Nausea squeezed her guts into a knot. She retched and retched, only distantly noting the vomit seemed awfully red.

"What's wrong?" she heard Veronica ask. "Mac…Mackenzie, can you hear me? What's going on? Are you okay? Answer me!"

Mackenzie slid into the waiting darkness.

She drifted in and out of consciousness, periodically waking to changing scenes like kaleidoscope views. When she slept, in strange, disturbing dreams she saw Annabel Coffin as the young woman had been in life: black hair, black eyes, fair complexion, pretty with a charming smile and a dimple in her cheek. The happy smile faltered when blood suddenly bloomed on the front of her pink skirt, the stain spreading until the fabric was saturated.

Rivulets of blood ran down Annabel's legs while she wept. More blood welled from her hairline and gushed over her face from brow to chin. Blood dripped from her hands, clung to her saddle shoes, clotted in her hair. Blood rose in a scarlet wave and—

Mackenzie opened her eyes to find a strange bearded man looming over her. The sight of his blue EMS uniform soothed her initial panic. Her gaze traveled to the IV bag he held in his left hand. A plastic tube connected the bag to a needle in her inner elbow.

He noticed her watching him. "You'll be fine, Ms. Cross," he said. "Life Line just landed. They'll be loading you in a minute for transport to Trinity General."

Life Line. The name didn't mean anything at first. The answer eventually surfaced from the confused tangle in her head. Emergency medical helicopter. Air ambulance.

She closed her eyes.

The next time she woke, she lay on a gurney surrounded by medical equipment. The fluorescent lights were too bright. Pain throbbed in her arms and legs, especially in her bitten leg, which lay outside the white sheet covering the rest of her body. Even the fingertip heart rate monitor's pressure hurt.

Veronica stood beside the gurney, her posture belligerent. Some of her hair had escaped the bun at the back of her head, and hung in messy strands around her flushed face. She looked rumpled, worried and downright furious.

"Now you listen to me," Veronica said in a low growl, surprising Mackenzie with her fierce glower. "She needs to be started on CroFab immediately. If you'd just read Russell's book, I have a copy right here, he recommends—"

"I beg your pardon," said the man in the white doctor's coat, stiffening in offense. "I'm not going to listen to advice given by someone who has no medical training."

"But—"

"The patient's vitals are steady. The swelling hasn't progressed. We're monitoring the situation and we'll give her something for the pain if she needs it. Frankly, I won't prescribe the antivenin treatment unless her symptoms make it necessary. I think I know more about medicine than you, *Deputy*." The emphasis he put on her title made it sound like an insult. "So I'll thank you to leave, or I'll have to call security."

Veronica leaned in, pushing her face close to his. "Apparently, I have more experience with rattlesnakes than you, *Doctor*, since I can see she's in trouble. She needs antivenin. If she dies because you're too arrogant to listen to common sense, I will—"

Mackenzie watched the doctor sneer. "Are you threatening me?"

"No, sir." Veronica poked a finger at him that didn't quite connect. Nevertheless, he flinched. In a flicker of a moment, she transformed from a woman with a personal agenda to a law enforcement officer. Her eyes glittered like winter sunlight on broken glass. "I'm informing you that due to your callous disregard for your patient's life," she said in her professional voice, "and your self-indulgent attitude, I'm forced to arrest you on suspicion of using or being under the influence of a controlled substance."

"You can't do that. You don't have a warrant."

"I don't need an arrest warrant. I have probable cause. Your erratic behavior leads me to suspect that you might be abusing drugs, Dr. Ingram, possibly narcotics, making you a danger to yourself and your patients. It's not an unknown problem. We won't know for sure until the results of the blood test come back. That could take a while and you'll stay in county lockup the entire time."

"My lawyer will have me out before breakfast!"

"Your attorney may file a motion, sir, and that motion may be granted by a judge. However, if the paperwork's been misplaced or misfiled, or if a prisoner has been transferred to a maximum security facility like Georgia State Prison in error…" Veronica shrugged. "Jail's a very unpleasant place full of very unpleasant people, or so I've heard. It might take a while before you're found, Dr. Ingram, because I'm the one who does the paperwork. No telling what might happen while you're at the mercy of hardened felons. A pity, but the law's the law and my duty is clear."

Veronica's threat was delivered in such a reasonable, conversational, almost gentle way, even Mackenzie was chilled.

Ingram stared at her. Suddenly, he backed off and fumbled his way through the curtains. Veronica watched him until he was gone, and then she turned around to look at the bed. For a second, a shadow crossed her face. Her shoulders slumped.

Mackenzie couldn't bear to see the defeated expression. She tried to lift her head.

"Hey, Mac, you're back with us," Veronica said in a completely different tone of voice: part relief, part concern, part resolve. She smiled. "How do you feel?"

Mackenzie felt Veronica's fingertips brush her arm. She flopped her hand over, palm up. Veronica took the hint and wrapped warm fingers around her wrist.

Her mouth was too dry to speak, as if she'd been eating sand. Mackenzie couldn't answer the softly spoken question. She closed her eyes and let go, secure in the knowledge that no matter what, Veronica would be right there, guarding her back and keeping her safe.

CHAPTER TWENTY

Mackenzie woke when someone jostled her gurney.

No, she realized, her bed in a proper hospital room, not the Emergency Room, though the medical equipment seemed similar. At least this place had a window.

Remembering the rattlesnake in the church, she did a mental assessment of her injuries. The IV site in the back of her hand itched. Careful exploration of her body led to the discovery of sensors attached to her skin. Leads fastened to the sensors trailed out from under the sheet to connect to a bedside monitor.

Further investigation showed she also had a catheter, which didn't exactly hurt, but the weirdness and sensation of pressure down there made her uncomfortable.

She shifted, biting back a gasp when a spike of pain flared in her leg from ankle to thigh. The pain ebbed slightly, but she felt it hovering on the edges like a feral cat, all vicious teeth and red-hot claws waiting to dig into her flesh again if she moved.

Veronica, seated in a visitor's chair next to the bed, put down the book she'd been reading and focused on her. "You're in the ICU at Trinity General Hospital."

Since a response seemed expected, Mackenzie nodded.

"Are you feeling any better?" Despite looking frazzled and as tired as Mackenzie felt, Veronica had never appeared more lovely or more luminous.

"Not really," Mackenzie wanted to say. She ached everywhere, as if she'd been beaten, but her wooden tongue prevented her from making more than a rasping sound.

"Here, this should help," Veronica said, taking a cup from the side table.

The ice chip Veronica spooned past her lips tasted like heaven. Mackenzie moaned when a shock of cold and wet filled the inside of her mouth and trickled down her throat. She moaned again, this time in disappointment, when Veronica shook her head.

"That's all for right now, Mac." Veronica returned the cup to the table. "You were throwing up a lot at the scene."

Mackenzie still couldn't speak. She tried anyway, managing to slur, "S-s-sur…" before she quit in frustration and made an impatient gesture.

Veronica scooted forward until her elbows rested on the edge of the bed. "Your leg is very swollen. The doctor in charge of your case, Dr. Cornsilk, is concerned, but he's had experience with snakebites and agrees with Russell's opinion. He ordered antivenin—you're getting the second vial of CroFab now—and he's keeping a close eye on you."

"Good," Mackenzie forced out. "Russ'l?" Another doctor, she supposed.

"Findlay Russell wrote *Venomous Snake Poisoning*." Veronica held up the book she'd been reading so the title was visible. "He's an expert toxicologist."

Recalling the confrontation she'd overheard between Veronica and Ingram, Mackenzie wondered what had happened to the ER doctor. "No Ingram?"

Veronica did not look in the least embarrassed. "Ingram's inexperienced, but snakebite's pretty rare around here. Fortunately, Dr. Cornsilk stepped in to educate him on when it's appropriate to administer antivenin. Ingram won't make that mistake again."

Her heart warmed by the memory of Veronica's fierce protectiveness, Mackenzie mouthed, "Thank you." Thank God Veronica had been there to act as her advocate.

"I notified your mother," Veronica told her. "She was here earlier and promised she'd come back in the morning with breakfast, if you're allowed to eat by then."

Mackenzie rolled her eyes. She knew Sarah Grace loved her as only a mother could love a daughter, but *Passion's Pastime* came first. "TV?"

"I'm afraid so." Veronica patted her hand, careful to avoid the IV needle.

"How...how long?"

"How long have you been in the ICU? They brought you up here the night before last. You've been out about thirty-six hours or so, probably because of the morphine."

Drugs. No wonder I feel like leftover crap, Mackenzie said to herself, briefly horrified at the thought of Veronica seeing her *sans* makeup, *sans* hairbrush, and—she sniffed, detecting a sour, bitter aroma under the medicinal smells—*sans* shower and deodorant.

As if reading her mind, Veronica grinned. "They say after three days camping, nobody stinks. I'm sure the same applies to hospitals." Her gaze softened, becoming almost unbearably tender. "I'm just glad you're alive, Mac. I was afraid—"

Veronica stopped speaking when a lean, older Native American man in a doctor's coat entered the room. His hair hung in fine black strands to the angle of a square jaw. He glanced at Mackenzie over the top of the gold-framed glasses perched on his nose.

"Good evening, Ms. Cross. How are you feeling? Dizzy? Any numbness or tingling anywhere?" When she shook her head, he went on, "How's your pain level?"

"Hurts," Mackenzie replied.

"On a scale from one to ten."

She held up seven fingers.

Veronica clapped a hand to her mouth, her eyes comically wide. "Oh! You've got a morphine drip hooked into your IV line. The button's right here. I'm sorry I didn't tell you."

Mackenzie mashed the button. After a few moments, the gnawing pain in her leg didn't so much go away as the rest of her moved to a slight distance from it, making the pain easier to bear. The tension tightening her shoulders relaxed a notch.

Cornsilk put on a pair of disposable, blue nitrile gloves and removed the sheet covering the lower part of her body, shocking her with the sight of her bloated calf which resembled a side of beef that had hung too long and gone off. The puncture wounds were very dark, as if the skin were bruised to the bone.

Veronica didn't seem fazed and actually craned her neck a little to get a better view of the injury. Mackenzie wasn't squeamish, but she averted her gaze after a moment, the sight of her swollen leg making her uneasy in the pit of her stomach.

"It's not quite as bad as it looks," Cornsilk said, examining her leg. "Every snakebite's different, but I'd say you received a moderate envenomation." His touch felt cool on her heated skin. "There's been no progression since last night. We'll keep monitoring, but if you continue to improve and there's no further swelling, we'll move you out of ICU tomorrow."

"How long?" Mackenzie asked.

Cornsilk seemed to understand the question without the need for elaboration. "Maybe three or four days," he said, giving her a sympathetic look. "We'll see how you do after we administer another vial of CroFab and do some blood work. Lucky for you, we could get antivenin doses delivered from Atlanta. Now you seem to be coming along quite well, but until further notice, I still want you to hold off on food or liquids. Nothing, understand?"

Mackenzie glared.

"Yes, I know your mouth is dry, but we're keeping you hydrated with the IV." Cornsilk removed his gloves. Behind the lenses of his glasses, his dark brown eyes were kind. "We'll revisit the idea of eating and drinking if the swelling continues to go down."

After the doctor left the room, Veronica said, "I thought I lost you, Mac."

"Sorry," Mackenzie said.

Veronica went on as if she hadn't spoken, "I got your call in the middle of directing emergency crews to people injured in the crash on I-85. At first, I figured it was an accidental call and I was about to hang up, but then I heard her."

"Who?"

"I heard Annabel."

A chill passed through Mackenzie at the mention of the ghost. She had a vague memory of seeing Annabel after the rattlesnake had bitten her. The memory had a lot of blood involved, so she dismissed it to concentrate on Veronica.

"Annabel kept saying, 'Help.'"

"I knew you were in trouble, so I didn't bother waiting for permission to leave. I just jumped in my patrol car and floored it to Sweetwater Hill," Veronica said. As she spoke, her voice grew thinner and thinner, like a thread unraveling. "Oh, Mac...you scared me. When I got to the church, you were semiconscious. Your face was so white. I didn't think you were breathing very well and you were dry heaving constantly. A couple of times while I was waiting for the ambulance, I thought you'd died, but the paramedics at the scene told me your vital signs were good. I guess I couldn't hold it together very well."

Mackenzie squeezed Veronica's fingers. "Sorry, Ronnie."

"Don't be sorry, just don't do it again!" Veronica cried. After a moment, she whispered, "Annabel stayed there, Mac. The whole time. I saw her in the car next to you, plain as day, and I wondered..."

She was silent so long, Mackenzie prompted, "What?"

"I wondered if she'd come to guide you to the Other Side." Veronica lowered her head to press her brow against Mackenzie's hand. "I'm glad I was wrong."

CHAPTER TWENTY-ONE

Four days later, Mackenzie paused at the top of the cement steps and braced a hand against the wall, fighting a wave of dizziness. Her vision blanked at the edges and she thought she might throw up. Eventually, the desperate panting eased. Once she was certain she wouldn't lose consciousness, she opened the door of her apartment and slipped inside.

Veronica wouldn't be happy she'd taken a taxi home, but she hadn't been able to stand being stuck in the hospital one more minute and she'd found out from Sarah Grace that her car had been driven from Sweetwater Hill by Veronica and left in its usual downtown parking space She had only waited for Dr. Cornsilk to give the all-clear before signing the paperwork and calling the cab company.

Her apartment smelled slightly stale when she entered, carrying a small bag from the hospital pharmacy. She moved to the living room and opened the windows before turning off the air-conditioner. The fresh air helped clear her head and invigorate her, no doubt aided by the delicious smells wafting from the bakery downstairs.

Going to the kitchen, she opened the refrigerator and eyed the nearly bare shelves. Her mother's work, she supposed. While she appreciated the gesture, she wished Sarah Grace hadn't bothered. The only items to survive the purge were three bottles of beer, an egg and several lemons. She had staples in the pantry, but didn't feel like scrounging up a meal even though she felt as if someone had scooped out her insides, leaving her as hollow as a gourd.

Faced with the hospital's gelatin, oatmeal and similar bland, ill-prepared institutional food, she hadn't eaten much. Sarah Grace had managed to bring her sausage biscuits once the eating restriction was raised, but she craved a hot, well-seasoned meal, preferably with a dessert afterward that wasn't wobbly or putrid green. Unfortunately, her injured leg throbbed too much to contemplate eating out.

Mackenzie sat on the sofa, her leg thrust stiffly out in front of her. The dramatic swelling had started to go down just after her second day and her seventh dose of antivenin, and all but vanished by her third day, but the muscles remained weak and painful.

No further necrosis at the bite site, thank goodness. Dr. Cornsilk had arranged for the damaged, dead tissue to be cleaned and debrided. She'd have a scar on her calf, but it could have been much worse. In the doctor's opinion and her own, she was a lucky, lucky woman.

Hearing a couple of knocks, Mackenzie levered herself off the sofa and answered the door. The bakery owner and the owner of her rental apartment, Sam, stood on the threshold smiling and holding a box emblazoned with his company's logo.

"Welcome back," he said, stepping into the apartment when she moved aside.

"Thanks. It's good to be back." Mackenzie liked Sam. Apart from being an excellent landlord, he was a distinguished baker and a generous soul.

"Hospital food is terrible," he said with a grimace. "I should know, I nearly starved to death years ago after my gall bladder surgery. Here." He thrust the box into her hands.

Mackenzie raised the lid. The box contained three hand-sized, flaky pastries that smelled savory rather than sweet. Her mouth watered. "This is new. Empanadas?"

He beamed, showing a gap between his front teeth. "No, baked sambusak with chickpea filling, or feta and kashkaval—a Bulgarian cheese—or beef and onions," he replied, pointing at each pastry in turn. "Nice and spicy. I just hired a new assistant baker and these are his grandmother's recipes. We'll try the fried variation next, see where it goes."

"I can't wait," Mackenzie said, meaning every word. Her stomach rumbled. She was so hungry, she could've eaten the box. "Thank you very much, Sam."

"I'd be glad to hear your opinion whenever it's convenient."

"No problem. You know I love being your test subject."

When he began to leave, she had a thought and stopped him. "You've owned the bakery a while, right?" she asked. "What do you know about the building next door?"

"This has to do with the lady's body they found in your office?" he asked instead of answering her question. When she nodded, he added, "Eat while we talk."

Without bothering to fetch a plate, she sat at the kitchen table and tried the cheese sambusak. Like an angel pouring blessings on her tongue, she thought. The pastry melted in her mouth and the cheeses were delicious. The spicier chickpea and beef fillings were equally good. She couldn't wait to try a crunchy fried version, and told him so.

The look on her face made him chuckle. "Okay, I guess they're all winners. Now as for the bakery, my father bought it in 'fifty six. It was just a warehouse and offices then, this building and the one next door. He had to convert this place for use as a retail bakery. At the same time, the other building's owner was also renovating his property, but who that was, I couldn't tell you." He seemed lost in his memories for a moment. "I was a kid, but I remember arguments Dad had with my mother about the costs running over. At one point, he ran out of money and had to stop work until my grandfather lent him what he needed. By that time, the building over there changed hands and the new guy halted the renovation work. No idea why. He left everything half-finished, rubble everywhere, broken windows, a real mess. Dad was pretty cheesed off. He used to complain to Mom that he'd never get customers in the bakery with that eyesore next door."

"When was this?"

"About nineteen 'fifty-seven or somewhere thereabouts." Sam opened the front door. "Got to run, Kenzie. If you need anything else, give a holler."

Her cell phone rang while she digested the sambusaks and Sam's information. Interesting that the buildings had been under construction in 'fifty seven, the same time as Annabel's disappearance and presumed murder.

"Cross speaking," she muttered into the phone.

"Hey, Kenzie, I hope this isn't a bad time," James Larkin said. "How are you feeling?"

The journalist had called twice while she was in the hospital and visited once when she'd been loopy on morphine. He hadn't stayed long, just dropping off a get well card and a bouquet on his way to his wife's appointment with her OB/Gyn. At the time, Mackenzie wished he'd brought her a chili dog and fries instead of flowers.

"Just got home, Little Jack," she said. "I'm fine. Thanks for the sunflowers. They really made the room a lot brighter."

"You're welcome. Listen, we're doing a story on your rattlesnake bite," he said.

"No."

"What you were doing, where it happened, the whole enchilada. My intern from Welcome College is already researching snakebite statistics in Mitford County."

"No."

"I'm angling to get hold of Deputy Birdwell to hear her side—"

"Absolutely not," Mackenzie interrupted. "Why, Jack? Slow news week?"

"Actually, your story has local interest and it's a link to the controversy with the Covenant Rock Church of God with Signs Following and the Antioch city council."

"What controversy? What the hell happened when I was laid up?"

"It's been going on a while. At the last city council meeting, some of the more conservative members talked about an ordinance against snake handling, but the proposal didn't receive majority support. You getting bit on church property is like a gift for them, Kenzie. Dearborn and his crowd will get a lot of mileage out of your accident."

"Jacob Dearborn?" Mackenzie blurted. "He's a city councilman?"

"That's right. I'd really like to get a quote from you," Larkin said.

Mackenzie considered the pain in her leg and made a decision. "Can you come over, Jack? I'd like to talk to you, but I'm not in any shape to traipse over to the newspaper."

"Sure, sure, Kenzie," Larkin replied. "I'll be there in ten minutes."

"I'll put the coffee on." Some nice person—probably Veronica—had replaced the coffee machine's broken glass carafe when she'd been in the hospital.

While she waited for Larkin to arrive, she thought about Dearborn, Wyland and what Larkin had told her about the Antioch City Council. Perhaps there was more to the situation than Kelly Collier had told her. Only one way to find out, she decided. She checked the time and picked up her phone. Luckily, she still had Kelly's number.

"Hey, Kelly, it's Mackenzie Cross—don't hang up," she added hastily. "I want to ask you a question and then I'll never call you again."

"Screw you," Kelly replied, making an obvious attempt to sound brave and cool. "And lose this number, bitch, or I'll call the cops. Mr. Dearborn says this is harassment."

"Just one question, Kelly, unless you'd rather I had Jack Larkin from the *Antioch Bee* ask you. I'm meeting with him in a few minutes. Or maybe I should just ask your father." Mackenzie crossed her fingers and waited, hoping the teenager wouldn't call her bluff.

Kelly sounded suspicious when she said, "One question. After that, you'll leave me alone and never, ever call me again or try to see me."

"Deal."

"Go ahead."

"Did you actually hear Rev. Wyland demand Mr. Dearborn's resignation after the park incident, or did Dearborn tell you about it later?" Mackenzie imagined crickets chirping in the background while Kelly hesitated.

"He told me after it happened. Why shouldn't he? I'm marrying his son, after all," Kelly finally said. "You were just supposed to deal with that freak on the hill, but you messed that up, didn't you?" she added spitefully. "I heard you got bit on the leg by a rattler. Maybe next time you'll do us all a favor and die."

Ignoring Kelly's insult—she'd known the girl had a nasty streak—Mackenzie pulled the phone away from her ear and disconnected the call.

If what she suspected was true, Wyland had wanted a great deal more from Dearborn than his resignation from the United Methodist Church.

CHAPTER TWENTY-TWO

"—and I'm very grateful to the Antioch Volunteer Fire Department and Life Line Air Rescue, and offer my sincerest thanks for their heroic efforts. They saved my life," Mackenzie concluded, watching while James Larkin scribbled in his notebook. "Happy?"

"Ecstatic," he answered.

"Thanks Jack." She refreshed his cup from the pot on the coffee table and sat back against the sofa cushions. "Now tell me about Dearborn and the city council."

Larkin flipped his notebook shut. "Why are you so interested, Kenzie?" he asked. "You've never given two hoots about local politics."

"I don't like the idea of some politician making hay out of my snake bite to further his own agenda," Mackenzie replied. "I'd like to get a little background on Dearborn, the council and the current situation before I go blundering into something."

"As a city councilman, Jacob Dearborn tends to go along with the majority except when it comes to issues that might affect his business concerns," Larkin said. "Remember last year when the city council was getting ready to vote on a change in the property tax laws?" At her blank expression, he went on, "If the change in tax laws had gone through, Dearborn would have owed a lot more money on several of his businesses, like the Lucky Strike Bowling Alley. He campaigned heavily and the proposal lost the vote, ten to two."

"Okay, I get that, but why's he so hot to ban snake handling? Rev. Wyland's church is tiny compared to the Methodist church in town," Mackenzie said, "and the congregation is certainly no threat to anybody but themselves."

"That's the part I can't figure out. God knows I've tried," Larkin confessed. "There's never been a cross word exchanged between Wyland and Dearborn."

"Dearborn's definitely behind the proposed ordinance?"

"Yep. The proposal on the table will make it illegal to display, exhibit and handle dangerous or venomous snakes or reptiles within the city limits. Offenders will be subject to a ten-thousand-dollar fine and up to twelve months in jail for each violation."

"But Sweetwater Hill isn't in the city limits."

"Sweetwater Hill was incorporated into Antioch a year ago, Kenzie. Try to keep up with the news," he said, shaking his head as if in despair at her ignorance.

Mackenzie was disappointed by the lack of a connection between the two men. Maybe they needed to dig deeper into the past. "Where's Wyland from, anyway?"

Larkin finished his coffee in a few gulps. "Good question. I've already looked into the possibility of them knowing each other As far as I can tell, Wyland sprang forth fully grown from his mother's forehead since the furthest I can trace him is nineteen eighty-six in Cochran—that's in the middle of the state in Bleckley County—when he was mentioned in the *Cochran Journal* as a guest speaker at a Holiness Pentecostal church down there. Before that, nothing. Wyland and Dearborn share no commonalities I've been able to find."

"I'm curious, what's Wyland's first name? I don't think I've ever heard it."

"Neither have I, but the *Journal* article listed him as Wilson Wyland."

Mackenzie thanked Larkin and saw him to the door.

He paused on the threshold. "You remember you mentioned Dr. Isaac Rush?" he asked. "Pastor Rush's son. You wanted to poke around the archives for information on him."

"Oh, right. I haven't had time." She'd almost forgotten. The doctor seemed to have some significance for Annabel.

"I thought I'd do it for you. Isaac Rush served eight years for violating the state's abortion law," he said. "He'd been performing abortions on the down low, made quite a bit of cash before he was caught and convicted. When he was released in 'sixty-six, he was diagnosed with lung cancer and died in a hospice. Mind me asking why you want to know?"

"Miss Laverne," Mackenzie lied. "She comes up with crazy stuff sometimes."

He gave her a suspicious look, but started down the steps after giving her a wave.

A half hour later, she heard a brisk rap on the door. Before she could get off the sofa and make her slow way to the door, Veronica let herself inside the apartment.

"Hey, Mac, I wanted to make sure you were okay. Hope you don't mind." Veronica held up the spare key. "I went to the hospital and they told me you'd checked out. Why didn't you call me? I'd have given you a ride home."

Mackenzie smiled. "You know me, Little Miss Impatience. I called a cab. Thanks for getting my car, Ronnie. I'd hate for anything to happen to Daddy's pride and joy."

"No problem. Visitors?" Veronica asked, glancing at the empty coffee carafe.

"Little Jack Larkin came by," Mackenzie replied, scooting over to give Veronica room to sit next to her on the sofa. "Jealous?"

"Of Larkin? No. He's not your type. Besides, Esmeralda would kill him if he strayed and she'd claw your eyes out to boot. What did he want?"

"A statement about my accident."

Veronica sighed, took her hand, turned it over and kissed the palm. "Are you okay?"

"I'm good." Mackenzie leaned over and kissed Veronica's lips, her cheek, her chin. They'd done this in the hospital, casual kisses that were more about affection than passion. She wondered when Veronica would turn up the heat. On the other hand, she wasn't exactly in the best physical shape to get her groove on. At the moment, kisses suited her fine. "Hi there. How's the hardest working deputy in Antioch?" she asked.

"Busy." Veronica sat up and unbuckled her duty belt, laying it on the sofa beside her. "I had to talk to Rev. Wyland today about his rattlesnakes. He insisted none of his regular snakes had escaped their cages, but I'm not sure he was telling the truth."

Mackenzie caught her breath at a sudden mental image of Wyland standing under a cherry tree, calmly watching her struggle to reach her car after she'd been bitten.

"What's wrong? Need a pain pill?" Veronica asked, starting to rise.

"No. It's fine," Mackenzie replied, touching Veronica's arm to make her sit down. "Just…well, when the snake bit me, I think I hallucinated about Rev. Wyland."

Veronica frowned and leaned forward. "Really?"

"Or maybe it was a dream. I don't know."

"Tell me."

Mackenzie related everything she could remember about Wyland leaving her to die, which wasn't much. "I don't believe he'd do something like that. Probably a hallucination. I saw Annabel too. She was crying and covered in blood." Feeling a bubble of excitement rising inside her, she thought she had a piece of the puzzle figured out. "Listen, a while back, I was buying a sandwich from Miss Laverne and she was telling me about Annabel Cross."

"Anything interesting?"

"Annabel appeared to me when Miss Laverne mentioned Isaac Rush."

"Who?"

"The son of Pastor Rush, the old head of the First Baptist Church," Mackenzie explained. "He went to jail for performing abortions in the late fifties."

Veronica nodded. "And how does he connect to Annabel?"

Mackenzie went on to tell Veronica about the "woodshed"— the shack in the woods off the Jefferson Lowe expressway—and how Annabel had repeated Rush's name there.

"Poor Annabel kept saying, 'my boy, my boy,'" she finished. "If you add in Rush doing illegal abortions and that vision I had of Annabel with all the blood on her skirt and everywhere else, we can probably guess what happened."

She waited for Veronica to exclaim she'd solved the mystery, but instead, the woman shook her head.

"Sorry, Mac, that dog don't hunt," Veronica said, giving her the sort of terribly kind, pitying smile a teacher might bestow on a dull student. "Annabel died of blunt force trauma. She didn't bleed out after a botched medical procedure."

"Damn it, I know that," Mackenzie said, bristling. "But what if Annabel started to bleed later, after she'd gone home, and she panicked and arranged to meet Billy in the 'woodshed?' It's plausible. How's that dog hunting for you now, Ronnie?"

"It's speculation, not evidence," Veronica pointed out. "And who killed her? Billy?"

"He was there according to her."

"What's his motive?"

"It was the fifties. Maybe she threatened to go to her parents about the baby—"

"Or maybe it was someone else with a different motive. Speculation is fun, but we need solid facts, Mac. We need to follow the evidence, if we can find any."

Annabel suddenly blazed to existence in front of them in all her silver-gray glory, her eyes glittering like shards of black, hateful ice. *He did it*, she whispered, her pale face distorted with rage. *Killed me. My baby, my boy. Dead.*

"Who, Annabel?" Veronica asked, scrambling to her feet. "Who killed you?"

Annabel screamed. The sound went on and on, rising in volume until Mackenzie feared the windows might break. When the freight train roar threatened to deafen her, the ghost winked out, the scream cut off and a loud crash reverberated through the apartment.

Mackenzie closed her eyes. Having Annabel around was bad for her nerves and her wallet. *Please, don't let it be the toilet*, she pleaded internally. Having to trek down to her office every time she needed to pee would be inconvenient to say the least.

Veronica left the living room. When she returned, she reported that every mirror in the apartment had been shattered.

CHAPTER TWENTY-THREE

The next day, Mackenzie sat behind the computer in her office, trying to find the website of the city assessor's office.

Though she hadn't learned from Larkin what she'd hoped regarding Dearborn, an idea had nibbled at the edges of her mind after Veronica left and she went to bed last night.

If Dearborn didn't have a personal reason to want Wyland's church shut down, perhaps something else prompted him to put his support behind the ordinance. Larkin had told her Dearborn didn't generally put himself forward in the city council unless his business interests were threatened. That bit of information could be the key.

After wasting time searching for a website, Mackenzie discovered the city's public assessment records hadn't been made available electronically yet. If she wanted to continue her research, she'd have to go to city hall and do it in person.

Her leg throbbed and ached like a rotten tooth. She didn't relish the thought of walking over to city hall, but driving a few blocks seemed a waste of gas. Rather than go immediately or dose herself with pain meds that made her groggy, she opted to take care of her personal business first. Maybe later, her leg wouldn't hurt so damned much.

She checked her inbox, finding mail from a few new clients as well as a message from Richard Chen, the Hong Kong art dealer. He had sent her the information that the '31 Bugatti Kellner was in the hands of Sheik Ahmad Salar of Saudia Arabia.

Looking up background information on Salar, her heart sank to her toes. The man was an obsessive automobile collector. In her experience, such people rarely, if ever, sold pieces from their collection and Salar certainly didn't need the money. If Forbes' annual billionaires list was correct, Salar could wipe his ass daily on fistfuls of thousand-dollar bills for the rest of his life and still leave a mighty fortune to his heirs.

No million dollar bounty for me, damn it. She sent an email to her client in Abu Dhabi with the news. If he wanted her to open negotiations with Salar, she would, though privately she considered the Bugatti beyond anyone's reach at this point.

Such terrible disappointment required soothing in the form of coffee.

Surrendering to necessity, she took half a pill to dull the edge of her pain before stepping out of the office and around the block to Mighty Jo Young's.

"Hey, Kenzie," Jo-Jo called from her place behind the monstrous espresso machine. Today, her lurid red curls were held back from her face by a floppy, candy-pink bow that bobbed each time she moved. The bow matched her dress, an A-line floral print covered with huge pink cabbage roses. "The usual?"

Mackenzie nodded and went up to the counter, bypassing the line and earning glares from other customers, which she ignored. "I'm about dead from caffeine deprivation," she said. "Get me a cappuccino, STAT…please."

Jo-Jo tamped espresso grounds into the filter, popped it into place and flicked the hot water knob while reaching for a milk pitcher. About a minute or so later, she slid a perfectly made cappuccino on the counter in front of Mackenzie.

"Beverage of the gods," Mackenzie said, collecting her cup.

"Let me finish up here and I'll join you at the table," Jo-Jo said over her shoulder, already working on an order for a latte.

Mackenzie chose a table close to the front, just beating out a high school student of indeterminate sex juggling a laptop bag, messenger bag, several books, a stack of flyers, a tablet PC and an iPod. The student gave her the hairy eyeball and wandered off.

Jo-Jo bustled over, wiping her hands on a kitchen towel. "So how are you doing?" she asked, sliding into a seat.

"I'm getting there." Mackenzie licked foam off her lips. She didn't know what Jo-Jo put in the cappuccino, but it was the best in Mitford County, bar none.

"I'm sorry I didn't get a chance to visit you in the hospital, honey," Jo-Jo went on, looking somewhat shamefaced. Her bright pink lacquered fingernails picked at a nick in the tabletop. "I meant to go, but I had two baristas quit on me without notice and another had to switch to part-time. I've been run off my feet. By the time I *had* time, visiting hours were over. At least we talked on the phone. Did you get the flowers I sent?"

"Yes, they were lovely," Mackenzie said, recalling the girlish bouquet of baby pink roses and daisies, so like the ultrafeminine Jo-Jo. "Really raised my spirits."

Jo-Jo scoffed. "Girl, I know you like I made you. Tell the truth and shame the Devil."

"The flowers were very pretty. Honest!"

"But pink's not your thing. I know. I can't help myself. Frilly stuff makes me drool."

A barista walked rapidly toward them, set down a caffè Americano in front of Jo-Jo and whisked away just as quickly.

Jo-Jo tasted her coffee and nodded. "Good. The boy can learn. Yesterday, his Americano was shocking, Kenzie. I nearly spit it out on the floor." She glanced at a clock on the wall. "Goodness! Break's over for me. Give me a hug, honey, so I have something nice to remember while I slave away to skin and bones over a steaming espresso machine."

Mackenzie drank the dregs of her cappuccino and stood to be crushed against Jo-Jo's vast, talcum powder and coffee-scented bosom. The lacy edge of Jo-Jo's apron scratched her nose, but she would never complain.

"Next time, I want to hear all about you and Deputy Birdwell," Jo-Jo said, holding her at arm's length. "Don't blush. I know you've been pining a while over her and I'm glad for both of you." She beamed. "When's the wedding? Can I be a bridesmaid?"

"For God's sake, Jo!" Mackenzie protested, chuckling at her friend's delight. "How the heck did you find out?"

"Honey, your mama told me the deputy hung around your hospital bed like a loyal puppy at her mistress' feet. I'm just saying, it's about damned time."

"Don't go too far. Ronnie and I are still sorting everything out. We haven't even been on a real date yet."

"Pooh," said Jo-Jo, pursing her lips. "Y'all make a cute couple. Anyway, I want to hear all about it, but later." She eyed the counter, nearly overwhelmed with customers, and made a face. "Right now, I'd better get back in there before the rest of my baristas quit."

After a final promise to meet for lunch on the weekend, Jo-Jo returned to her work and Mackenzie to hers—namely, paying a visit to the city assessor's office in city hall. Since the pill had kicked in, she felt able to walk the short distance.

The clerk was an elderly man with oiled gray hair and a nose like a cauliflower. Mr. Bryson didn't look like much in his shabby suit, but there was nothing wrong with his mind. He didn't consult the computer when she inquired about the ownership of parcels on the newly incorporated Sweetwater Hill, but nodded and came out from behind his desk.

"This way, miss," he creaked in his dusty voice.

With shuffling steps, he led the way through a door and into a large room. The space was full of floor-to-ceiling shelves. Each shelf was loaded with boxes.

"We have records from as far back as the original Spanish settlement in the mid-sixteenth century," Bryson went on, his voice hoarse and barely audible. "Sweetwater Hill, you said? Wait one moment."

He shuffled away and returned several minutes later carrying a box, which he put on a small table. "Now, miss, here's the rules: you can look at the records, but they can't leave this room. If you want to make copies on the machine downstairs, I'll do it for you and it'll cost fifty cents a sheet. If you don't find what you're looking for, come get me. Don't return the box to a shelf and don't touch any of the other boxes." He waited for her reply, staring at her with a sharp brown eye. The other was clouded and milky with a cataract.

"Yes, Mr. Bryson, I understand," Mackenzie said. "Do you mind if I take pictures of the pages with my cell phone?"

He didn't answer, but turned his back and began shuffling out of the room. She took his dismissive wave as permission.

Taking a seat on an uncomfortable metal chair and elevating her bad leg on another, she removed the lid from the box, took out a file and began to read, snapping pictures with her cell phone of crucial data like legal descriptions of property, parcel numbers and other information.

Several hours later, Mackenzie returned the last file to the box and stuck her cell phone in the pocket of her jeans. She still didn't know who owned the parcels of land on Sweetwater Hill, but she'd found what she needed to further her search.

She left the room to talk to Bryson.

CHAPTER TWENTY-FOUR

"Excuse me, sir," Mackenzie said, walking to the desk where Bryson sat reading a newspaper. "Where can I find deed records?"

"Mitford County Register of Deeds," he said, "which ain't here."

"Where is it?"

"Downtown Laxahatchee City."

She swallowed a groan. A trip to Laxahatchee City would only take a half hour, but the downtown area was a maze of one-way streets and confusing parking zones that seemed to change hourly. Few non-natives escaped without at least one violation.

The last time she'd had to visit Laxahatchee City, it had cost her two hundred and eighty bucks in parking tickets, her car had been towed, requiring another four hundred to get it out of the impound yard, and she'd been given a further citation for speeding when she left town.

Bryson wheezed. It took her a moment to realize he was laughing. "You look like you've been sucking lemons, miss," he said. "If you don't want to make the trip, you can order a copy of recorded deeds for a dollar a page."

"From you?"

"No, the Internet. Takes two weeks, if you're lucky."

"Do you know any way I can expedite things?" Mackenzie asked with faint hope.

Bryson regarded her with his bird bright eye. "Maybe," he said.

"And how could I do that, sir?" she asked, leaning an elbow on the counter. She recognized a man willing to make a deal, or at least open negotiations. The trick was to avoid any overt offers and take her cue from his opening move.

"Well, as it happens, as chief clerk of the city assessor's office, I have access to county deed records right here." He jabbed a thumb at his computer.

Mackenzie nodded. "And would you be willing to look up the records for me?"

He rubbed his stubbly chin. "Maybe I could." He smiled. "For two dollars a page."

Petty larceny at its pettiest, she thought, but worth the expense. Mackenzie took out her cell phone. "Deal. I'll give you the liber and page numbers, you print out the deeds."

The documents, run off on the office's cheap printer, were good enough for her needs. When Bryson added the last deed to the stack on his desk, she ran through the pages twice to be sure she had everything, and reached for her wallet.

He watched her count out the fee with poorly disguised greed.

"That's fifty dollars," she said, handing him two twenties and ten one-dollar bills.

Wordlessly, Bryson accepted the money and gave her an empty manila file folder.

Mackenzie put the sheets in the folder, thanked him and left the office.

Returning home, she sorted through the deeds. The result of her study was unexpected, though not exactly surprising. It seemed Jacob Dearborn owned almost the entirety of Sweetwater Hill apart from two parcels, both belonging to Wilson Wyland.

She didn't bother sorting through the entire history of the parcels, but picked up her cell phone and dialed James Larkin. "Hey Jack, I came across something interesting today," she told him when he answered the call.

"Can it wait? I'm up to my ass in alligators, Kenzie," he said, sounding distracted.

"Do you think the *Antioch Bee* might be interested in running a story about corruption on the city council?" Mackenzie asked.

The line went silent. At last, Larkin asked, "Are you sure? I mean, are you absolutely sure?" in a slow, deliberate way that left no doubt she had his undivided attention.

"I'm not a hundred percent sure, which is why I need your help."

After another long pause, he sighed. "Okay, tell you what… come over to the newspaper and we'll talk. I can't leave right now and I promised Esme I'd come home at a Christian hour, so take it or leave it."

"I'll meet you in ten minutes." Mackenzie ended the call.

As she left the apartment, the downstairs door opened to admit a uniform-clad Veronica, who glanced up at her. "Hey, Mac, I was coming to see you."

"I'm on my way out, Ronnie. I've got a meeting with Jack." Mackenzie paused and really looked at Veronica. Even the awful deputy's uniform couldn't hide the woman's prettiness. She groaned internally. This romance of theirs was going nowhere fast, but pain and opiates had struck her libido dead for the moment. She hoped Veronica still wanted her, because when she felt better, there would be naked happy time. *Swear to God.*

"Little Jack Larkin at the *Bee*? I thought he already interviewed you," Veronica said, pushing her hat back from her brow.

"He did. This is for something else."

Veronica waited for her at the bottom of the steps. "Anything I can do?"

Mackenzie shook her head. "Not unless you can pick me up and carry me to the newspaper. My pain pill's doing its best, but I'm starting to feel it." She kept a tight hold on the banister as she walked down step by step on her stiff leg.

"Want a ride in the patrol car? I can run and go get it," Veronica offered, holding the door open and letting her pass outside.

"The newspaper's not that far." Mackenzie took Veronica's offered arm and started in the direction of the *Antioch Bee*. "Do you know anything about Jacob Dearborn?"

"Apart from the complaint he tried to file against you?"

"What?"

Veronica nodded. "He came into the station the other day claiming you were harassing a high school student, Kelly Collier. But Miss Collier is eighteen years old. If she wants a complaint filed, she needs to do it herself, as I told Mr. Dearborn. I also advised him that making slanderous statements to an officer of the law wasn't a very bright move."

Fuming, Mackenzie said, "I'd like to wring the old bastard's neck."

"Don't make threats, Mac. Did anything happen between you two I should know about?" Veronica asked mildly, but the question rubbed Mackenzie the wrong way.

Her temper flared. Was Veronica insinuating something improper had occurred with her and Kelly Collier? Recalling Dearborn's threat to make trouble for her on the day she visited him at home, the question from Veronica seemed like an insult. "You too?" she asked, wrenching her arm away. "Do I need a lawyer before I answer?"

"Take it easy, Mac," Veronica said, giving her a concerned look. "If there's a situation between you and Dearborn, I want to help. Or don't you trust me?"

Oh. Me and Dearborn, not me and Kelly. Mackenzie's anger abruptly dissipated, leaving her deflated. "Yes, of course I trust you. Sorry. I'll tell you about my conversation with him, but I don't want to be late for my appointment. Mind if I talk to Jack first?"

"Fine by me," Veronica said. "I'll drop you off at the *Bee*, since I guess you'd rather have your meeting with Larkin in private."

"Yes, thank you."

"What would you like for dinner? I can cook, if you want."

"Ronnie, the only thing you know how to cook is spaghetti," Mackenzie said, shuddering at the memory. "I hate to tell you this, but the jury's still out on that claim. The last time, you burnt the pasta to a cinder and the sauce was made of ketchup."

A flush crept up Veronica's neck to stain her cheeks. "You said the crunchy bits added texture. And you told me you liked the sauce."

"Mama raised me to be polite. Know what? How about you pick us up a couple of 'to go' dinners from Pontefract's boarding house on St. Mary Street?" Mackenzie suggested. "Just get me anything off the daily menu. And double corn bread."

"Will do. I'll meet you back at your place. Or would you like to eat at my house?" Veronica paused and glanced at her shyly. "If you're feeling up to it, that is."

Mackenzie pretended to think about the invitation while she and Veronica continued walking to the newspaper. "I don't know," she said when they reached the door of the *Antioch Bee*. She joked, "I don't want you to get the idea that I'm one of those 'fast' girls."

Veronica chuckled, leaned over and kissed her cheek. "See you later."

The brush of soft lips against her cheek made her long to turn her head and take Veronica's kiss on her mouth. For the first time since the rattlesnake bite, she found her desire rising—a welcome surprise. She reached out, her hand faltering in the air when Veronica continued walking away.

"Your house, Ronnie," Mackenzie said loudly, willing herself not to grab Veronica and wallow in her touch. "I'll meet you there, all right?"

On the corner, Veronica stopped and called to her, "Bring an overnight bag," before disappearing around the corner.

Oh, my God. Mackenzie felt as though her insides had melted like ice cream on a hot day. "Take that, Dilaudid," she murmured.

If her leg behaved, she was pretty sure she and Veronica would do more than kissing tonight. She bit her lip hard to distract herself from the sudden flush of warmth between her legs and pushed through the door into the air-conditioned atmosphere of the *Antioch Bee*.

CHAPTER TWENTY-FIVE

Seated in a chair at the side of Larkin's desk in the busy newsroom, Mackenzie laid out the facts she'd found in the county's public records. "My question is: when did the city council vote to incorporate Sweetwater Hill?" she asked at last. "Was it before or after Jacob Dearborn started buying parcels left and right?"

He shook his head, eyeing her over his steepled fingers. "I see where you're going and that's interesting, Kenzie, but to be honest, it's not so much corruption on the city council as much as blatant self-interest, which is not against the law."

Disappointed, Mackenzie slumped in her chair. "Okay."

"Sure, the city council voted to annex Sweetwater Hill into the Antioch city limits after Jacob Dearborn started acquiring parcels of land up there," Larkin explained, giving her a sympathetic pat on the arm. "Dearborn has supporters on the council who made a tidy profit selling their land on the hill to him. I'm sure they'll also get favors in return. None of this is illegal, Kenzie. Political *quid pro quo* is just business as usual."

"Crap. I thought I was onto something."

"Don't despair, my friend. There's one thing you said that piques my curiosity."

"Oh?"

Instead of answering her immediately, Larkin nodded a greeting at Marilyn Hayes, the young, brown-haired junior journalist and "copy boy." She dropped papers and envelopes into his in-box before wheeling the mail cart away.

"The two parcels you mentioned that are owned by Wilson Wyland," he said to Mackenzie when Marilyn was out of earshot. "Those pieces of land are probably the reason Dearborn's trying to push through his snake handling ordinance. He wants those parcels. No, I take that back. He *needs* those parcels. I'll bet Wyland has refused to sell. Or maybe he's holding out for a better price and Dearborn's using the threat of the ordinance as leverage."

"Why would Dearborn want to buy up Sweetwater Hill anyway?" Mackenzie couldn't think of a single motive. "There's damned little up there but scrub pines, a few wild fruit trees and hardscrabble." *And venomous snakes*, she added silently.

"At a recent city council meeting, there was a vote to change the zoning of Sweetwater Hill from unincorporated agricultural to residential," Larkin said.

Mackenzie snorted. "Agricultural? You can't even grow weeds up there. As for residential, there's no power, water, or city sewage lines."

"Not yet. The change in zoning presents Dearborn with an excellent opportunity to add to his fortune," Larkin said, rubbing his thumb in circles over the tips of his index and middle fingers in the classic "money" sign. "Probably millions."

"How so? No, wait, let me guess," Mackenzie said, not bothering to conceal her disgust. "The day after the proposal passed, Dearborn filed plans to develop Sweetwater Hill."

"Actually, he filed with the city planner's office the same day for permission to build an exclusive 'wilderness' community of vacation homes."

"What the hell's a 'wilderness community?'"

"The outdoors carefully sterilized and packaged for rich people who enjoy the pretense of roughing it in the great outdoors. Faux log cabins with satellite hookups, all the modern luxuries and conveniences, perched on Sweetwater Hill so the owners can look down at us little people in Antioch. And of course, armed security patrolling twenty-four/seven to ensure none of us little people pester those rich folks with our proletariat ways."

"Bastard." Mackenzie hated the idea of Sweetwater Hill being ruined. As long as she'd been alive, the hill had squatted unsullied on the skyline. Generations of Antioch's citizens had gone there berry picking, hunting deer and the occasional wild boar, digging for arrowheads, camping and other fun activities unpowered by electricity or batteries.

"Since Dearborn's very good friends with more than half of the city planning commission, I suspect he'll get approval of his plans as soon as he can persuade Wyland to sell those parcels to him," Larkin concluded.

"If Wyland won't sell, what will Dearborn do?"

"Dearborn has to have those parcels, Kenzie. His property development scheme won't go through without them. And if the scheme doesn't go through, he's ruined. He needed a lot of money to finance his real estate purchases. Right now he's in debt up to his eyeballs. I'll go out on a limb and suggest that Dearborn is in talks with Wyland right now, promising him the ordinance won't go through at the next city council meeting if he agrees to sell."

Fat chance, Mackenzie thought. *I wonder if Wyland demanded that Dearborn resign from the church because of the whole Sweetwater Hill and ordinance thing, or because he really saw something hinky going on between Dearborn and Kelly.*

"I thought a pastor would be above all this...this..." She waved a hand.

Larkin answered her with a fondly amused look underscored by a knowing cynicism. "Underhanded deal making? Kenzie, pastors are mortal, fallible and subject to greed like everybody else. Dearborn saw an opportunity to make a killing and seized it. As a businessman, using his influence wherever he can is a smart move."

"Don't get me wrong, I'm not too wild about rattlesnakes," Mackenzie said, "especially after what happened to me, but Dearborn shouldn't mess with another man's religion in the name of profit. That doesn't sit right with me. Not at all."

"You're a better person than Dearborn," Larkin said, "which is why I find it so surprising he tried to make a complaint against you to the police, claiming you were harassing a cheerleader over at the high school."

Horror stiffened Mackenzie's limbs, froze her mouth and stopped her heart. How had he found out? A wave of rage exploded in her chest, stealing her breath. Several moments later, she was able to respond, though she kept her fury to herself.

"That is slander and a vicious lie," she painstakingly enunciated, mindful to choose her words with care. Larkin was a friend and she trusted him to a large extent, but he was also a reporter. She never forgot that fact. "If you print any such thing, it's libel."

"Kenzie, slow down," Larkin said with a shocked expression. "I wasn't implying anything. I have a source at the sheriff's office who told me about Dearborn's bullshit accusation. My source also told me Dearborn withdrew the complaint without actually filing anything. I just wondered why he was attacking you. Did you bust his dolly?"

She put her head in her hands and closed her eyes. In the darkness behind her eyelids, she sought calm. Dearborn had withdrawn the accusation, but she knew how people thought. If a rumor started that she was "bothering" young girls in some way, even folks who had known her since she was a gap-toothed tomboy would put the worst interpretation on it. They'd exchange significant looks and whisper sagely to one another, "Where there's smoke, there's fire." That's how lynching parties started.

"Jack, I went to talk to Kelly Collier at her school once and only once," Mackenzie said when she lifted her head. "My visit had to do with business. There's nothing else to tell you. Is the paper planning a story?" She couldn't imagine a less newsworthy event, but perhaps George Wyatt, the *Antioch Bee's* owner and publisher, had other ideas.

"Consider the matter dropped," Larkin said, rolling his chair closer so he could put an arm over her shoulders. "There's no story. I wanted to make sure you weren't in trouble. But you know, Kenzie, if you need anything, just ask, okay?"

Gazing into his eyes, taking in his concern, Mackenzie was glad he was her friend. "Thanks, Jack. I don't know what I did to get on Dearborn's shit list. My people are Episcopalians and as far as I know, I only met the man once."

"Do you own any land on Sweetwater Hill?" Larkin joked. "No, seriously, if Dearborn keeps on giving you grief, I'll have a chat with him. He's a pastor and I'm a journalist with lots of contacts, mad search engine skills and a front page to fill. I'm sure there are skeletons in his closet he'd rather not come out in the newspaper."

"I don't mean to sound ungrateful, but is there really anything worth printing?"

"Men of God sometimes have a little more dirt in their pasts than others. I shouldn't be telling you this, but the paper is going to run a series of stories about Sweetwater Hill, Dearborn and the city council. Not an exposé, Wyatt would have a fit, but more in the line of keeping the public informed of new developments in Antioch's economic growth, yadda, yadda. I had to research Dearborn for the story, of course."

"You found the skeleton in Dearborn's closet."

"Could be. Not many facts I can print with confidence, not unless the paper's lawyer suddenly lost all her marbles, but let's say Jacob Dearborn has an interesting past."

"Really? Do tell."

After Larkin told her what he'd discovered about Dearborn, Mackenzie left the newspaper in a very thoughtful mood, especially since she'd seen a silver-gray spark hovering just over Larkin's shoulder while he spoke.

CHAPTER TWENTY-SIX

When Mackenzie stepped outside the newspaper building's air conditioning, the late afternoon heat slammed into her. Sweat instantly beaded her upper lip. She felt her hair frizzing worse in the humidity, beginning to stand out around her head like a halo crafted from black, fuzzy, kinky springs. She tried to smooth the strands down, but her hair stubbornly refused to cooperate.

Just as stubbornly, she refused to let herself be bothered. Her chin lifted in the air. She and Veronica had known each other a long while. Hell, Veronica had seen her in the hospital unwashed, practically naked, stinking and swollen with poison, and had even helped her to and from the bathroom when the nurse finally removed the catheter. She doubted her unruly hair would cause even a nanosecond of consternation.

Mackenzie returned to her apartment, put together an overnight bag and scraped her hair into a ponytail. She hadn't replaced the mirrors broken by Annabel yet, so she peered at the various bits of her reflection caught in a tiny compact mirror until she was satisfied.

The clock on the bedside table read five twenty-three p.m., which meant Veronica was probably at Pontefract's boarding house right now ordering their dinner. She took a quick shower and applied some very light makeup, sparing a moment to be thankful her pain had faded to a bearable ache so she didn't need medication. Falling asleep in the middle of sexy fun times would be a sure-fire mood killer.

White denim pants, a lime-green tank top worn with an unbuttoned white shirt over it, and white sandals completed her outfit. She grabbed her bag and went out the door, only to stop halfway down the steps and hobble back for the bottle of pain pills, just in case her leg flared up.

With everything she needed finally in hand—including a towel to sit on since her car had been parked in the sun all day— she left the building.

Veronica lived on Carter Crescent in a two-bedroom house at the end of a cul-de-sac, close to a historic Antioch landmark: the oldest continuously operating, family-owned business in Mitford County. The Loveless gristmill on Wahusi Creek had been producing grits, cornmeal, flour and animal feed since a decade before the Revolutionary War. Mackenzie had to drive past the mill on her way to Veronica's working-class neighborhood.

As a child, she had been fascinated by the great red wheel spinning round and round as the water rushed past. According to local legend, the mill was haunted by the ghost of a worker who'd had his arm crushed and torn off when it got caught in the wooden gears. Pre-Annabel, she'd believed the legend of Arm-Gone Charlie was just a story to frighten kids. Post-Annabel…well, anything was possible, she supposed.

A creeping chill touched her spine. She averted her eyes when the Loveless mill came into sight, keeping her gaze firmly fastened on the road.

Reaching the house, Mackenzie parked on the street rather than behind the patrol car in the driveway, in case Veronica had an emergency callout. The screen door opened when she exited her car. She paused, torn by a sudden, nervous urge to drive away.

"Hey Mac, I just got here. Come on in," Veronica called from the doorway.

Mackenzie mentally shook herself by the metaphorical scruff of her neck. *Don't be a dumb-ass. This is what you want.* She'd been cherishing lustful thoughts about Veronica for months and squashing said thoughts into the deepest, darkest corner of her mind. Now that the moment had come when her desire seemed within reach, she hesitated. What if they weren't compatible? What if something went wrong? What if their first sexual encounter was as big a disaster as their first date at Swine Dining? She didn't want to lose her best friend.

Idiot! No matter what happened tonight, she knew Veronica would never reject their friendship. There might be a little awkwardness at first, but they'd manage. Impatient with her dithering and determined not to second-guess herself any longer, she took hold of her bag, slammed the car door shut and marched up the driveway to Veronica's house.

Inside, the air was stuffy and sultry with heat, seemingly much hotter than outside. She let out a low whistle, hoping her deodorant wouldn't fail.

"Sorry," Veronica said, moving from behind her. "The A/C hasn't had a chance to kick in yet. Would you rather eat in the backyard? It's still light enough."

Grateful to Veronica for acting normally, Mackenzie nodded.

Veronica disappeared into the kitchen. Mackenzie went to the living room to drop off her bag and walked through the kitchen to the backyard where she took a seat on a lawn chair positioned to face the rear of the property where vegetables grew in neat rows.

She recognized tomatoes, cucumbers, runner beans, crowder peas and bell peppers. Crookneck squash plants spread broad green leaves over the ground. Other rows held onions, sweet potatoes and cantaloupe vines, and at the very end of the plot, a luxurious growth of rhubarb. She'd helped Veronica work compost into the ground and plant those crops...

Little by little, her stress faded and she began to relax

In a little while, Veronica joined her outside, carrying two plates in her hands, a third balanced on her arm and bottles of Snakehead ale in the crooks of her elbows.

The touch of nerves hadn't affected Mackenzie's appetite. Very little ever did. Her metabolism meant her body burned food as fuel at a fast clip. Some people, mainly women, thought she was lucky not to retain fat, but she had her share of health problems like borderline anemia and an immune system that surrendered to the first flu virus every season.

She surveyed the contents of the plates with happiness. The boarding house owned by Cornelius Pontefract and his mother, Belle—ninety-six years old, nearly blind and famously sharp-tongued—had an open buffet dinner six days a week for anyone who wanted to pay eight dollars a plate. Veronica had chosen a meatless menu: macaroni and cheese, black-eyed peas, collard greens, a piece of corn on the cob, and as requested, two of Belle Pontefract's crispy corn bread sticks made in an ancient cast iron pan. In addition, Veronica had added a plate of sliced ripe tomatoes from her garden.

"We can have a cantaloupe for dessert," Veronica said, placing the plates and bottles on a table near Mackenzie's lawn chair. She dragged over another chair. "I picked one this morning. It's in the fridge."

"I think I love you." Mackenzie took her plate and dug in until she realized Veronica wasn't eating, just sitting in the chair and staring at her. She swallowed. "Um...do I have food on my chin or something?"

Veronica snapped out of her trance. "No, no, just thinking, that's all." With a determined air, she began forking macaroni and cheese into her mouth, though from her gloomy expression, she might as well have been chewing goat droppings.

Mackenzie thought she certainly didn't look like a woman anticipating a night of sinful pleasure. "Is anything wrong?" she asked, setting down her beer bottle.

"No," Veronica answered, too quickly and far too cheerfully. "Everything's fine."

Shit. Mackenzie's stomach curdled. *I knew this whole thing was too good to be true.*

Suddenly, the food tasted like ashes. She put her half-eaten dinner aside. Clearly, Veronica already regretted her impulsive invitation. What to do? Should she make an excuse and go home to spare Veronica from embarrassment? Or should she stay and brazen it out? Frustration and annoyance warred with sympathy and insecurity. At last, she cleared her throat to capture Veronica's attention.

"Hey, if you're not in the mood," she said, "we can do this some other time." When Veronica's big green eyes widened further, she added, "I mean dinner, you know, just a nice, artery-clogging dinner between two good friends."

Veronica blinked. "You don't want to...?" Her voice trailed off.

"Yes, I want to!" Mackenzie babbled. "But goddamn it, Ronnie, you look like you're about to swallow a dose of cod liver oil instead of...well, instead of have a good time. If you don't want get together, that's fine. I've got some things to do at home anyway—"

The instant the words tumbled out of her mouth, she knew she'd made a mistake.

Veronica's face turned ashen, her pinched nostrils white around the rims. "I apologize if I've put myself forward where I'm not wanted," she said, her voice like chipped ice, her spine ramrod straight. "Please, by all means, don't let me detain you."

Appalled, Mackenzie lurched out of her chair, ignoring the twinge from her injured leg. "No, Ronnie, no, I swear to God, I do want you. I want you so much, my guts hurt." She nearly fell to her knees.

To her relief, the corner of Veronica's mouth twitched, and she began to regain some color. "I've never been compared to a stomachache before," she said.

"Not very romantic, huh?" Mackenzie sat down a bit shakily.

Veronica put her plate on the table, stood and held out a hand. "Let's go find out if we can make tonight a little more romantic, okay?"

Mackenzie took the offered hand. Where they touched, she imagined sparks flying.

In the bedroom, the sparks turned to a bonfire.

Mackenzie let everything slide out of her mind except the reality of the beautiful woman next to her. Heat bloomed where bare flesh met bare flesh.

She glutted herself on Veronica's tanned skin, on the round breasts and long thighs she'd wanted to touch for so long. In her turn, she surrendered to Veronica's hands, to the fingers and mouth that trailed fire in their wake, and found release at last.

CHAPTER TWENTY-SEVEN

The next morning, Mackenzie woke filled with drowsy lassitude and aching a little, her muscles stretched and warm. *Rode hard*, she thought, slowly grinning. *But what a ride!*

She hummed and rolled over to poke Veronica, but found herself alone in the bed with the tangled sheets. Her grin turned into a frown. She sniffed. The scent of coffee hung in the air. Perhaps Veronica was making breakfast.

Mackenzie leaned her back against the headboard and rubbed a palm over the curve of her hip, remembering the strength and sureness of Veronica's touch and the gun calluses that had caught on her skin. Her fingertips slid over her belly. She'd been so greedy for kisses…sweet kisses, biting kisses, soothing kisses, tender kisses, every one a delight.

A giggle escaped her. How could she have jumped to the idiotic conclusion that Veronica was straight? If last night was any indication, Veronica was about as straight as a pretzel, and knew how to please and be pleasured. Mackenzie sighed in fond remembrance.

An unwelcome subject abruptly intruded on her happiness: Debbie Lou Erskine.

Veronica hadn't exactly explained how or why she'd ended up in a clinch with the Lesbian Antichrist. Pricked by the thought of her ex-girlfriend, her bubble of gloating satisfaction popped. Mackenzie threw off the sheet and swung out of bed in search of her clothes, coffee, Veronica and an explanation, in that order.

Veronica wasn't in the kitchen. The coffeemaker was on, the pot about half full. A mug sat on the counter, holding down a piece of paper.

Recognizing Veronica's handwriting—neat and schoolgirl round, so unlike her own indifferent scrawl—Mackenzie snatched up the note to read:

Dearest Mac,

I'm sorry. I had to leave early this morning on an emergency call. There's coffee for you. Milk's in the fridge. Bagels and low fat cream cheese if you're in the mood. Thank you for last night. I had a wonderful time. I'll call you later, promise.

Love, Ronnie

P.S. We owe each other a good morning kiss. Consider this my IOU.

Mackenzie was touched by the postscript, but also a bit irritated at the demands of the job taking Veronica away before she could claim a morning cuddle. She poured a cup of coffee and added milk. The bagels looked okay, but she needed caffeine first. Before she could take her first sip, her cell phone rang.

She picked up the phone. "Cross speaking."

"Hey, Kenzie," said James Larkin. "You awake?"

"No, I'm sleep talking," Mackenzie grumbled. "What's up?"

"I guess you haven't seen the news this morning."

"What news?"

"Turn on the TV. Channel Ten."

"Can I not have a cup of coffee and a chance wake up first?" Mackenzie moved to the living room and found the remote control. She spent a moment admiring and being envious at Veronica's tidy housekeeping skills. Not a speck of dust to be seen anywhere.

Clicking on the television set, she navigated to Channel Ten, the home of Antioch's local news station.

The news anchor, Charlene Wyatt—granddaughter of George Wyatt—was a bubbly, personable, blue-eyed, peroxide blond whose bland good looks belied her intelligence. Time and plenty of money spent in an orthodontist's office had given her a television-friendly smile. Mackenzie had gone to school with Charlene when she'd been pudgy, worn glasses and had an overbite. Sarah Grace, slightly tipsy on sherry, had once said Charlene could eat corn on the cob through a knothole, bless her heart.

"To recap our top story," Charlene said, looking and sounding somber as she gazed out of the television screen, "this morning, the body of Jacob Dearborn, pastor of the United Methodist Church, was found at his home. The police have not yet issued an official statement, but an anonymous source close to the department has revealed the circumstances of Dearborn's death are suspicious and police are treating it as a homicide."

The screen behind Charlene flashed a picture of Jacob Dearborn: his iron-gray hair swept back from his brow, his face creased in a smile. He wore a dark blue suit and teal silk tie. His right hand was lifted in a friendly gesture reminiscent of a benediction.

Mackenzie turned off the television. Jacob Dearborn was an important man in Antioch. As the Methodist pastor, he was well respected. He owned a lot of property, more now that he'd purchased most of Sweetwater Hill, and had a lot of influence. If he'd been murdered…Rubbing her hand across her mouth, she broke off the thought.

Dimly, she heard Larkin's voice. She'd never disconnected the call on her cell phone. She lifted the instrument to her ear in time to hear the end of his question.

"—you there?" he asked

"I can't believe Dearborn's dead," she said.

"Murdered," Larkin corrected. "It's true. Charlene Wyatt isn't the only person with sources in the police department. I had it straight from the horse's mouth, as it were. And I'm not going to tell you who it is, so don't ask."

"Who's the lead investigator?"

"I'll give you three guesses and the first two don't count."

"Probably Maynard, right?"

"Right." Larkin paused. "Do you have an alibi for last night?"

Mackenzie turned around, walked to the kitchen, picked up her abandoned cup of coffee and finished it in a couple of gulps before she answered.

"I spent the night with someone," she said cautiously, unsure if Veronica wanted their fledgling relationship to be public knowledge or not. For all she knew, Veronica was firmly in the closet at work. They'd never discussed the subject. "Jack, why do I need an alibi?"

"Not that long ago, Dearborn tried to file a complaint against you with the police. Someone will remember that fact, Kenzie. Someone always does," he said. "You may not be a suspect, but you'll certainly be a person of interest."

"I'm not worried." But Mackenzie didn't feel very confident. "Do you know any more about what happened to Dearborn? Channel Ten didn't have any details."

"No official statement yet."

"You have a horse's mouth inside the station, Jack, so give."

He huffed, the sound loud in her ear. "Okay, you did *not* hear this from me, understand?" He didn't wait for her to respond, but went on. "His son Tucker found Dearborn's body on the back porch this morning when he came downstairs. No obvious cause of death. Dearborn wasn't shot or stabbed, but it wasn't an accident. The case is too high profile for Hightower and the local morgue, so the Georgia Bureau of Investigation's medical examiner will do the postmortem. The body's on its way to Decatur right now."

"Poor Tucker," Mackenzie said. She had never met the young man, but that didn't matter. Finding his father's body had to be traumatic. She hoped Kelly Collier was up to the task of consoling her fiancé.

Her cell phone beeped. "Jack, I've got another call waiting."

"I've got to go, too. Take care, Kenzie."

"Thanks." Mackenzie switched to the new call. "Hey, Ronnie, I missed you."

"Sorry, Mac. Have you heard about Jacob Dearborn?" Veronica asked, getting straight to business and annihilating what little was left of Mackenzie's postcoital mood.

"I just saw it on the morning news."

"Detective Maynard wants to talk to you. Can you come down to the station?"

The back of Mackenzie's neck prickled. The lack of emotion in Veronica's voice meant one of two things: either she regretted what had happened between them last night, or someone else was listening to their conversation and she couldn't speak freely.

Mackenzie would bet her savings that the cause was the latter, not the former.

Would James Maynard eavesdrop? He might, she decided. He knew she and Veronica were friends. The suspicious bastard probably wanted to make sure she was kept in the dark so he could try to startle a confession out of her or something like that.

"Sure, Ronnie, I'll drop by the station this morning on my way to work," she said, her voice dripping venomous honey for Maynard's benefit.

"Thanks, Mac. See you in a little while." Veronica ended the call.

Putting her cell phone on the uncluttered coffee table, Mackenzie wished Kelly, Dearborn, Wyland and her cousin Jimmy to perdition for complicating her life.

CHAPTER TWENTY-EIGHT

The moment she entered the police station, Mackenzie saw James Maynard lurking around the sergeant's desk. She went straight over to him.

"Hey, Jimmy, terrible what happened to Mr. Dearborn, isn't it?" she asked, taking the wind out of his sails. "You have a little girls' room around here, I hope. My bladder's about to bust." She leaned closer and lowered her voice to add, "And Aunt Flo's paying her monthly visit, if you know what I mean. I need to freshen up."

His expression went from stern to uneasy. "Over there," he said, pointing.

She turned her back to hide her smirk and walked across the room to the indicated door. Inside the white tiled restroom, she was unsurprised when Veronica came out of a stall.

"We need to make this quick," Veronica said hurriedly. She looked as though she'd dressed in a hurry that morning. Her uniform shirt was wrinkled, her pants legs lacking the usual sharp crease. Even her hair wasn't pinned back as tidily as usual.

Two long strides and Veronica was right there, almost pressed against her. Mackenzie's pulse quickened. Her body yearned toward Veronica, whose warm presence blotted out the sterile restroom atmosphere. She blinked when she realized her hand had lifted of its own accord, poised to touch.

Withdrawing her hand, Mackenzie cleared her throat and told herself that now was not the best time to indulge. "We need to get our story straight," she countered.

Veronica stared at her in confusion. "What story?"

"Look, I figure I'm a person of interest in the Dearborn case, right?" At Veronica's hesitant nod, Mackenzie went on, "I assume I'm here so Jimmy can question me. I don't want to mess you up at work, so what do I tell him?"

"What do you tell him?" Veronica took a moment to process the question. When the light dawned, her mouth flattened into a thin line. "The truth, Mac. You were with me last night." Her severe expression changed. "Oh! I'm sorry. I guess you have reasons for not wanting him to know about us. I understand completely, in which case—"

"Hush!" Mackenzie enforced her command by covering Veronica's mouth with hers.

For a moment, Veronica's lips moved under hers as if she were still speaking. Mackenzie kissed harder, tasting bitter coffee and artificial sweetener. To her relief, Veronica finally responded with an urgent growl and an eager tongue that nearly unhinged her knees.

All too soon, Veronica's body stiffened. Strong hands took hold of Mackenzie's wrists and pulled her away, even as she made a wordless whine for more.

"Not now," Veronica said, her face flushed, her mouth wet and red. She turned to the sink, wet a paper towel in cold water and began to pat her flushed cheeks. "Anybody could come in. I'm not ashamed, but finding us together right now might raise ugly questions."

Mackenzie leaned a hip against the counter, trying to catch her breath and calm her racing heart. "It's okay for me to tell Jimmy about us?"

"He's just covering his bases. I doubt he really considers you a suspect," Veronica said, glancing at her reflection in the mirror. "Tell the truth. We'll be fine."

"Will do." Mackenzie kissed the side of Veronica's neck, just a quick brush of lips over the smooth skin above her collar, before heading toward a stall. "If Jimmy sees you, tell him you came in to check on me and I'm still doing mysterious female things. Bring up menstruation. He'll be so embarrassed, he'll probably go into a coma on the spot."

"Mac!" Veronica protested, but she laughed. "I can't do that to my boss. On the other hand, I have no problem asking him where the janitorial staff keeps the tampon refills." She nodded at the feminine sanitary products vending machine standing at one end of the room.

"Not unless I'm there, cell phone in hand, to preserve the moment for posterity," Mackenzie said, grinning. "See you in a few, Ronnie."

When three minutes had passed, she rinsed her hands and left the restroom.

Maynard escorted her to an interview room about ten feet square, the walls painted a light blue that looked almost white under the fluorescent lights. The thin, royal blue industrial carpet underfoot smelled as it had been recently cleaned. An unseen fan whirred quietly.

"Take a seat," Maynard said, closing the door behind them.

Only two chairs in the room, she noted, both the kind of molded orange plastic, armless, uncomfortable horror usually found in office waiting areas. One of them sported a small, hinged writing surface that could be swung up or down.

Of course, Maynard sat on the chair with the writing surface. "Sit, Kenzie. I just want to ask you a couple of questions," he said. He sounded mild, but she didn't miss the keen glance he shot her from under his dark brows.

She dropped down in the other chair. "Can we get this over with, Jimmy, please? I have work waiting for me at the office."

"I won't keep you long." Despite his words, Maynard spent a few minutes removing a little spiral-bound notebook from his jacket's inner pocket, locating a ballpoint pen in another pocket and raising the hinged desk and fixing it in place. His preparations made, he thrust his legs out in front of him with every sign of settling in for a while.

Mackenzie vowed to revenge his behavior at the next family reunion.

"Do you know why you're here?" he asked.

She shook her head.

"I believe you know Jacob Dearborn."

"You know I do, Jimmy," she replied. "He's the pastor of the United Methodist Church, as anyone knows who's lived in Antioch longer than five minutes."

Maynard scribbled in his notebook as if she'd said something profound. "And you and Mr. Dearborn had a confrontation recently."

"What do you mean by 'confrontation?'" she asked.

"He filed a complaint against you, said you were harassing a teenager in his church." It was clear to her Maynard thought he'd scored a point.

Mackenzie answered evenly, "Get your facts straight, Jimmy. I met Dearborn once, at his home, for about one minute. That's it. As for the harassment..." She shrugged. "I've never been officially informed about this so-called complaint, so you're lying. Why, I don't know. I mean, okay, I put depilatory in your shampoo bottle when we went to summer camp that time, but you set fire to my favorite stuffed unicorn, so I thought we were even."

"Kenzie, you could be in trouble. I urge you to take this seriously," he said.

"Oh, screw you, Jimmy!" Mackenzie shot to her feet, not concealing her annoyance. Something about him, a personality conflict perhaps, had irritated her since they were children. She didn't hate him, but he could rile her up like nobody else. "I watched the news this morning. I know Dearborn's dead. Is that what this is about?"

"You have to admit it looks bad—"

"You are so full of shit, James Austin Maynard, the septic tank's jealous."

He slapped the notebook closed. "If there's anything, Kenzie, *anything* at all to the complaint Dearborn tried to make, you'd better tell me now because everything will come out. In a murder investigation, every connection to the victim has to be checked. Secrets have a way of coming to light no matter how deep they're buried. Straight up: if I start inquiring about you, Kelly Collier and Jacob Dearborn, what will I find?"

Indignation drained out of Mackenzie. On the one hand, he was doing his job. On the other, he acted like she'd been caught red-handed doing something immoral or illegal.

"Straight up, Jimmy: I'm not sure what you're thinking, nor do I think I want to know what's rolling around in the gutter of your mind," she said. "Are we done?"

"So be it." Maynard stood. "I'll give you some friendly advice, one relation to another: don't come to the police station again to answer questions in a murder inquiry unless you have a lawyer with you. Had I known you wouldn't have the sense God gave to a goose, I'd have told Birdwell to pass the word along."

A lawyer? Mackenzie's mouth dried.

He went on, "I can't officially question you because we're cousins. This interview's a courtesy, so to speak, but I wanted to talk to you first. I'm trying to protect you."

"I don't need your protection."

"Where were you last night between midnight and two a.m.?"

"With Veronica Birdwell, at her house, all night." The words were more difficult to say than Mackenzie had anticipated, especially with Maynard glaring at her.

"Fine. Someone other than me will check out your story," he said, looking more weary than surprised. "I know you like to be contrary for kicks, but if you're lying now, I can't help you. Last chance, Kenzie. Is that the truth?"

"Yes, it is. And fuck you very much." As a parting shot, it came out too thin and strained to be satisfactory. Nevertheless, Mackenzie flounced from the interview room.

As she left the police station, she spotted Veronica, who gave her a significant look, raised one finger, pointed it down and made a stirring motion. *Meet in one hour for coffee.*

Mackenzie nodded tersely and continued out the door.

CHAPTER TWENTY-NINE

Too agitated to go to the office or return home, and in desperate need of time to think, Mackenzie went across the street to Stubbs Park instead.

A mobile kiosk standing by the fountain sold coffee drinks, doughnuts and muffins. She ignored the lure of cappuccino to settle herself on the cement lip of the fountain, preferring to concentrate on her thoughts rather than her empty stomach.

First and foremost: was Veronica in trouble because of their relationship? Mackenzie doubted it. She and Veronica had done nothing wrong, nothing against the law.

Next question: who killed Jacob Dearborn? From what James Larkin had told her, the suspect list might contain more than a few names. Dearborn had hidden his past well, but not well enough to prevent a determined reporter from finding out the truth.

She reflected on what she'd learned from Larkin the previous day.

Dearborn's real name was Samuel Jacob Dearborn Bledsoe, son of a petty thief and a drug-addicted prostitute from Atlanta.

Dearborn had been born in 1957, the same year Annabel Coffin met and fell in love with Billy Wakefield.

Dearborn hadn't always been a man of God. Bad choices had taken him from troubled youth to career criminal. In fact, he and Billy had met in prison in the eighties.

Under the name J.D. Bledsoe, Dearborn was convicted in '81 as an accomplice in a jewelry store robbery—he'd driven the getaway car—while Billy was serving time for assault in the Fulton County Jail. They'd been cellmates for four years before Dearborn's conviction was overturned on a technicality. Billy was released a few months later in the same year, 1985.

She regretted not having the information earlier that Dearborn and Billy had known each other. The pastor might have been able to shed light on Billy's ultimate fate...*if he hadn't been so agitated about Kelly Collier*, she thought ruefully.

A shadow fell across her face, startling her. Glancing up, she saw Veronica. The sight gave her a fluttery, excited feeling in her chest. A slight worry intruded. They'd agreed to meet in an hour. Had she been musing over Dearborn that long? No, the clock in the courthouse cupola showed just fifteen minutes had passed since she left the station. Getting to see Veronica early wasn't a bad thing, but she wondered why.

"I've got the rest of the day off," Veronica said, correctly interpreting her glance across the street. "Hey, Mac, if you don't mind, I'd rather not go to Mighty Jo Young's." The breeze picked up, blowing loose strands of brunette hair that had escaped her messy bun.

"Why not? I mean, don't you like their coffee?"

"I love the coffee there, but we need to talk in private."

"My place it is."

At the apartment, Veronica walked straight to the living room, removed her duty belt and sat on the sofa. "Could I have a glass of water, please?" she asked.

Mackenzie worried about Veronica's apparent weariness, the bruised purple of her eyelids and the rigid set of her shoulders. She went to the kitchen, returning moments later with a glass of ice water.

"Thank you," Veronica said, taking the glass. She drank deeply, her throat working.

Mackenzie waited in tense silence until she could stand no more. "What's wrong?"

"I'm taking a few days off. It's okay, Mac. I have a lot of vacation time and Detective Maynard reminded me I've got to use them before the end of the year." Veronica drained the rest of the water and rolled the sweating glass over her forehead. "He's in a tough spot."

"Oh, Jimmy can go take a flying leap—"

"You don't know," Veronica interrupted, sitting up and speaking earnestly. "Detective Maynard wants to protect you. He doesn't believe you had anything to do with Dearborn's death, which is likely murder, by the way. The ME's preliminary report suggests death was caused by asphyxiation due to a poison like cyanide or strychnine. He's waiting for toxicology results while he completes the autopsy. Nobody believes Dearborn committed suicide, most of all his good friend, the mayor, who is applying a lot of pressure on Sheriff Newberry and the department to find the person responsible."

Mackenzie recalled Mayor Mosley was a member of the Methodist congregation. "Who'd want to murder Dearborn?"

"Your guess is as good as mine." Veronica shook her head. "Your cousin was under a lot of scrutiny with this case. If there was the slightest hint of misconduct or impropriety, he could have lost his job. But as of this afternoon, he's off the investigation."

"Who's taking over?" Mackenzie asked.

"Detective Robert Davis, the other detective in the department. A fair man, a good investigator. Davis is verifying our alibis. Don't look like that, Mac. It needs to be done. Detective Maynard and I are connected to the case by our relationships with you."

"So you and Jimmy got the boot. I understand why, but I don't like it."

"Well, it was either that or spend the next couple of weeks patrolling the hollow in Stubbs Park," Veronica said ruefully.

"What hollow?" Mackenzie asked, settling on the sofa next to Veronica, who still appeared overheated. She undid the top buttons of Veronica's uniform shirt, hiding her amusement at the pink flush brightening the newly exposed skin.

Veronica swallowed. "There's a spot in Stubbs Park called the Hollow," she replied. The emphasis on the word made the capitalization evident. "It's behind the bandstand where the landscaper miscalculated with the climbing trellis that supports the wisteria. There's a space back there, small, but real private. You can't be seen, you can't be heard except from inside the bandstand. We sometimes catch drug dealers there, but mostly it's used for…well, I guess the nicest way to put it would be outdoor liaisons. When the weather's warm, we have to send a deputy over to check the Hollow every hour or so. You'd be surprised."

"That many nature lovers, huh?" Mackenzie grinned.

"You know how it is, Mac," Veronica said, sudden mischief shining in her eyes. "Making love outdoors can be very nice." Her voice dropped an octave. "Very nice actually, with all that fresh air and sunshine."

"Quit that." Mackenzie mimed a swat at her.

Veronica finished unbuttoning her uniform shirt, untucked it from her pants and whipped it off. Underneath, she wore a sleeveless white undershirt that showed off her smoothly muscled arms. "In fact, not long ago we had someone come into the station complaining about the sinners in the bush, as he put it. Sheriff Newberry wasn't very happy. His grandchildren play in the park. We ran extra patrols that day, but didn't catch them."

Fascinated by the little divot where the wings of Veronica's collarbone dipped—she knew from experience the skin there tasted extra salty and it was currently exposed by the undershirt's low curved neckline—Mackenzie asked absently, "Who complained?"

"Rev. Wyland." Veronica sighed. "He kept quoting a Bible passage, something about cords and sin. I didn't quite take his meaning."

Mackenzie wasn't paying that much attention. She leaned forward to press a kiss right above the shirt's neckline, on the little crease that marked the beginning of Veronica's cleavage. In last night's mutual haste and hunger, she regretted not taking even more time to truly appreciate every glorious inch of her lover's body. She thought Veronica had been satisfied with her, too, despite her thinness, lack of hips and her almost nonexistent breasts—what Grandma Maynard had meanly called "two fried eggs on a plank."

She thrust aside all thoughts of grandmothers and bent her head to continue scattering kisses over the base of Veronica's throat. Her increasingly lustful thoughts evaporated in a flash when what Veronica said penetrated her brain.

She raised her head. "What did you say?"

"Wyland complained about discovering a couple having sex in the Hollow," Veronica replied, each word pronounced with the prim precision that meant she was annoyed.

Mackenzie spared a thought to wonder why and felt her face grow hot. "Sorry," she murmured. "Want me to…" She made a vague gesture in the air.

Veronica chuckled. "No, Mac, you're distracted. Maybe later."

"Sorry," Mackenzie repeated, sitting up and taking off the white shirt she wore over her tank top. "Didn't mean to break the mood. Say, what was Wyland doing inside the bandstand anyway? He must've been in there if he saw or heard this fun-loving couple."

"Do you remember the afternoon right before our date at Swine Dining?"

"I remember that date, all right. You were as nervous as a bag of chips on Super Bowl Sunday. You got drunk, Ronnie. Drunk! On a couple of beers," she teased,

"It was Snakehead Ale and please don't remind me," Veronica said, her voice squeaky with embarrassment. She coughed. "Moving on, okay?"

Mackenzie nodded, keeping a straight face despite the smile twitching the corners of her mouth. "Go for it."

"Rev. Wyland has a habit of preaching in Stubbs Park, which is fine, a perfectly legal use of a traditional public forum," Veronica said, "Problem is, Wyland wants to exercise his freedom of speech from the bandstand, which is privately owned by the City of Antioch and requires a permit to use. He has no permit. We keep rousting him out, but he's stubborn. When he came into the station to report seeing the couple breaking the decency laws that day, I thought I'd talk to him, try to make him see sense. I think it worked since he hasn't been back to the park since—"

"Oh, my God," Mackenzie muttered, interrupting the rest of Veronica's narrative.

She knew what Kelly Collier and Jacob Dearborn had been doing in the park.

CHAPTER THIRTY

Rather than risk another confrontation with Kelly at the school, Mackenzie called her, hanging up when the call went to voice mail.

"What's up, Mac?" Veronica asked. She had followed Mackenzie to the kitchen and settled at the table. "You look like a cat at a mouse hole who heard a squeak."

Mackenzie put down the phone on the counter and opened the refrigerator door. "Did I tell you why Dearborn accused me of harassing Kelly Collier, Ronnie?" she asked, taking out a jar of homemade ginger syrup and a lime.

"Not exactly," Veronica answered, leaning back in the chair. "Although if this has to do with the Dearborn case, Mac, you'd be better off talking to Detective Davis."

"When pigs have propellers, maybe. I'm involved enough as it is." Mackenzie spent a moment adding ice cubes to the glasses. Taking a knife from the drawer, she cut the lime into quarters and squeezed juice over the ice. "The same day you were talking to Rev. Wyland on the police station steps, Kelly called to ask for an emergency meeting at Sampson's Diner. She told me she and Dearborn had been in Stubbs Park discussing the wedding when Wyland confronted them, demanding that Dearborn resign as pastor of United Methodist Church."

Victoria's indrawn breath made her smile tightly.

She drizzled a spoonful of ginger syrup into each glass. "Kelly wanted me to make Wyland leave Dearborn alone. I agreed because her father owns my office building and it didn't seem like a big deal. She wouldn't tell me what happened, though. Now I know why."

"Mac, are you sure?" Veronica asked, her eyes wide.

"I don't need proof," Mackenzie said. "Proof is for a court of law. What I've got is a damn good theory." She cracked open a bottle of sparkling water and filled each glass to the brim while gently stirring with a spoon in her other hand. "If I'm right—"

"If you're right. That's the problem, Mac. Why would Kelly have an affair with Dearborn? She's young, attractive and engaged to his son."

"Offhand, I have no idea." A few memories surfaced, things seen and half forgotten. "No, wait. Kelly drives a new Corvette Stingray convertible. I saw it at the diner when we met the first time and again at the high school. I'm pretty sure her father can't afford a fifty-thousand-dollar price tag on his preacher's salary."

"Doesn't Mr. Collier own real estate around town?"

"My office building, a couple of others. I can tell you from the rent I pay the man, he's not getting rich. Hell, he doesn't even own the house he lives in," she recalled. "That belongs to the church. Can you find out who put up the money for the 'Vette?"

Veronica accepted the glass she offered. "I suppose so. Let me make a call."

While Veronica talked on her cell phone, Mackenzie took a long swallow from her glass, letting the slightly sweet, slightly spicy, delicious and tooth-achingly cold water slide down her throat. Her mind worked over the puzzle she faced, tracing paths of possibilities, dredging up facts, gathering hazy recollections.

Fifteen minutes and two calls later, Veronica put down her phone. "There's only one Corvette Stingray registered in Antioch. The vehicle belongs to Kelly Collier. It was purchased by Jacob Dearborn at the luxury car dealership in Laxahatchee City."

"That's interesting, considering Little Jack told me Dearborn was drowning in debt." She told Veronica about Sweetwater Hill and the development project. "Now why would Dearborn, in the middle of a deal that's going to make him stinking rich or ruin him completely, buy such an expensive car for a pretty blond cheerleader?"

"Because his son asked him to? I don't know, Mac. What are you thinking?"

"When I saw Kelly at the school, she was wearing a diamond tennis bracelet."

"Maybe a gift from her fiancé?"

"Maybe. We ought to hear what Dearborn's son has to say."

"That's a matter for the investigating officer." Veronica swallowed the last gulp of water from her glass. "Although I guess it can't hurt to speculate."

"Maybe Kelly killed Dearborn herself," Mackenzie pointed out. "What if she was about to lose her sugar daddy?"

"I still can't believe Kelly Collier was having an affair with Mr. Dearborn. I'm sure there's a less lurid explanation, Mac."

Mackenzie persisted. "What if Dearborn Sr. regretted their relationship, wanted to break it off with Kelly? Or he was afraid of exposure? That might explain why he tried to come after me with that bogus charge."

"All right, I'll play along. If Kelly didn't tell him she was contacting you, he would have wanted to make sure you couldn't go after him. The best defense is a good offense," Veronica said, rattling the ice cubes left in her glass. "He tried to discredit you."

"He didn't succeed." Mackenzie paused. Something she'd said earlier poked at her. She went back over the conversation.

The light flickered and finally dawned. "Okay, bear with me… you and Rev. Wyland on the police station steps."

"He'd been preaching in the park's bandstand again, which isn't allowed."

"He quoted from the Bible right before he left. Do you remember what he told you?"

"Something about sin."

"*Cords* of sin. I've heard that quote before. Hang on."

Momentarily leaving the kitchen, Mackenzie found her copy of the King James Bible—a childhood Christmas gift from her Uncle Dillard, her mother's other brother—on a bookshelf in the living room and returned to Veronica.

She leafed through the thin, onionskin pages, thinking she'd never believed her mother's insistence that she attend Sunday service would come in handy. When she found the passage she wanted, she handed the Bible to Veronica, her finger on the page to mark the verse. "It didn't really register with me at the time, but I think this is what Rev. Wyland was trying to tell you."

"'And why wilt thou, my son, be ravished with a strange woman, and embrace the bosom of a stranger?'" Veronica read from Proverbs. "'For the ways of man are before the eyes of the LORD, and he pondereth all his goings. His own iniquities shall take the wicked himself, and he shall be holden with the cords of his sins. He shall die without instruction; and in the greatness of his folly he shall go astray.'"

"Adultery Ronnie," Mackenzie said, feeling somewhat satisfied with her theory. "If we're right, then when he was preaching in the bandstand one day, Wyland must have caught Kelly and Dearborn together in the Hollow—the sinners in the bush. I'll bet you a hundred dollars they weren't playing Scrabble. Oh sure, Tucker and Kelly aren't married yet, but do you suppose Tucker would just laugh it off if he found out his father was diddling his fiancée behind his back? In a public park, no less. If you ask Wyland directly, I'm sure he'll tell you exactly who and what he saw that day."

Veronica laid the Bible on the table. "Detective Davis needs this information, Mac," she said earnestly. "It's an important lead. You should go into the station and tell him."

"You tell him. I can't talk to a man nicknamed Pee Wee."

"Nobody uses that nickname. His first name is Robert."

"Everybody calls him Pee Wee, even his own mother. I ought to know. I've heard deaf, old Mrs. Davis shouting for him at the grocery store."

"You're being silly. I can't make an official statement about events I didn't witness myself."

"I hate this," Mackenzie whispered harshly. "What if Kelly Collier tells Davis lies about me to protect herself? Who will Davis believe? Pretty cheerleader Kelly, daughter of a respected church minister, or me, the lesbian, loud-mouthed bitch?"

"Mac! You shouldn't talk like that." Veronica rose, only to squat next to Mackenzie's chair and put a comforting hand on her thigh. "I'll go with you. Your cousin Maynard is on your side. You're not alone. It'll be fine."

Mackenzie set down her glass. How could she explain when Veronica gazed up at her with infinite patience, waiting for her to make the right decision? She just didn't trust the police— present company excepted. But she wasn't prepared to go into her reasons yet. Someday, perhaps. Not today. "All right, all right, call Davis and tell him I've got some information for him," she said with grudging acceptance of her fate. She let out a muffled, "Oof!" when Veronica sprang up to give her a soft kiss, sweet with ginger and warm with emotion.

She leaned into the embrace, but Veronica released her, too quickly in her opinion.

"Everything will be fine," Veronica said.

"Hope you're right," Mackenzie said, the last word ending on a gasp when Veronica suddenly took her face between both hands and stared down into her eyes. The devotion in Veronica's expression nearly undid her.

"Mac, it will be fine," Veronica said, leaning down to brush their mouths together a second time before she straightened and headed toward the living room.

Mackenzie listened to Veronica talking on the phone. Now that she wasn't mesmerized by the woman's presence, a cold sensation began stealing through her belly at the thought of sitting in that uncomfortable orange plastic chair in the interview room with a suspicious Pee Wee Davis giving her the stink-eye. She'd rather eat tacks.

Speaking of which, she hadn't had a meal since last night.

For once, Mackenzie had little appetite. After rummaging through the cabinets and finding nothing more inspiring than cereal or oatmeal, she tried the refrigerator. Not even eggs stirred her interest. As she scanned the shelves looking in vain for inspiration, her father's voice echoed in her head: *For God's sake, girl, quit standing there and shut that fridge! I'm not paying good money to air condition the rest of Antioch!*

Mackenzie closed the refrigerator when Veronica, now wearing her uniform shirt buttoned to the throat and tucked into her pants, her duty belt securely in place, came into the kitchen. She had even tidied her hair.

Looks like the deputy is on duty, Mackenzie thought gloomily.

"Detective Davis is waiting for us," Veronica announced, skewering the knot of hair at the nape of her neck with a final bobby pin. "Are you ready to go?"

"No," Mackenzie answered, but she moved to accompany Veronica to the front door.

"And please, Mac, don't call him Pee Wee."

"No promises." Mackenzie gestured for Veronica to precede her out of the apartment.

Veronica paused on the way down the steps and turned to face her. "Is your leg bothering you? Do you need a pain pill?"

Mackenzie opened her mouth to protest. As though the question had triggered a sympathetic response, her calf suddenly throbbed. "No. The pain medication takes the edge off and I need to be sharp for this interview."

She managed to walk down the steps, hissing under her teeth each time her leg was jarred. Still, she got to the bottom without bursting into tears, which she considered a triumph.

Outside on the pavement, Veronica said with a pained expression, "My personal time's been canceled. I have to pick up

Kelly Collier and Rev. Wyland and bring them to the station. Detective Davis's orders. Are you okay to go to the station by yourself?"

Mackenzie nodded. "I'll manage."

Veronica smiled and squeezed her arm before striding away.

CHAPTER THIRTY-ONE

"Let's make sure I haven't made any mistakes," Detective Davis said. He began reading her statement aloud, stopping now and then to cock an eyebrow at her.

Mackenzie nodded each time he paused. So did Maynard, she noticed, who had silently brought another chair into the interview room and sat behind Davis. Her cousin might be off the case, but he was clearly keeping an eye on her.

At last, Davis finished his recitation and looked at her.

"Yes, that's correct," Mackenzie said on cue. She took the pen Davis offered and signed and initialed the statement. "Are we done?"

"You can go," he said neutrally, his face expressionless.

She rose and left the room, followed by Maynard.

"Why the hell didn't you say anything when I asked you about Dearborn before?" he asked in a furious whisper, grabbing her arm when she ignored him and continued walking.

"Because I hadn't put it together yet," Mackenzie replied. She resisted his grip, which tightened until the bone in her arm began to ache. It was worth the bruise to see him rattled. "You're hurting me. Keep it up and I'll sock you in the eye."

He let go. "Kenzie—"

"Jimmy, I told you everything I know," she interrupted. "I'm going home now."

"Fine, but do me a favor…next time somebody asks you to do them a favor, say no!" He appeared equally exasperated and relieved. Ruffling his dark hair with a hand, he sighed. "I don't want to fight, Kenzie. Just so you know, Rev. Wyland has already given us a statement that corroborates yours."

"And Kelly Collier?"

"Not a word, but I suspect your statement and Wyland's will have some effect. At this point, her credibility's shot, which won't help her much at all."

"She's a suspect."

"Her and Tucker. Deputy Buzzard is bringing him in now."

Mackenzie turned to leave the station, happy that she wouldn't have to deal with Kelly or the whole Dearborn mess any longer. She halted in her tracks when she recognized James Larkin standing at the front desk, chatting with the sergeant.

"Crap." She ducked back around the corner. "Larkin's here."

She owed Larkin for the information he'd had dug up on her behalf and intended to repay him someday, but now wasn't the best time for a chat. After a quick glance around showed Maynard talking to a couple of deputies down the hall, she opened a nearby door and went into the room, which turned out to be an office. Maynard's office, she realized, recognizing a framed photograph of Aunt Ida Love and Uncle Anse—her cousin's parents.

Given the opportunity to snoop, Mackenzie resisted the temptation for a full minute before sitting down behind Maynard's desk. His computer was off, so she concentrated on the manila folders stacked neatly beside it.

The first folder had the name "Jacob Dearborn" on it. She bypassed that one. The next few files were disappointingly mundane. Another sighting of the mythical Bear-Man—Mitford County's answer to Bigfoot. A third citation for drunk and disorderly by Ella "Minnow" Pease. Marvin Beanblossom had started a fight at the Get-R-Done Roadhouse on Saturday night. However, the fourth folder was marked, "Coffin, Annabel."

Mackenzie debated a split second with her better half, but the argument was short-lived. Curiosity won. She opened the folder.

Inside, she found photographs of the skeletal remains *in situ* and in the morgue. To her amazement, Maynard had also dug up a black-and-white picture of Annabel Coffin from when she'd been alive in the fifties, her black hair in a ponytail, her black eyes dancing, her pretty face animated as she laughed with someone off-camera.

She was so happy here, Mackenzie thought.

In the background of the photo she recognized some of the other people including her father and mother, standing so close together, she assumed they must be dancing. Since Maynard had a copier wedged in the corner of his office, she ran off a copy of the photo, folded it into a small square and stuck it in her pants pocket. Perhaps Sarah Grace would remember where and when the picture had been taken.

In Maynard's report, she read that he was aware of the Annabel Coffin-Billy Wakefield affair. His efforts to trace Billy's current whereabouts hadn't been much more successful than Larkin's. However, as a law enforcement officer, he had access to Billy's criminal records. From his notes, she learned Billy had found religion during his time in Fulton County Jail, eventually joining a Christian organization, the Love Jesus Foundation, that ministered to convicts. According to the warden, Billy's conversion seemed genuine.

Also, prior to his release from prison in '85, the last time he'd surfaced on the official radar, Billy had told another convict— whom Maynard had interviewed—about his plan to visit his sweetheart, identity unknown.

Coming to the end of the file, Mackenzie closed the folder and leaned back in the chair, propping her feet on the desk to ease the ache in her leg.

After Annabel's death, who was Billy Wakefield's sweetheart? she wondered. *Must be some woman he met between prison stints.*

The temperature inside the office chilled, though she hadn't touched the thermostat.

Goose bumps pebbled her arms as a silver-gray face formed in midair on the other side of the desk. Annabel's familiar form quickly followed. She looked like the photograph in the file except for her expression—cold, hard, angry, and somehow also sad.

Billy, the ghost whispered.

Something rattled inside the closed desk drawer.

Startled, Mackenzie nearly fell off the chair. She put her feet on the floor. "Quit that," she complained even as she grasped the drawer pull. "It's locked. Now what?"

She heard a click. The drawer opened a few inches.

"Remind me to call you if I ever need to break in somewhere," Mackenzie said, sticking her hand in the drawer.

When something slithered under her questing fingers, she snatched her hand back, her heart thumping. A vision of the rattlesnake in the church filled her mind. Her calf muscle spasmed. She gritted her teeth and massaged the cramp away. Telling herself not to be a coward, she reached inside the drawer again and felt around among the papers and miscellaneous objects.

She pulled out an evidence bag with a heavy silver charm bracelet inside. She'd seen Annabel wearing the bracelet in her fevered dream after she'd been bitten by the rattlesnake.

Billy, Annabel whispered.

Through the plastic bag, Mackenzie studied the bracelet with its array of charms. An ice cream cone, a hamburger, a tiny movie ticket, a roller skate—she thought the charms might represent Annabel and Billy's dates. There'd been a roller rink in Antioch until the end of the seventies, so it was conceivable the two lovebirds had gone out for an evening at the Roll 'R' Rock when it had been new.

The four-leafed clover, horseshoe and "wheel of fortune" were self-explanatory, as were the little moonshine jug marked with triple Xs, the tiny diary with key, a red enameled heart, mini cigarette lighter and the hourglass filled with pink sand. The final charm was a three-quarter inch square picture frame holding Annabel's photo.

Mackenzie squinted at the three lines of tiny letters on the photo charm's flip side, hard to make out through the bag. *A. Cross, Burton Lemoyne Class of '57.* Poor Annabel. She'd never graduated, of course.

The photo was protected by a minute sheet of glass covered with a spider's web of cracks. While Mackenzie studied the picture, she heard a crackling sound and something gave under her fingertips. Tiny bits of glass fell to the bottom of the bag. Alarmed, she shoved the bag into the desk drawer. If Maynard returned and found she'd messed with his evidence, he'd skin her alive and sell the rest to science.

Billy, Billy, Billy, Annabel repeated.

The drawer jerked open. Mackenzie slammed it shut.

"Goddamn it, do you want me to end up in jail?" she snapped.

Hearing the doorknob turn, Mackenzie jumped up and ran around the desk. When Maynard entered, she stood at the window, looking at the parking lot.

"You're free to go, Kenzie," he said pointedly.

"Oh! Thanks!" she replied, keeping a sidelong eye on Annabel, who hadn't vanished. She hesitated. What did the spirit want? Would Annabel attack Maynard?

"Well?" he finally prompted. "Do you need a map to the front door?"

Realizing he couldn't see Annabel and the ghost didn't seem inclined to pester him, Mackenzie fled his office.

As she rushed through the doorway, she imagined she heard a rattle from the desk.

CHAPTER THIRTY-TWO

On Monday morning as promised, following a quick breakfast sandwich from Miss Laverne's Luncheonette—egg, sausage and cheddar cheese on a French toast bagel, pinned together with a Bible verse from Ephesians: "Let not the sun go down upon your wrath"—Mackenzie picked up her mother to drive her to the hospital in Trinity to visit Aunt Ida Love.

"And how's your leg, baby?" Sarah Grace asked, settling into the passenger seat.

Mackenzie pulled the car away from the house and headed for the expressway. "Much better, Mama. The swelling's gone down a lot and I don't have nearly as much pain."

"I'm glad to hear it. You should be more careful."

"Yes, Mama."

"My mother killed a rattlesnake. Did you know that? Longer than a man's arm. She ran over it with the lawn mower."

Mackenzie had heard the story many times before, but she just nodded.

"My, my, my, today's a genuine scorcher!" Sarah Grace plucked at her flowery blouse, drawing the material away from her bosom. "Is the air-conditioning on?"

"Yes, Mama." Thank God Daddy had paid extra for the factory A/C option back in the seventies, Mackenzie thought. Her mother's irritation grew in direct proportion to the outside temperature. "Takes a few minutes to get really cool."

Sarah Grace spent several moments fanning herself with one of the magazines she'd brought for Ida Love. "These chocolate turtles will melt in the heat," she fretted, shifting the candy box from her lap to the dashboard and back.

"Mama, stop fussing."

"I'll thank you not to tell me what to do, missy, since I do believe *I* gave birth to *you*, not the other way around."

Mackenzie sealed her mouth shut against a groan, which would only antagonize her mother further. Instead, she turned on the radio to an oldies station.

Sarah Grace craned her neck to squint at the speedometer and let out a dissatisfied harrumph. "Are you going over the speed limit?" she asked.

"Yes, Mama, just a little bit."

"Well, you slow down 'cause I'm not in a hurry to go home to Jesus today."

"Yes, Mama."

At this rate, Mackenzie thought as she eased up on the gas pedal, they'd be in Trinity sometime tomorrow. To give her mother something to do, she took the photocopied picture of Annabel Coffin out of her pants pocket where she'd shoved it that morning.

"Hey, Mama," she said. "Do you know where and when this was taken? I'm guessing nineteen fifty-seven or before."

Sarah Grace unfolded the piece of paper and studied the picture, holding it close to her face, and then at arm's length. Tutting in annoyance, she rummaged in her big black leather purse, finally locating her glasses in their needlepoint case. Her eyes were magnified a bit behind the lenses.

"That's Anna Coffin all right," she said at last. "Pretty girl. Such a tragic thing to happen. I felt sorry for her mother, God rest her soul."

"Uh-huh. You and Daddy are in the background," Mackenzie said, taking a hand off the steering wheel to point out the figures behind Annabel.

"Yes, I see that," Sarah Grace replied tartly. "I'm not senile yet."

"No, Mama." Mackenzie waited for her mother to elaborate.

Sarah Grace peered at the picture. "Let me see...do you remember Axel Cushman?"

"Who?"

"Axel Cushman. He used to run the penny candy counter at the drugstore."

"Mama, I have never in my life bought a piece of candy for a penny."

"Oh, hush." Sarah Grace flapped a hand in dismissal. "Maybe by the time you were old enough to have an allowance, the candy was five cents or something like that, but we're talking about Axel Cushman. Sure you don't remember him? Tall fellow. Had three long, long hairs. He used to grease them with Brylcreem and—"

"Comb them over the top of his bald, freckled head," Mackenzie finished, chuckling at the mental image. "Us kids called him Mr. Shine."

Sarah Grace gave her a sharp look. "I suppose it doesn't matter now. Anyway, Axel's family ran a social dance club over where the old theater used to be. The Cakewalk, they called it. Me and your father and a lot of the other boys and girls from school and from the college used to go over there on Friday and Saturday nights. We'd dance until dawn."

"So I guess Annabel and Billy Wakefield went there, too."

"I recall seeing them there a few times before Ann just up and disappeared. I think I told you, didn't I, that Billy used to sell moonshine out of his truck before he got thrown out of town? He'd bring Mason jars of 'shine to the Cakewalk. Sell it for ten cents a swallow. Some of those boys would get blind drunk. Some girls, too."

"Did Annabel get drunk often?" Mackenzie asked, checking the rearview mirror before switching lanes in preparation for the Trinity exit.

Sarah Grace considered the question. "I don't know about Ann specifically. She was usually there with Billy. I know some of the rowdier boys would go buy a bottle of Coke for their girlfriend, then pour some out and replace it with Billy's moonshine." Her voice lowered. "At least one girl, a friend of mine from church, got pregnant after her boyfriend played that trick on her. There was a place behind the Cakewalk where couples went, you know. To be private. Your father and I never did, but I heard about it from my friends."

Mackenzie grimaced. Of course she knew date rape wasn't a modern invention, but she still found it slightly shocking that such immoral behavior happened in an "innocent" era. "Could Annabel have been 'tricked' by Billy that way?" she asked.

"I doubt it," Sarah Grace said. "She doted on that boy. She loved him to distraction. See?" She brandished the picture. "Ann never took off her charm bracelet. Those charms meant something to her and Billy. Oh, Lord, how I coveted that bracelet! All those silver charms! But your daddy didn't have two nickels to rub together most of the time. We were saving for the wedding." Her eyes went soft. "The bracelet was so romantic. Even had a picture of Billy in a sweet little frame."

"Here's the exit, Mama. We'll be at the hospital in about ten minutes," Mackenzie said, turning off the expressway and onto the exit ramp. While stopped at a traffic light, she went on, "You're wrong, Mama. It's a picture of Annabel in the frame. I saw the charm bracelet at the police station."

To her surprise, Sarah Grace laughed. "Baby, I know what I said and I know what I meant! Mr. and Mrs. Coffin didn't approve of that no-account Billy Wakefield, so Annabel put a picture of herself over his to keep it hidden. I saw her showing it off one day in the girl's bathroom at school. She thought herself quite clever."

Mackenzie's heart leaped. A photograph of Billy might not help her locate him, but it couldn't hurt. At least she'd have a face to put with his reputation.

As soon as the light turned green, she drove through the intersection and straight to Trinity General and the visitors' parking lot.

After helping Sarah Grace gather an array of magazines, crossword puzzle and Sudoku books, candy and a canvas bag of miscellaneous items including knitting, nightgowns and a small bouquet of bright yellow Gerbera daisies, Mackenzie led her mother into the hospital and through the maze of hallways to the orthopedics department.

"I'll pop in to say hi to Aunt Ida Love, but I can't stay," she told Sarah Grace when they stood outside the right room. "I need to talk to Veronica. You know, Deputy Birdwell. Call me when you're ready to go home and I'll pick you up, okay?"

"That's fine, baby. Ida Love and I can have a nice, long talk and I'll make sure those nurses are treating her right." Sarah Grace kissed her cheek and gave her a little push toward the room. "Go on, the sooner you make your polites to your aunt, the quicker you can leave. Though you ought to at least send Ida Love flowers or a card later."

"Yes, Mama."

On the way back to Antioch, Mackenzie tried to figure out how she could persuade Maynard to let her examine the charm without giving away her reason for wanting to do so in the first place, or letting him know she'd snooped around his office. She was certain if she asked, he'd refuse to let her see if a photo of Billy lay behind Annabel's picture. *Probably cite some stupid rule of evidence.*

She retrieved her cell phone and speed-dialed Veronica. "Hey, Ronnie," she said when Veronica answered the call, "any way you can get your hands on that charm bracelet y'all found on Annabel's body?"

"Detective Maynard's keeping the evidence in his office right now," Veronica replied in the fastidious tone she used when she suspected Mackenzie was up to no good.

"Just five minutes," Mackenzie wheedled. "Please?"

Veronica sighed. "May I ask why?"

"I have an idea."

"I want details."

"I have reason to believe there's a photograph of Billy Wakefield on Annabel's charm bracelet. It's under her picture in the frame."

"Mac, where are you? Are you in your car? Using a handheld phone while operating a moving vehicle in Mitford County is a misdemeanor offense punishable by a fifty-dollar fine."

"Only if you get caught."

"Mac!"

"It's fine, Ronnie. Can you sneak me a peek at the bracelet or not?" Mackenzie held her breath, hoping for a positive answer.

At last, Veronica said, "I have a break in a couple of hours. Meet me at the Hot Spot."

Mackenzie grinned and ended the call.

CHAPTER THIRTY-THREE

After speaking to Veronica, Mackenzie decided to get some work done in her office. The repairs had been completed quickly once police released the scene. As she was fumbling with her door key, Paul Collier stopped on the sidewalk to speak to her.

"Ms. Cross," he said, blinking his pale blue eyes. His brown hair seemed to have a little more silver at the temples than the last time she'd seen him. "I believe you know my daughter, Kelly."

Mackenzie nodded warily, unsure what he meant to do. Would he break their lease agreement and throw her out of the building? She could work from home, but as long as her finances permitted, she preferred to keep work and home separate.

"I wanted to offer you an apology," Collier went on, gazing at her steadily despite a quiver in his jowls. He stuck out his hand. "I'm sorry you were put in a terrible situation. I don't know what happened to Kelly. I tried to raise her right after my wife, June, passed away, but my daughter's always gone her own way, not necessarily the Lord's way."

"I'm sorry, too," Mackenzie said, shaking his hand. "Have the police told you anything yet? I know Kelly was brought in for questioning. Is she all right?"

"The police let her go this morning. She sinned with Jacob Dearborn and she will have to bear the consequences, but she did not kill him."

Mackenzie offered the man a nod, although in her opinion, most teenagers believed consequences were for other people. "How about Tucker? How's he taking the news?"

"As you might expect, Tucker called off their engagement." The sad, somewhat bewildered expression ill-suited Collier's normally cheerful face. "The boy's devastated. None of us knew what was going on. My girl hasn't been thinking straight for a long time."

"What do you mean, if you don't mind me asking?"

"As I understand it, Tucker planned to leave Antioch after graduation. The boy wanted to make his own way in the world and told Kelly he wouldn't take a penny from his father. Said he'd rather work hard and live simply until he earned his success. That didn't suit Kelly." Collier gestured helplessly. "She admitted seducing Jacob Dearborn to get at his money. The foolish man forgot himself. He gave her the things she coveted: jewelry, designer clothes, an expensive new car. I didn't know. I swear to you, I did not know."

"I'm sorry, Mr. Collier." At a loss for what to tell the man, Mackenzie gestured at the door. "Would you like to come inside and have a cup of coffee?" Her leg had settled to a dull ache so she didn't need a pain pill, but she'd love to sit down for five minutes.

He ignored her, his gaze turned inward. His shoulders sagged. "How could my daughter, my own flesh and blood, sell her body for trinkets? Condemn her soul for dross? And on the eve of her marriage to a fine young man. I don't understand her. I never did."

Your daughter's a selfish, spoiled teenager who's been indulged by everyone in her life to the point where she wouldn't know a sound moral decision if it smacked her on the nose. Mackenzie didn't voice her opinion aloud. The poor man was suffering enough. Why add to his pain? "Sir, I'm sure when Kelly grows up a little more, she'll feel different."

His eyes refocused on her. He shook his head. "My daughter is lost. Perhaps she'll return to Jesus someday. I'll pray for her. However, it wasn't my intention to take up your time with my woes, Ms. Cross." He attempted a smile. "In the interests of full disclosure, perhaps you'll want to know that Kelly told me she enlisted your help to cover up her affair with Jacob Dearborn because, in her words, you were 'dumb enough to do what you were told.' I don't believe that, not for a moment."

Mackenzie flushed and bit her tongue.

"I'm sorry for my daughter's attitude, I truly am," he went on. "I hear you think you owe me something on account of the work I'm having done on the building to fix the storm damage. I want to reassure you that you shouldn't feel obligated in any way. The repairs are my responsibility. If I ever gave you the impression otherwise—"

"No, sir, not at all," Mackenzie hastened to reassure him.

"I'm glad to hear it." He shook her hand again. "Good day, Ms. Cross, and God bless."

Mackenzie turned to make a second attempt at opening her office door, but this time, her cell phone's ring interrupted her. "Cross speaking," she answered, tucking the phone between her ear and her shoulder while juggling her set of keys.

"I'm told you do appraisals?" asked an unfamiliar, hesitant, older female voice. The rising inflection made each sentence seem like a question. "You know, of antique furniture and so forth?"

"Yes, ma'am, I can give you an appraisal," Mackenzie replied, finally unlocking the door. A gust of hot air rushed out. Sweat beaded her face. She'd forgotten to set the timer on the air-conditioner. *Must be a hundred degrees in there*. She hesitated.

"My mother recently passed, and my sisters and I inherited some furniture?" the woman said. "You know, old wooden stuff?"

"Uh-huh," Mackenzie encouraged, standing on the pavement under the broiling hot sun, holding her office door open in a futile attempt to cool the interior enough so she wouldn't bake like a muffin when she went inside.

"Mother always said they were Chip and Dale?"

An image of cartoon chipmunks flashed through her mind. "You mean Chippendale?" Mackenzie asked, coming to attention.

The woman sniffed. "I suppose? Real old, Mother said?"

Mackenzie thought about the eighteenth century Chippendale Bombe Chest-on-Chest that sold about a decade ago for nearly two million dollars at auction. Some of her regular clients would love to add antique Chippendale furniture to their collections. "Well, I can give you a valuation of the pieces, ma'am," she said. "When would be a convenient time?"

"When's the soonest you can come? I have the address here, if you want?"

Mackenzie dashed into the heated office to fumble a pen and notepad off the desk in the reception area. She had a little time before she was supposed to meet with Veronica. "I can come out right now, if that's convenient."

"Yes, I suppose that's fine?"

"Where do you live?" Mackenzie scribbled the address the woman gave her. A drop of sweat rolled off her nose and splashed on the notepad, smearing the ink. She straightened and made a grab for a tissue from the box on the corner of the desk to blot her face. "I can be there in twenty minutes, Ms...?"

The woman hung up without giving her name.

"Damn it." Mackenzie slipped the phone into her pocket, wiped the sweat from her face with the tissue and went to adjust the thermostat on the wall.

The air-conditioner kicked in with a subtle whoosh. It took a few moments before cool air began to flow from the ceiling vents. She didn't have time to bask, so she hurried out of the office, making sure to lock the door behind her, and climbed into her car.

During the drive, Mackenzie found herself excited about the prospect of discovering genuine Chippendale furniture as opposed to "Chippendale style." Even an experienced appraiser might have difficulty telling the difference, but she knew an acknowledged expert who could provide a second opinion if needed. Of course, if the woman had provenance for her late mother's furniture pieces, that would be even better.

The address raised her spirits even higher. The house was in Dawn Rise, the wealthiest neighborhood in Antioch, populated by lawyers, doctors, bankers and other people with money to burn on luxury real estate. No doubt the woman's mother had lived in one of those pseudo-Antebellum mansions built in the seventies with graceful Palladium architecture, tall columns, classical lines and manicured lawns.

When she and her friends had been driven to the Rise as kids on Halloween to go trick-or-treating, Mackenzie had learned a couple of important lessons. Having money didn't make you a nice person—she'd had more than one asshole slam a door in her face after screaming at her to get lost—and rich folks were too cheap to hand out name brand candy bars. The best she'd received on the Rise had been discount lollipops, tiny boxes of stale raisins, apples and once a lecture on the merits of dental hygiene.

At least Jacob Dearborn's scheme to transform Sweetwater Hill into another Dawn Rise had died with him, she hoped.

She turned onto Troy Avenue, checking the numbers on mailboxes. The driveway she wanted led uphill off the street and seemed long, perhaps a quarter-mile or so, lined on either side with hickory trees. Sunlight flickered through the leaves as she drove, creating patterns of dark and bright on the windshield that made her blink. At the end of the driveway, she saw the huge, gleaming white *Gone With the Wind*-style mansion she'd expected.

Mackenzie parked the car. As she emerged into the stillness and heat, she sensed movement behind her. She spun around, catching a glimpse of Annabel's oddly sorrowful, silver-gray face before a canvas bag was yanked over her head.

Hands pinioned her arms roughly behind her back. She fought against the hold, trying to head-butt her captor, but someone else grabbed her ankles and wrenched her feet off the ground. Pain flared in her leg. Still she twisted in panic, her screams muffled by the fabric.

She sucked in a terrified breath, accidentally inhaling a mouthful of canvas tasting of mothballs and dust. A cough turned into retching that tore something in her chest. The burning pain felt as if her sternum had crumpled.

Suddenly, she was free, she was flying, and when she crashed, her head struck something solid. The lights bursting inside her skull faded to black.

So did her consciousness.

CHAPTER THIRTY-FOUR

Mackenzie woke slowly, her head hurting, her leg on fire, her mind fogged.

What the hell happened? She wanted to rub her aching skull, but her arms wouldn't move. Her body felt like dead weight, slumped in a seated position on her tailbone. *Did I have too much to drink last night? I guess Jose Cuervo is not a friend of mine.*

She cracked open an eyelid and recoiled.

Rev. Wilson Wyland stood in front of her. He looked old, thin and vulturine in his customary black suit and string tie. His white mane of hair was tousled. He saw her staring up at him and gave her a grave look in return, bending over so they were face-to-face.

"Glad you're awake, Ms. Cross," he said in his beautifully modulated baritone. His breath smelled faintly of peppermint. "I hope you aren't too uncomfortable. I apologize for my colleagues, who were supposed to deliver you unharmed. Your wounding was an accident, so I've been given to understand. Please find it in your heart to forgive them."

Mackenzie remembered the assault on Dawn Rise. The woman's call about an appraisal must have been fake, meant to lure her out of her usual haunts, away from potential witnesses into a trap. She glared at Wyland, realizing she was unable to speak because of the duct tape over her mouth, and unable to leave or defend herself because her wrists and ankles were bound with it as well.

"I wish it hadn't come to this," Wyland said, shaking his head.

He straightened and walked away a few paces, giving her a better view of her surroundings. She immediately recognized the cross on the wall, the upright piano in the corner. She'd been assaulted, kidnapped—by whom, she didn't know yet—and taken to the Covenant Rock Church of God with Signs Following, where she'd been put on the dais floor and concealed behind the pulpit. Wyland must be behind it—but why?

"When you approached me the first time, I thought you were a Christian woman," he said, rubbing his wrinkled dry hands together with a sound like old paper rustling, "until I learned you were doing the bidding of that young whore and her panderer. We must forgive the trespasses of sinners, but you wouldn't let it go. And then God gave me a sign."

Mackenzie wondered what he meant, since he had made a complaint to the police.

"I saw you enter my church that day," Wyland said. "I saw you leave after being bitten and I knew the Lord had punished you. God used one of His own creatures to deliver His judgment. I saw the signs and knew my faith had been rewarded."

She recalled her rattlesnake bite in this same church and how she thought she'd seen an indifferent Wyland watching her from a distance. In the hospital, she'd believed his silent presence was an hallucination, but she'd been mistaken.

Wyland paced a few steps, stopped and turned back to regard her. His gaze held an unnerving conviction. "But you survived. I thought the Lord's grace had saved your life, for did Jesus not say the very hairs of a man's head are numbered by God? God's eye never wavers upon us. All happens according to His plan."

Deciding to play along and encourage him to think God had spared her, Mackenzie nodded, unsure if he registered the motion.

"And that thief J.D. Bledsoe, calling himself Dearborn, came trying to buy my land, trying to destroy my church—!" His fists clenched, the sole outward sign of his anger. His expression remained placid. "Threatening me and my ministry. Bledsoe was no man of God. He worshipped Mammon. He was steeped in vice. But the blackest sinner may have a change of heart. I gave him a chance to prove his faith."

Abruptly, Mackenzie heard Veronica's voice in her head telling her about the cause of Jacob Dearborn's death: *a poison like cyanide or strychnine*. From her position, she had a good view of the table along the left wall with its stacks of hymnals, screen-topped wooden boxes where rattlesnakes rested and jars of colorless strychnine. She cursed herself for not thinking about a possible source for Dearborn's poisoning sooner.

Why was Wyland telling her what he'd done? Why confess to murder? The answer made her stomach twist tight around a knot of ice. Sickness rose in her throat to choke her.

He had nothing to lose. She wasn't a witness. She was his next victim.

Wyland appeared oblivious to her struggles. "Divine providence...I had only to offer Bledsoe the poison. He drank, believing the strychnine was water and my faith was as much of a sham as his own. And so perishes the false prophet. Thank you, Jesus!"

The sound of a car engine filtered through the church walls. Although Mackenzie knew logically that the driver couldn't hear her, she sucked in air through her nose and began to make loud, inarticulate grunts behind the duct tape sealing her mouth.

Listening hard above her galloping pulse, it seemed to her that the car had turned off the road and parked on the grass outside the church. She redoubled her effort to break free, drawing back her legs to kick out at Wyland and thump her heels on the floor though fresh pain shot through her bad leg.

When Wyland's admonitions failed to silence her, he stalked off the dais toward the table. Hearing another car, Mackenzie continued grunting, kicking and pulling at the tape binding her wrists together. She felt certain most of the Reverend's genuinely Christian congregation wouldn't approve of kidnapping and he was no Jim Jones.

He returned with a long, sinuous form dangling from his hand. He draped the snake over her neck. She stiffened in sudden terror at a familiar rattling buzz.

"I find you troublesome, Ms. Cross," he said, "and I've prayed for an answer. Did God spare you before, when you came to my church, or was it the Devil's luck? I was shown the way to test you as I tested Bledsoe." He reached down a long fingered hand to stroke the rattlesnake's head where it rested against her flat chest. Instantly, the buzz intensified. "Let this be a test of *your* faith. Armor yourself with salvation, put your trust in God and you'll not be harmed. Let your faith falter and you'll die. Whatsoever He wills, so it shall be."

Sweating, Mackenzie rolled her eyes, trying to glimpse the snake. The vibrating tail tickled the side of her arm. She dared not move, not so much as a hair. She sat perfectly still, every inch of her skin crawling, while she heard more cars arriving and people entering the church chatting softly among themselves. Wyland left the dais to greet them.

He must have called for a special meeting. Nobody here would think twice about attending church when the Spirit moves their pastor.

A shimmer caught her eye, a silver-gray manifestation to one side of the dais. *No, Annabel, not now!* Mackenzie desperately thought.

The apparition appeared, looking more solid than she'd seen at any time before. Annabel's black gaze was filled with blistering hate. Her form glowed brighter. The gray bled out of the ghost until she shone like molten silver in a forge. Mackenzie had to avert her gaze. Always in the past, Annabel had been cold, but now she burned.

Billy, Annabel whispered in a voice like dust.

After a short while, the congregation took their seats. Wyland mounted the dais. He launched immediately into his sermon. The subject was lost on Mackenzie, but she was keenly aware that his jerky movements and pacing, and the occasional slaps of his Bible against the top of his pulpit, kept the diamondback around her neck in a state of restlessness. Its blunt, wedge-shaped head quested over her chest to her shoulder, but for some reason, the snake didn't seem inclined to bite. Perhaps it didn't feel threatened enough.

She started to flinch when the snake's tongue flicked softly against the skin of her neck, but caught herself. Fear wrung a stifled whimper from her throat.

Annabel waited in perfect silence, her dark gaze fixed on Wyland, who became increasingly agitated as he preached. In the corners of the room, shadows stirred.

Mackenzie heard someone in the congregation fall to the floor, babbling nonsense while others praised Jesus. She also heard rhythmic scuffling footsteps—no doubt women coming forward to perform a rocking step-dance in front of the pulpit. A guitar played. A few voices began to sing a hymn, "I'm Gonna Let It Shine."

"A joy unspeakable it is, to be obedient to God's will!" Wyland cried, his hair further disordered and falling over his brow. A patch of sweat darkened his shirtfront.

"Tell us!" bellowed a man in response.

"There's no power but God," Wyland thundered. "Every soul here is subject to God's power. Resistance is damnation. I tell you, I feel the power today! Let it come!"

"Bring it!"

"In this moment, in this hour, I feel His power! Can you feel it, brothers and sisters?"

"Amen!"

"I do not fear death—no, sir, I'm ready to go. We all need to be ready to go. I tell you, you can't be ready for Jesus and hang on to the world. Trust in Him and you will go to a better place." Wyland pulled off his jacket, tossed it on the piano and rolled up his shirtsleeves. He extended his arms outward, out of Mackenzie's line of sight.

When he drew his arms back, he held several fat rattlesnakes coiling and squirming in his grasp. "No matter what comes," he shouted, raising his arms high, "I'll glorify God!"

Mackenzie saw the crude sailor girl tattoo on his wrist—on *Billy Wakefield's* wrist, she realized—at the same time Annabel Coffin darted forward, no longer human-shaped, but a blue-white blaze of fury, hotter than a sun, more brilliant than a flash of lightning.

The rattlesnakes held by Wyland began to bite him in a frenzy, striking his hands, his forearms, his face, his neck. The snake around her neck slithered off to join the rest in their crazed attack. He screamed and tried to drop the snakes, but they clung to him, strike after strike, while he turned pale and staggered.

The sudden disappearance of the bright light left spots dancing in Mackenzie's vision. She glanced around, finding no trace of Annabel.

Wyland collapsed, his tongue protruding blue and swollen between his lips.

CHAPTER THIRTY-FIVE

"What happened?" Veronica asked much later.

Mackenzie glanced around her apartment, glad to be home and safe. "The rattlesnakes just went crazy, Ronnie," she replied, settling more comfortably on the sofa. "They kept biting the reverend even after he was dead. They ignored everybody else, including the Animal Control officers who rounded them up."

Veronica kept touching her as if unable to believe she was actually there. "Detective Maynard and I found Billy Wakefield's picture in the frame on the charm bracelet, just like you said. Wakefield and Wyland were the same person. Dearborn must've recognized him."

"So did Annabel. I should have known. Wilson Wyland. 'Will's son,'" Mackenzie explained. "William Wakefield Sr.'s criminally inclined boy, Billy. I guess Billy didn't just vanish in '85, but changed his name and went to Bible school. Had a daughter of his own. By the way, what will happen to Alafair?"

"From what Detective Maynard told me, relatives on her mother's side offered to take her in," Veronica said. "They're Holiness Pentecostals, too."

"Poor girl. At least she'll find comfort in her religion. Hey, let me do this one thing before I forget." Mackenzie took her cell phone from the coffee table and made a quick call.

When she finished, she answered the unspoken question in Veronica's eyes. "Sam the baker," she explained, waving the phone for emphasis. "I had an idea in the patrol car on the way home. I wanted to know if Sam recalled what company did the renovations on my office building next door back in '57. Turns out it was Young Construction Company."

"Didn't Billy's father work for Young?"

"He sure did. Billy could have gotten access to the worksite."

"If Billy killed Annabel in the shack in the woods, why not leave her body out there?"

Mackenzie shrugged. "Somebody was making moonshine at the site. If a 'shiner was brewing out there at the time, Billy couldn't risk Annabel's body being found. Hiding her behind the drywall of a building under construction probably seemed like a good bet to give himself a head start out of Antioch."

"His luck held a lot longer than that." Veronica shifted a little, drawing her legs under her. "But eventually, his bad deeds caught up with him."

"I'd say so."

"I'm unclear on why he'd kill Annabel, though. Didn't he love her?"

"Perhaps he did, but Annabel got pregnant. Billy had promised her they'd run away to New York City together. Whether he meant it at the time, I don't know, but when she told him she was expecting, he persuaded or forced her to go to Isaac Rush for an abortion. After the procedure, she started to hemorrhage. She called Billy and arranged to meet him in the shack in the woods. Maybe Billy panicked when he saw all the blood. Maybe he never loved her as much and she became a complication he didn't need. Either way, he hit her on the head with a pipe or something else heavy enough to do the job."

"As a theory, it hangs together, but there's no evidence."

"Ronnie, we'll never know the whole truth. That died with him."

"Dearborn's murder?"

"Wyland said he arranged a test of Dearborn's faith by giving him strychnine to drink," Mackenzie said, moving to a more comfortable position that also brought her closer to Veronica. Their shoulders touched. She leaned her head over, letting out a little sigh when Veronica hooked an arm around her. "Dearborn thought the stuff was water, not poison."

"Strychnine is colorless, odorless, tasteless. Not hard to imagine Dearborn might think Wyland was just trying to frighten him with a bluff."

Mackenzie nodded. "Wyland told me Dearborn threatened him over that land on Sweetwater Hill," she went on. "Dearborn needed the land to avoid financial ruin. However, Dearborn had a false identity and a criminal past, too. If he exposed Wyland as Billy Wakefield, he exposed himself, so he didn't dare go to the police or try to discredit Wyland. But if Wyland told him he'd sell the parcels in exchange for Dearborn proving his faith by drinking what he thought was fake poison, he'd do it in a hot second."

"Why did Wakefield/Wyland go after you?" Veronica's expression remained pleasant, but her hand tightened on Mackenzie's thigh.

Mackenzie found the possessive gesture endearing. She considered the question. "I don't know for sure," she finally replied. "Remember, I told you I thought I'd seen him when I was bitten by the rattlesnake."

Veronica looked stricken. "Oh, Mac, I'm sorry, I thought you were hallucinating—"

"Hey, it's okay." Mackenzie put her hand over Veronica's. "I thought the same thing. Anyway, he told me that since Dearborn failed his divinely inspired test by dying of strychnine poisoning, he decided to find out if I was really a righteous person or not by using another test, this time trial by rattler. He wasn't making a whole lot of sense at that point. I got the feeling he wasn't shamming about his conversion, though. He really *was* a devout man of God. So devout, he saw signs everywhere."

"The man wasn't in his right mind," Veronica declared flatly. "What about his followers? The ones who kidnapped you and put that bump on your head?"

Mackenzie had given up trying to figure out the identities of the "Chippendale woman" and her accomplices. "No idea. He called them 'colleagues,' whatever that means."

"I don't like the sound of that."

"Well, Wyland's gone. I suppose the church will disband now."

"Or get a new preacher."

"Don't say it. I've had enough of rattlesnakes to last me a lifetime."

Veronica turned her head to bring their lips together. "You stay off Sweetwater Hill, Mac. I don't want to lose you."

"I don't want to be lost." Mackenzie kissed Veronica. The angle was wrong, her lips were sore from the duct tape gag and she suspected her breath could've peeled wallpaper, but Veronica didn't seem to mind.

Suddenly realizing she *had* forgotten something important, Mackenzie tore her mouth away and gasped. "Oh, my God!"

Veronica sat bolt upright. "What's wrong?"

"Mama! I was supposed to pick her up at the hospital in Trinity. She's going to have a cow, Ronnie. A herd of cows," Mackenzie went on, imagining the horrors an angry Sarah Grace would inflict on her. "A herd of mad, bloodthirsty, vindictive cows with—"

"It's okay," Veronica interrupted, visibly relaxing. "Your mother called me when you didn't answer your phone. I was worried, Mac. I dispatched a patrol car to pick her up in Trinity and started calling around town looking for you. I was about to put a trace your cell phone's GPS when someone at the church called nine-one-one to report Wyland's death."

"And you guessed I was involved? I don't know whether to be insulted or not," Mackenzie teased.

Veronica smiled. "What happened to Annabel Coffin?"

"She disappeared. One second she was there, going for the old man like she meant to tear him apart, the snakes went wild and the next minute…poof. She was gone."

Although Mackenzie appreciated Annabel's absence, a small part of her also missed the spirit despite her anger and her destructive habits. She picked up a glass of peach iced tea, raising it in a salute. "To Annabel Coffin: may she rest in peace."

"World without end, amen," Veronica said, raising her own glass.

Holding her breath, Mackenzie waited for a flash of silver-gray to appear in the corner of her eye to contradict her, but none did. The apartment remained quiet and undisturbed.

Veronica joked, "Alone at last," but Mackenzie didn't feel like laughing.

"Yes," she replied, wondering if Annabel had really found peace.

Who knew why the dead returned as shades to haunt the living, or why some murders cried out to be revenged and other old grudges moldered in the grave?

Annabel had chosen her, tormented her, saved her, and she still didn't understand why. She blew out a breath. Perhaps one day she'd understand, but not today.

She and Veronica sat in silence for a long moment, just looking at each other. Finally, Veronica leaned over, offering her mouth for another kiss.

Mackenzie obliged.